DEKE

FAKE BOYFRIEND BOOK 3

EDEN FINLEY

DEKE

DEAR READER

I am an Australian girl, so please excuse my serious lack of knowledge when it comes to ice hockey. I grew up on soccer, cricket, and rugby. Although, to be honest, I know jack shit about those sports too.

Research can only get an author so far, so I blame that movie *The Mighty Ducks* for any inconsistencies. Because even though that's where I learned the term *deke* from, it turns out a triple deke is not even a thing. My whole childhood was a lie. Damn you, Emilio Estevez and Joshua Jackson.

TRADEMARKS USED IN DEKE.

This is a work of fiction. As such, NHL team names—like the Dragons and the Bobcats—are completely made up. The views in this book in no way reflect the views and principles of the NHL or any of their real teams.

While Boston's team is referred to as "the B's," for my story, the B stands for … Beavers. Yes, let's go with Beavers. Colleges have also been fabricated so not to misrepresent policies and values, curriculum, or facilities of existing universities.

Names, characters, businesses, places, events, and incidents are either the products of the author's imagination or used in a fictitious manner. Any resemblance to actual persons, living or dead, or actual events is purely coincidental.

DEKE

Verb:
to fake an opponent out of position
(hockey)

CHAPTER ONE

OLLIE

There are only so many times I can hear that coming out will solve all my problems. Like saying the words "I'm gay" to the entire world will somehow give me unicorn powers and I'll start farting rainbows and scoring on the ice.

I love my family, but for the love of Gretzky, they need to get over it. I have.

I think.

Okay, probably not.

My boyfriend left me because he hated being referred to as my roommate all the time, and somehow, that makes me the bad guy. I mean, I know I'm not the good guy, either, but Ash and I didn't deliberately set out to hurt each other. We were just really good at it.

My family—especially my ma—thinks if I come out to the world there'll be a domino effect, and I won't be the only gay guy in hockey for long.

There's more chance of me farting rainbows.

It didn't happen when Matt Jackson came out in the NFL a few months ago, and I have no delusion it'll happen for hockey when my time comes. I followed Matt's story, and it wasn't pretty.

The NHL was one of the first leagues to support LGBTQ players with their You Can Play project, and yet not a single player has creaked open the closet door, and my career doesn't need the added pressure of being the first one.

I don't want to be the NHL's first pancake.

Last thing I want to do is yell out in the middle of the locker room, "Oh, by the way, I'm gayer than a leather daddy convention."

No matter how many times I say I need to be in a good place before bringing shit on my career, it all falls on deaf ears when it comes to my family. And Ash.

I'm not out, so I shouldn't get shiny things like happiness to play with. That's what they seem to think.

And that's why I'm hiding in the bathroom of this dingy bar-slash-restaurant before we've even been served dinner. We came to the Honey Bee so the whole family could be together. Ma already complains she doesn't see us all enough, but in our defense, we're five dudes with shit going on in our lives. I think she's more upset she doesn't get to dote on all of us now we're grown-ups. And by dote on, I mean butt in.

She's a meddler through and through, but I get the brunt of it. I'm her baby—the youngest—and also the gayest. My whole family has been overprotective of me ever since my mom outed me to myself when I was fifteen.

Yup. *That happened.* Because Ma knows everything. Apparently.

Tonight, all I've heard is how lost Ash is without me and how relationships need compromises to work.

"Be the person that you needed growing up, struggling to

believe you could be anything you wanted to be," she'd said not ten minutes ago.

Changing Gus Kenworthy quotes to suit my situation doesn't help, Ma.

When I'd stared at my brothers to get any of them to back me up, they all sipped from their drinks and avoided eye contact. Dad grunted and nodded but didn't take sides.

Switzerland-loving asshole.

Okay, my dad's not an asshole. I'm just frustrated.

The door to the bathroom opens, and I assume it's one of my brothers come to check on me as per Ma's orders.

"I've been waiting for you—" I turn and come face to face with someone who is definitely not one of my brothers.

This guy who is the spitting image of a blond Superman, even down to the wild curl across his forehead and an adorable chin dimple, stares at me with wide, pale blue eyes. He's smaller than me but still probably six foot easy. My gaze travels down his slim build, and when I meet his eyes again, I replay my words and take in our location—a gay-friendly hangout in the South End—and I think I might've just come onto someone for the first time since Ash and I split. Unintentionally, but still.

Oops.

"Not you. I thought you were my brother."

The guy screws up his face. Oh, fuck, now it sounds like I'm waiting in the bathroom to hook up with my brother.

"No. I wasn't waiting for … that." My face burns, and I pray to God I'm not turning red. "I'm hiding."

He cocks an eyebrow. "From your brother?"

"From my entire family."

His warm gaze trails over me and lingers on my tattooed arms. His heated stare causes a stirring in my groin, reminding me that I haven't had sex in six months.

"I'm guessing you belong to the giant Norse gods out by the bar?" he asks.

My brothers and I often turn heads, especially when we're all together. I'm the runt, and I'm six four. My brothers always joke that I took up hockey so I could add height with my skates.

We're seated in one of the restaurant's private rooms, but I'd say my brothers are about due for another drink.

"Yeah, that'd be us."

"You mind if I ..." He points to the urinal behind me and adjusts the strap of his messenger bag on his shoulder.

"Oh, right. Sure." I move toward the sinks so he doesn't think I really am creeping in the bathroom for a hookup.

"So why are you hiding?" he asks, and I don't know if he's actually interested or just trying to break the awkwardness over the sound of him taking a leak with me lurking here.

"They're on my case about my ex."

After he's zipped, he turns around and eyes me from top to toe again, and I can't say I hate it. If anything, my instinct is to puff out my chest and flex my biceps.

"They want you to take him back?" He moves beside me to wash his hands.

Interesting that he assumes I'm gay. Although, the whole accidentally hitting on him thing probably helped him come to that conclusion. This is where I should normally deny it—where, under any other circumstance, I would—but for some reason, I can't bring myself to lie to this cute stranger. He just scrutinized me hard enough that if he was going to recognize me as a winger in the NHL, he would've already picked up on it.

"They want me to come out at work so he'll want me back," I say. That's a vague explanation, because it's not like I'd be coming out to an office of twelve people; it'd be coming out to the entire world. Tabloids would jump on it faster than a drug-addicted popstar.

The guy winces. "Tough situation. One that rarely works without resentment."

"The thing is, I'm twenty-four. I have a long career ahead of me, and I don't want anything to throw me off. I want to be established first."

"What do you do? Let me guess ..." He mockingly assesses me this time, his finger rubbing across the thin layer of blond scruff on his chin. I wonder if he's using this as an excuse to rake his gaze over me again. His eyes seem to lock onto my arms a lot, which are covered in so many tattoos there's no bare skin anymore. "I think, despite the tats, you're gonna be a contradiction. You're bulky and tatted up, but I bet you're in something like corporate business."

I know way better than to tell him the truth. "Something like that. Very much a man's world, anyway."

"Right. Real men don't like dicks," he says dryly.

"Real men don't know what they're missing."

Our eyes lock, and he relaxes into an easy smile as he reaches for the paper towels. For the first time in a long time, I find myself appreciating a man who's not Ash. Not just in a *he's hot* kind of way, but in a way where I actually feel a flutter of something in my gut. A couple of months ago, I didn't think that'd ever be a possibility.

I hold my hand out for him to shake. "I'm—"

The door opens again, and this time it *is* one of my brothers.

I drop my hand fast.

"What the fuck is taking so—" Vic spots the guy next to me. "Oh. Gotcha. Hurry up and do what you gotta do. I'll stall." After dropping *that*, Vic turns on his heel and walks out.

"So, that was one of your brothers," the guy says, his tone amused.

"You see what I have to put up with?"

"He didn't seem so bad."

"You know why we're *here* at all?"

"At the Honey Bee?"

"It's because they want me to be comfortable in my surroundings, as if I can't be okay at a restaurant that's not a gay hangout."

He tries to keep his face passive, but a hint of a smile comes through. "It's great they love who you are."

"You go have dinner with them then," I grumble.

He stares at the door and then back at me. "All right."

"Uh ... what?" I can't have heard that right.

He steps closer. "You need them off your back about your ex, and I'm utterly fascinated by this odd family dynamic you claim to have. Doesn't hurt your brothers are hot. Any of the others gay too?"

I feign offense. "What am I, chopped liver?"

He blatantly checks me out again, and I'd totally call him out for having the subtlety of an enforcer pummeling another player, but I like him looking at me.

"Not a big fan of guys on the rebound. Sorry." Yet, he's still staring at me.

"Hey, I'm over Ash. It's my family who has the issue with him."

That might be a tiny lie. I'm still dealing with being single, but I'm not pining after the guy or anything. I made my choice, so now I have to learn how to be an adult. Ash and I got together when I was nineteen, so I went from living in my parents' house to a billet family while I was with the AHL, and then into an apartment where Ash took care of everything. These past six months have been the first time in my life I've been truly alone.

A part of me will always love Ash, but childhood fantasies coming true don't always end in happily ever afters. *That* should be in fairy tales. Prepare for reality, kids, because when all's said and done, Prince Charming will throw you an ultimatum.

"Here's an idea. Why don't you introduce your family to a new boyfriend?" This guy gestures to himself. "I could totally be in love with you." His mouth drops open. "I mean, I could totally pretend … if you needed me to. To, you know, get them off your back."

I kinda love that he's fumbling all over himself. "They won't believe it. I woulda told them if I was bringing someone to meet them."

He shrugs. "Make something up. Tell them you wanted to bring me, but I got stuck at work and didn't think I'd make it. Being an awesome boyfriend, I decided to surprise you."

"What do you do for work?"

"I can do anything you want your boyfriend to do … Uh, that sounded a hell of a lot less sexual in my head. I swear I'm usually good with words."

I laugh.

"We could tell them I'm in business like you," he suggests.

I eye his chinos, which have been rolled up to the ankle, and his shoes with no socks. He looks more nerdy than someone who's in the corporate world, but that's not really what I should be focused on.

"Why are you offering to do this? No, why do you *want* to do this?" I ask. "It's … weird, and my family is nuts."

"I'm not a serial killer if that's what you're worried about."

"Well, I wasn't, but *now* I am. What kind of person introduces themselves as *not a serial killer*? Like, you're not gonna meet one who goes around saying 'Hi, I'd like to wear your skin as a suit.'"

"Good point. But let's call my offer a morbid fascination with a family who doesn't tell you to *hide* the gay so you're not jumped. I want to know what that's like."

And there it is—the usual flare of shame that hits me when I complain about my family. They want to march in parades by my side and want me to be a good role model for gay kids growing up in this shitty world that still doesn't always accept them.

"Way to make me feel wicked guilty for having it better than a lot of other people."

His warm hand touches my upper arm through my short-sleeved T-shirt. He squeezes my biceps, and his eyes focus on my muscles and my tats again before he shakes his head and stares up at me. "I'm not diminishing your experiences. It can be hard for any of us for multiple different reasons, but hey, if you don't want a get out of jail free card, I'll be on my way."

Before he gets two steps, I reach out to pull him back without giving it proper thought. His chest presses against mine, and it's nice to be close to someone again.

It's amazing what you can take for granted when you're in a long-term relationship. Not coming home to affection has been a big adjustment for me. I never realized how much a simple touch could reassure me that everything was going to be okay until it wasn't there anymore.

And it's not like I can go to a bar or meet someone and say *Mind if I press myself against you for a while?*

What this stranger is offering … it's a stupid idea—one that probably won't work—but if I can deke my entire family into thinking I'm happy, it might be worth it if it makes Ma stop saying shit like I could never truly find someone while being closeted. If only for a dinner.

"Thank you. It, uh, would help me out a lot."

A slow smile spreads across his face as he links his fingers through mine as we exit the bathroom.

I can't stop staring at our joined hands. A thrill rushes through me. I should be concerned someone will see or recognize me, but the lighting is dim, and the novelty of holding a guy's hand—in public or not—is too much for me to resist.

When we get into the busy part of the restaurant though, I drop his hand and lead him to where our private dining room is hiding in the back.

My family's large table accommodates my brothers—minus Max—Nic's wife, their two kids, and my parents. This guy doesn't seem to care he's walking into a lion's den. Then again, he doesn't know my family and probably thinks I'm overreacting.

When we get to the table, all eyes lock on us.

"Welcome to the jungle," I mutter out the side of my mouth.

Before any of them can start tormenting this guy who's doing me a favor, I cut them all off.

"Guys, this is …" Fuck, I didn't even ask him his name, and all I can think about is how much he looks like a blond Superman. "Clark."

I knew this was a bad idea for a reason. Pulling it off is going to take more than saying *This is my boyfriend, so now you can stop acting like dicks.*

He glances in my direction, and I want to apologize for panicking, but what kind of boyfriend doesn't know his partner's name?

"And who is … Clark?" Ma asks, giving him the same stare down she gave Amanda when Nic first brought her home.

"He's, uh—" My voice cracks like it did when I was twelve years old, and I have to clear my throat. "This is my boyfriend."

Everyone's eyebrows shoot up in surprise, even Vic, who saw us in the bathroom together.

The guy now known as Clark lifts his hand and waves awkwardly, which makes me chuckle.

"Umm, I wasn't going to tell you because it's fairly new"—*like, ten minutes new*—"and he said he had to work—"

"But it turns out I didn't," Clark says with a warm smile. "Plus, this guy offered to take me to a football game if I could make it."

Oh, shit. A voice in the back of my head screams *Abort. Abort!* But we're too far gone now. Can't exactly turn around and be all *Ha-ha, gotcha.*

How did I think I could get through this dinner without my profession coming out?

I'm never going to hear the end of this. Not that I sprung a boyfriend on them but that he's a football fan.

"*Football?*" Vic teases. "Ollie, you have to end it *now.*"

Yup, right on cue.

"Why is that a big …" Clark's words trail off as something akin to recognition crosses his face. He's able to quickly cover his reaction, but everyone in my family is looking at us like they're about to pounce. "What? Can't a hockey player take his boyfriend to watch a football game every now and then?"

And that's when it's confirmed. He does know who I am.

CHAPTER TWO

LENNON

Sweet Neil Patrick Harris, I'm fucked.

Ollie looks like he's going to throw up, and I'm kicking myself for not recognizing him sooner. I should've known he was a jock with the way I immediately wanted to climb him like a tree. If he really was waiting in the bathroom for a hookup, I wouldn't have hesitated. Closeted meatheads are my kryptonite, and apparently, I don't even need to know that fact anymore before being drawn to them.

Maybe I have some sort of beacon or tracking system for them now.

What's worse is I'm a sports journalist who didn't recognize Ollie Strömberg immediately. Although, in my defense, I mainly cover football and baseball. Kevin does hockey.

While I don't know much about the sport, I do know Ollie and his teammate Tommy Novak are an unstoppable force, but Novak gets all the credit for it, because he's usually the one sealing the deal and getting the puck in the net.

If Ollie had any idea who I was, he wouldn't only be nauseated but in full-on freak-out mode. He outed himself to me, and no fucking way would I ever run that story, but he doesn't know that. I work with the bloodsucking journalists we're notorious for being, but I'm not like that … most of the time. The one time I tried being sneaky to get a story, it blew up in spectacular fashion when Matt Jackson's boyfriend tried to punch me out.

That was intentional. This whole situation has been brought on by some twisted turn of fate.

What am I supposed to do here?

"Can't believe you're dating a football fan," Ollie's dad says. "I've never been more disappointed in you, son."

At his serious tone, I blink at him, wondering if he really said that to his kid. His face is stoic, giving away nothing. When Ollie laughs, his dad finally breaks and cracks a wide smile.

"Please don't scare him off with your horribly dry humor where people can't tell if you're joking or not." Ollie turns to me. "Which he totally is. Dad played college football back in the day. Like, you know, when they used to wear those leather helmets."

"Watch it, boy. I'm not that old."

There's a round of sarcastic "Mmmhmms" from all the sons at the table, and there's a lot of them.

Four boys. *Four.*

Not to mention the fucking genes in this family. Their hair ranges from light blond to strawberry, and Ollie was blessed with the darkest shade out of all of them, but even his ashy blond hair is still blond. His dad is gray, but I'd bet my left nut he used to be blond too.

I wasn't joking when I said they all looked like Norse gods. As soon as I walked into the restaurant, the group of tall and wide —not to mention hot—guys by the bar caught my eye. Two of them, twins by their resemblance, look like John Cena on steroids.

The other is the polar opposite. He's tall and lanky.

"Take a seat," Ollie's mom says, and it occurs to me what a bad idea this was.

Faking a relationship for a dinner didn't seem like a daunting task, but now I realize we know nothing about each other.

Under the scrutiny of so many people, I begin to think Ollie's family could be secret spies or something because their burning gazes make me want to break down and confess everything.

And all they've done is looked at me and cracked a joke.

Intimidating much?

I blow out a loud breath. No backing out now.

I. Can. Do. This.

Ollie and I take a seat next to each other after bringing an empty chair from the other end of the table.

"How did you meet Ollie?" Ollie's mom asks.

Hmm, *in a bathroom* is probably not the best answer here.

"Mutual friend," I say vaguely.

"Ollie has friends?" the smartass brother says—the one who caught us in the bathroom.

Ollie leans closer to me. "If you haven't worked it out yet, I'm the one they pick on because I'm younger, half their size, and earn about ten times as much as all of them combined."

Simultaneously, three middle fingers face our direction.

"I'm going to call my mother tonight and tell her she shouldn't complain about me and my sister anymore," I say.

The woman at the other end bounces a sleeping baby in her arms and wipes a toddler's face. "Don't worry. You get used to their antics pretty fast."

One of the twins—the non-smartassed one—stands and takes the baby from her and gives the woman a kiss on the forehead. "Antics. Pfft. No antics here. We were always good boys growing up."

Ollie's mother lets out a loud "Ha!"

The conversation breaks into normal family ribbing, and it gives me a false sense of security, because as soon as I start to relax, everything turns back to the topic of me.

"So, what do you do for a living?" his dad asks. Let the interrogation begin!

"Uhh, you know, business." That's the lie we came up with in the bathroom, so I'm sticking to it.

"What type?" his dad asks.

"Uh, you know. Acquisitions. Accounts. Tax. Mutual funds. Dividends." Great, now I'm just saying words that sound businesslike. "It's super boring. What do all of you do?" A good boyfriend always asks questions—especially when he doesn't want to answer their questions that have no answers.

"Leo coaches basketball," Ollie says, and the tall, lanky brother nods. "The twins, Nic and Vic, are personal trainers for MMA fighters."

"Nic and Vic?" I ask.

"Nicklas and Victor," Ollie says and points to each of them. They're obviously not identical, but it's still hard to tell them apart. "I don't think my parents chose rhyming names on purpose …" He looks at his parents. "Right?"

"We thought it was cute," his mom says.

"Yeah. Super cute," Vic grumbles.

"Didn't cause teasing in school or nothin'," Nic adds.

"Where do you think we got the idea to learn MMA?" Vic says to their parents.

"Anyway," Ollie says, "Max is a tattoo artist."

I balk. "Wait, there's *more* of you?"

Everyone at the table laughs.

"There's five of us," Ollie says.

"All boys?" I squeak and give his parents the most sympathetic look I can pull off.

Ollie's mom puts her napkin in her lap and smiles demurely. "God blessed us with all boys because He wouldn't give me anything I couldn't handle."

Leo laughs. "If I remember correctly, you used to threaten military school on us if we acted up."

Nic chimes in. "And when that didn't work, you'd cry about God testing you."

Ollie leans in and whispers, "By the way, we're barely religious."

I snort.

"Whatever," Ollie's mom says, sounding more like the age of her sons than the late fifties she'd have to be. "We all survived."

"Just," Vic mutters.

Waiters and waitresses come out with plates full of food, and my stomach rumbles. My first stop after the bathroom was supposed to be the bar where I could order something fast. Guess fast isn't part of the deal now. I still have a family grilling to endure. Karma better pay me back with something awesome. Like hot, naked men fawning over me. Actually, things have been so slow lately, I'd settle for just a man. Singular. See, Karma? This is me not being greedy. Then again, doing someone a favor in hopes of good karma defeats the purpose.

When they finish dishing the appetizers out, Ollie has three plates in front of him.

"You want?" he asks, gesturing to the food.

"Were you psychic and knew I'd be here or ..." Looking around the table, I realize everyone has at least two plates in front of them. "Did you guys not order mains?"

Ollie laughs, but it has a nervous edge to it. "Come on, you should be used to my appetite by now."

Right. Athletes and their insane amount of food intake.

Another thing I should know. I think Ollie makes me stupid, because I'm usually smarter than this.

Wouldn't be the first time my brain has jumped ship over a cute boy with muscles.

I turn to Ollie's parents. "I'm guessing food in your household costs more than rent?"

"We were able to retire once all the boys had flown the coop," his dad says. "No longer had to feed them all."

There are muffled grumbles from Ollie and his brothers, but they're too busy shoving food in their mouths. I'd laugh if it wasn't frighteningly eerie watching them eat. It's like watching a nature program showing a pack of lions ripping into a poor animal.

I eat a bacon-wrapped shrimp from Ollie's plate and a couple of pieces of calamari before the dishes are empty because Ollie scarfs all the ribs before I get a chance to try them.

When the mains come out, I shouldn't be shocked that Ollie's ordered two. He grabs the waitress's attention but then quickly turns to me. "Which one do you want to eat?"

"I'm good with either," I say.

"Pick one."

"The salmon looks good."

Ollie passes over the plate and then orders another salmon.

"You seriously could eat half of this," I say.

"I'll probably take you up on that too."

Damn, if his appetite is this ravenous, I wonder what else he's insatiable for.

Nope, won't be thinking about that.

Had he been anyone but Ollie Strömberg, I'd allow myself to think of those things. But jocks and nerdy Lennon have never played well together.

After we settle in, dinner becomes a quiet affair, probably because it's feeding time at *Jurassic Park*.

I begin to think Ollie's family isn't as bad as he makes them sound, but then his mother finishes her meal and turns to me.

"Did he ever tell you the story of how he came out?"

Ollie almost chokes on his food. "Here we go." He turns to me. "I'm sorry. I'm sorry, I'm sorry, I'm sorry. Please still like me after you hear this story."

"Well, now, I *need* to hear this story."

The brothers snigger. Ollie groans.

"So, when he was fifteen," his mom says, the green in her hazel eyes sparkling. "He brought home his very first girlfriend."

I try not to smile but fail miserably.

"I knew they didn't like her immediately," Ollie says. "One thing you should know about us is if we're silent something is seriously wrong. I think that was the quietest dinner we'd ever had."

"Oh, honey, we didn't hate her. We were just so confused." His mom continues, "After she left to go home, we sent the other boys to their rooms."

Ollie shifts uncomfortably in his seat. "I thought they were about to give me the sex talk. I was kinda hoping the world would open up and swallow me whole."

"We were not so delusional that you didn't already know everything," his dad says. "You had four older brothers."

"So, Mom's there, telling me how if I'm straight she'll accept me and love me anyway." Ollie shakes his head.

My hand flies to my mouth as I try to stifle a laugh.

"Granted, I had some idea, but until that moment, I didn't realize how ridiculous it all was. My parents were there telling me they'll love me no matter what but they couldn't help thinking my girlfriend was a phase."

My gaze flies to theirs. "But … why? I mean … how …"

Ollie's mom smiles. "Telling us at four years old that he likes boys was the biggest tip-off, but there was no one certain thing he did or said. He didn't have much interest in girls at all. Like, the other boys all came home at one point during elementary school talking about some girl or another. Ollie never did. It was just a hunch, so the girlfriend was a shock."

Ollie turns to me. "That's when they decided it was time to give me the gay sex talk. Seriously scarred me for life."

His brothers snigger, and I can't help joining in. "Better you than me," I say.

Ollie's brothers tell me how they heard the whole thing from the top of the stairs while trying to keep their laughter at bay—not at Ollie being gay but about having to endure a more than awkward sex lesson from their parents, including the lecture about still needing protection even if you can't get your partner pregnant.

My eyes tear up from laughing so hard when a brown-haired guy covered in tats walks in and takes the last spare seat at the table. "Hey, sorry I'm late."

"Honey, we thought you couldn't make it," Ollie's mom says.

Ollie stiffens. "Max."

Ah, the other brother. And the odd one out with his brown hair. Interesting.

Max settles in his seat and glares at Ollie. "Oliver." Then his eyes meet mine and he freezes. "Who are you?"

"Umm … C-Clark." Because I'm Clark now. Apparently.

Ollie warned me that when the Strömbergs are quiet you know something's wrong, and right now, dead silence falls. It must freak out Ollie's nephew or something, because he starts wailing.

The sister-in-law goes back to bouncing him and settling him with shushing sounds.

Ollie, Max, and I are in some sort of three-way stare-off.

"I don't get what the big problem is," Vic says out of nowhere. "It's not like Ash isn't moving on with as many guys as possible. Ollie's allowed to have a boyfriend." The remaining two brothers glare at Vic, and Ollie's silverware clatters on his plate as it falls from his hands.

Max's eyes narrow. "Boyfriend? Really …"

Ollie ignores Max and instead stares at Vic. "Ash is doing what?"

"You have a *boyfriend*." Vic throws his arms up in the air in defeat.

"And that's why I'm the married twin." Nic slaps his brother over the back of his head. "Because this one doesn't understand shit about relationships."

Vic looks like he's going to defend himself, but then he gives up. "Yeah, okay, that's true. I just didn't think Ollie or Ash would care. Like, they're both living separate lives now."

Just because their relationship's over doesn't mean they're over it I want to say, but it's not my place.

And if anything, I totally see where the ex is coming from. Dating someone who's closeted? Not fun. I should know.

Max stands. "I knew I shouldn't have come here." He storms away.

In perfect timing, Ollie's salmon is delivered to the table, but as it's placed in front of him and his other plate is removed, all he does is stare at the new dish with no intention of eating it anymore. "I'm … I'm gonna go find Max."

He pushes away from the table and chases after his brother.

And when I think it's safe to keep eating my food, his mom needs to have her say.

"Ash, Ollie's ex, is Max's best friend. They grew up together, so Max is … defensive. We all thought they were going to get married, but with hockey and his unwillingness to come out—"

Unwillingness? Like he's being stubborn about it?

"While I appreciate you trying to explain to me, you don't need to. Like Ollie said, we're new, and I know the score. I'm well aware of the industry he's in."

I'm only in sports journalism, and the amount of shit I get from coworkers annoys the crap out of me. Like them saying I should be writing fashion instead of sports because, you know, the fashion and gay gene are one and the same. It's mainly said in jest, but they don't understand how it's insensitive and inappropriate—probably because they've never had to deal with being put in a box and told that's where they belong.

"But—"

"Ma!" Leo, the tall, lanky, basketball coach snaps. "Just … let it go, okay? You hover over Ollie's life enough as it is. Don't scare his new boyfriend away."

"She wasn't—" I start, but then I get more glimpses of the family Ollie was hiding from.

"You don't have to take on that tone," his dad says to Leo.

"I didn't mean anything by it, but come on—"

Nic and Vic join in, and the table is surrounded by so many strong Boston accents, I end up not knowing what the hell they're talking about.

I'm thankful when my phone vibrates in my pocket, and I don't even have to fake an incoming phone call. I don't hesitate when I see my editor's name on screen.

"Sorry, I have to take this," I say, but I don't think they can hear me.

I leave my laptop bag but make my way to a quieter corner of the restaurant. By the time I reach somewhere I can hear, Harry has hung up. But a few seconds later, a message pops up.

The Pat's IR list got updated. Get your ass to the stadium ASAP. They're holding a conference. They lost Johnson.

I quickly type back: *On my way.*

Their star quarterback, who was recruited to replace Marcus Talon at the beginning of the season, is on the injured reserve list. What the hell happened?

Part of me wonders if the coach is up to old tricks. He's known for updating the IR list close to games to throw off the opposing team's strategies. Still, it can't be ignored. If Johnson really is injured, that could mean the defending Super Bowl champs are done for the season.

Rushing back to the table, I grab my bag, and the bickering between the family members stops.

"Oh no, sweetie, you don't have to leave," Ollie's mom says.

"Thanks, but there's been an emergency at work, and I've got to go."

I'm not sure they believe me, but I can't stay to reassure them. Won't matter anyway because after the game I'm flying back to Chicago, where I live, and I'll never see the Strömbergs again.

I tell myself this is a clean break. I don't have to tell Ollie who I am, and I don't cover hockey, so I won't be running into him anytime soon. I don't know if this little charade has done him any favors or created more family drama, but I hope I've at least achieved them getting off his case about the ex. Or maybe with the way Max stormed out of here, we've made things worse.

"Uh, if I don't see Ollie on the way out, can you tell him work called? Thanks."

We say our quick goodbyes, and I make my way out of the private room. The Honey Bee is one of Boston's underground hangouts, and as I make my way upstairs, Max passes me the other way, "accidentally" bumping his shoulder with mine.

It's like I'm back in high school being picked on by everyone who was bigger than me, which was, well, everyone. I hit my growth spurt so late I thought I was going to stay five eight forever. The last few inches came a year too late—my freshman year of college.

Ollie appears at the top of the stairs. He smiles down at me and comes to meet me halfway in the middle of the stairwell. "I'm sorry about Max. He's … uh …"

"A dick? I figured that one out on my own. Thanks." Then I realize how harsh that sounds. "Sorry, I probably shouldn't say that about your brother."

"He's not that bad. He, uh, well, he's my ex's best friend. He's still mad over the breakup."

"It doesn't sound like it was your fault though. Situations like yours …"

"Well, it wasn't Ash's fault. He went back into the closet for me for four years."

My eyes widen. "*Four years*? That's like ten times the longest relationship I've ever had."

"I think that says more about you than me."

I laugh. "That's probably true. Like, really true."

"Were you looking for me, or—" Ollie's gaze goes to my bag.

"I got an emergency call from work, and I have to go."

His downcast hazel eyes make me want to quit my job, but I also can't be sure what I'm seeing is actual disappointment or if I'm hoping it is. Plus, in the past, I've been known to read into things, thanks to the Jefferson High football team for fucking with me and making social cues so much harder to trust.

The stairwell is narrow, so we're practically pushed up against each other, and I really wish I didn't have to go.

Stupid closeted jock magnet.

Ollie shuffles from one foot to the other, and he's so freaking adorable with his hands in his pockets. This giant, muscled hockey player is shy and a little bit awkward, and I can't help loving it.

I take a step closer, which makes him raise his head.

His brow scrunches. "What are you—"

"Shh. I'm seizing an opportunity." I don't know where my courage or the idea to do this comes from, because it's backfired so many times in the past, but I lean in and kiss his mouth gently. It's quick and chaste but well worth it. "Mmm, I've always wanted to kiss a jock. Lifelong fantasy. Guess I can cross that off my bucket list."

Technically, I've been there, done that, and have the scars to prove it, but maybe once I'd like for it not to end badly.

I wait for the situation to turn, but it doesn't.

Instead, Ollie looks left and right to make sure no one's coming and then steps closer. "Well, in that case, better make it worth it." He grabs me around my waist and brings me fully against him and then pushes his tongue into my mouth.

None of my teenage athlete fantasies live up to the reality of Ollie Strömberg running his hands up my back to cup my face and dive in deeper.

His tongue tangles with mine, and we stumble until Ollie's pushed against the handrail of the staircase.

It's hard to tell which one of us groans, but it breaks something in Ollie, and he pulls back, hitting his head against the wall.

"Damn, I wish things were different," he whispers. "I'd love to take you on an actual date."

"I live in Chicago."

Ollie pulls back. "What?"

"I'm only in town for a few days for work."

"Oh." That's definite disappointment I hear, and I shouldn't like it as much as I do.

"Besides, you're getting over your ex and can't come out

because of hockey, and I'm, well, me. I'd love to go on a date with you too, but that sounds like a whole lot of nope."

"About the hockey thing—"

"Yeah. About that." *Tell him who you are. Promise you won't print anything.* "You should probably know ..." *Don't tell him. Why ruin this and make him paranoid when you'll never see him again and you don't report on hockey anyway? Don't ruin your perfect kiss with reality.*

"Know what?"

"I won't tell anyone. I promise."

He lets out a relieved breath. "Thank you. You did me this huge favor today and put up with my family, and then I basically ask you to shut your mouth."

I lean in for another kiss: a slow, soft kiss. "I understand one hundred percent. Probably more than you know. I hope everything works out with your family. At least they won't be talking in your ear about Ash anymore, right?"

"Here's hoping."

"Sorry I couldn't stay." My phone vibrates again. "I have to go before I get fired." Or someone else beats me to the scoop.

As I get to the top of the stairs, Ollie calls out, "Wait ..."

When I turn, I hope he asks for my name, which I shouldn't give, or my phone number, which I really shouldn't give.

Instead, he puts his hands in his pockets and whispers, "How did you know? In the bathroom, I mean. How did you know I was gay?"

I smile wide. "Totally wishful thinking on my part."

I turn and leave before I do something we'll both regret, but that doesn't stop me from online stalking him as soon as I get home. Or from reading and watching his career highlights and games. Or from perhaps building an unhealthy obsession with a hockey player I'll never see again.

CHAPTER THREE

OLLIE

SIX MONTHS LATER

The Rainbow Beds benefit is packed with people, soft lighting, and loud music. It's not the first time I've been asked to attend something like this, but this particular fundraiser makes me antsy. Not because it's an LGBTQ charity, but because it's run by Matt Jackson's husband.

When I got here, I took a selfie outside and sent it to Ma with the caption. "I can be closeted and still support the community." Passive-aggressive, maybe, but I know it'll shut her up ... for like a week.

Matt's proof gay athletes can have it all, but I don't think I'm ready to deal with that. He announced his marriage the night he won the freaking Super Bowl.

Sports have been a certain way for so long that when I see other people living the life I thought I'd have one day, I can't help being bitter and somewhat intimidated by them. Not to mention jealous.

"You're, like, the worst closeted guy ever," my best friend says.

I'd laugh at Tommy if he didn't have a point. "Say it louder. I don't think the people in the back heard you."

"No one's hearing anything, drama queen."

I pretend to be offended, because Tommy's right. Everyone is standing at the other end of the bar—where all the servers are tending. We'll probably never get service at this end. "Did you call me a queen?"

He ignores me, like he always does when I fuck with him. "You're staring at every ass that walks by."

"Just because I can't eat at the restaurant doesn't mean I can't look at the menu." But God knows, I really, really, *really* miss sex. Like, really.

Tommy screws up his face. "I don't even want to think about what that means."

Ash once accused me of being too comfortable and that's why I refused to come out for him. I had my cake and got to eat it too. I argued with him constantly that if I wasn't with him, I'd be with no one because it was too risky, and while I've stuck to that, after a year of celibacy, I'm starting to see his point.

It might be getting to the time when I need to seriously consider coming out, but I can't right now. Not until I win the Cup.

Ash's voice rings through my head loud and clear. *Not right now. It's never right now. It's been* not right now *for years, Oliver, and I'm sick of waiting and holding my breath for the day where you realize I'm more important than your career.*

Even a year after our breakup, I continue to be haunted by our arguments. At least I'm no longer in the apartment filled with Ash's ghost thanks to being traded to New York two months ago.

"I'm still pissed you were traded, man," Tommy says as if

reading my mind. "I miss you. This season has totally sucked ass."

"And you think *I* say inappropriate things, yet you're talking about sucking asses."

Tommy sighs in that big-brotherly way that annoys me. He practically adopted me when I made it to the NHL after slugging it out for a few years on Boston's farm team. He treats me like the little brother he never had, and I treat him like my four brothers back home. *Like I need another one.*

"They did the right thing." The lie is thick on my tongue as I try to hide my bitterness over the trade, even months later. I hate that Boston traded me, but it's part of the game, so I have to suck it up.

The joys of a nonexistent no-trade clause in your contract.

According to the media, Boston got the better part of the deal by scoring Ilya Malik for their defense, but without me and Tommy together, their offense is struggling. We could sense each other on the ice almost as if we could read each other's minds. With us being torn apart, both our games are suffering, and he's right. It totally sucks.

It doesn't help that bloodsucking reporters like Lennon Hawkins write slanderous articles in reputable sports magazines that the only reason my stats were so good last year was because of Tommy.

What the hell kind of name is *Lennon*, anyway? It's probably an alias to hide behind so he can be candidly asshole-y about the fact he could never make it in sports.

I'd like to see you chase around a puck while wearing skates, asshole.

It wouldn't surprise me if I found out Lennon Hawkins is a washed-up has-been in the sporting world but probably in a sport like baseball or football. I've pretty much stalked the man online within an inch of breaching privacy laws, and up until recently, he only reported on football and baseball.

The reason for his switch hasn't been printed or publicized, but my guess is he got tired of terrorizing ballers and decided to switch to puck chasers. And for some reason, he's been on my ass from day one.

Tommy says I'm reading into it and to let it go—block the site and move on—but there's something about this reporter guy I don't like, and I can't put my finger on it.

In all my stalking, I couldn't find a photo. He's probably a fat balding dude who looks as bitter as his articles, and that's why the magazine won't post his picture.

"You're doing that thing with your face again," Tommy says.

"What thing?" I snap.

"Looking angry and sulking at the same time. Didn't know it was possible to look like a badass and a bitch, but here you are."

I cock my head. "Why am I friends with you again?"

"Are you thinking about those stupid articles for the billionth time?"

"No," I lie and know he doesn't believe me.

"That guy doesn't know what he's talking about, and don't make me go on and on about there being no *I* in *team*. Without you, I wouldn't have had the highest scoring stats last season. You set them up, I seal the deal. That's how it is … err, *was*."

"Exactly. It still wasn't good enough for the GM."

And I'm still convinced one of Lennon's articles had something to do with my trade. I've read over it so many times I could recite it if I had to, but there's one line I can't get out of my head:

Strömberg would thrive if he was in the encouraging environment he requires to grow into a player who doesn't need to hide behind a sniper.

It's as if that Lennon guy knows all my secrets and is teasing me with them. Tommy says I'm being paranoid, but I dunno … something about that article doesn't sit right with me. Not only does it call me out for being a mediocre player, saying I'm being overshadowed by Tommy and even implies I'm using Tommy's talents to my advantage, but it also points out I have a reason to hide from the limelight. A reason no one in the NHL knows apart from Tommy. And the only reason he knows at all is because he overheard me on the phone to Ash when we roomed together once. I was still in the AHL at the time but had been called up for a few games. All he had to say about it was "My brother-in-law has a boyfriend, so I'm cool with it." He promised to never tell a soul, and he never has.

"You know what you need?" Tommy says.

"Here we go."

"You should take some guy home tonight and do things to him that I don't want to hear about tomorrow."

"Brilliant idea. While I'm at it, I'll call a press conference and out myself to the entire world."

"There you go being all dramatic again. Aren't gay guys all about the anonymous hookup?"

"Stereotyping, for the win," I say.

Again, he ignores my snark. He truly is like one of my brothers. "Where better to find the perfect candidate than a gay and lesbian charity event?"

Well, there's Grindr for one … "I'm not ready."

"It's been a year since Ash—"

I grit my teeth. "Really? It's been a year? Had no idea." It's been three hundred forty-two days to be exact, but if I say that aloud, I'll never hear the end of it. And in those three hundred and forty-two days, I've only wanted one other man, and he disappeared without a trace and without giving me his phone number. Or real name for that matter.

"You need to move on," Tommy says. "Even if it's only a quick blowjob in a bathroom stall."

I'd give him a lecture about not every gay man being into casual sex, but I think that might go against the gay rule book. Thou shalt not let anyone know we can be monogamous, loving, and all we want is to find that one person who makes our whole world complete. Someone who doesn't throw ultimatums and guilt trips.

"I've seen it," Tommy says. "Your tension on the ice. You're hesitating. Your head's too in the game, and you need to turn your brain off for a while."

"That's the last thing I need. I need to focus more. The team is in a slump. The Dragons were on track to make the playoffs easily. Now … if we don't win against Toronto this week, we're out. It's like we still haven't gelled even though I've been with them for two months. It's not like you and me where we clicked right away."

Tommy leans against the bar. "Why do you think that is? Could it be that I knew your secret since before you were called up?"

For all I know, our bond does have something to do with my game. Tommy and I had trust. I've been playing for New York for only two months. I don't know the guys on my team well yet, and it shows.

"So, you're saying I should come out," I say. "At least to the team."

"At least to someone on your line. Hell, start small. Come out to Maddox or Damon."

Tommy is married to Maddox's sister, and Maddox happens to be my agent's boyfriend. The reason I met Damon was because of Tommy's connection to him.

"I know they're, like, your family, but it's weird hanging out with my agent. I'm scared I'm gonna say something or do something stupid in front of him. I need to be professional."

"Pfft, he works for you."

"Doesn't mean he won't drop me faster than you can say *power play* if I fuck up. Until I'm ready to make it public, Maddox and Damon aren't an option."

"Fine then—a complete stranger who doesn't know who you are or what you do. Maybe it's time to start taking those steps—"

I eye him suspiciously. "Have you been talking to my mother?"

He chuckles. "No, but I'm saying it could help your game."

"You should worry about your own game, old man. You're at seventy-five percent of the points you had at the same time last year."

Tommy ruffles my hair as if he finds my heckling cute instead of the wicked trash talk I'm trying for. "Just think about it."

We're finally served drinks, and I gulp mine down so fast I order another one straightaway before the bartender can run off again. My defenses are down for all of five seconds while I'm distracted with the bartender, and I can only blame myself for not anticipating Tommy's big brother antics.

Someone brushes by me, and next thing I know, Tommy hip-checks me into them.

"You're a dead man," I say through gritted teeth.

"What did you say?" a masculine voice says behind me.

Shit. I put on a smile and turn to face the poor guy Tommy's picked as some sort of target for me. "Sorry. My friend can be a bit—"

My words die when I come face to face with my blond Superman. Strong jaw, nerdy framed glasses that he didn't have in Boston and don't suit his pretty boy face but somehow make him look even better, and a chin dimple that could make anyone—man or woman—want to touch it. Or lick it.

With the glasses, he's no longer Superman but an actual Clark Kent. And that makes him hotter.

Huh, who knew I liked nerd kink?

Recognition sets in for him too. His mouth hangs open.

We both forget how to use our words. I suddenly can't remember how to talk, what I was saying, or what my name is.

Clark composes himself first. "A bit …"

"Uh …"

"Rough," Tommy says for me. "Sorry about that." He claps my shoulder. "This guy here can help you with getting a new drink."

It's only then I notice the beer dripping off the lapels of Clark's tux jacket. He fills out the royal blue suit perfectly with tight lines wrapped over an even tighter body. He's tall—well, still shorter than me, but most people are—and lean, and I try not to stare.

"My brother-in-law is waving me over, so I'm out," Tommy says.

He's totally lying. Maddox is at the other end of the bar talking with Matt, but I don't care. I practically shove him in their direction.

Before Tommy goes, he leans in to whisper in my ear. "At least make a friend, you loner." With a slap to the back of my head, Tommy walks off.

Clark watches Tommy leave. "Did he call you a loser?"

The tips of my ears burn, and I can only hope they're not bright red, but being a loser is probably less sad than being a loner. "Smack talk," I say, finally finding my voice. I shrug. "Hockey players."

"You both kind of look more like corporate businessmen."

I laugh and shake my head. "You. It's … *you*."

He points to his chest. "Clark. Did you forget your boyfriend's name?"

"Ooh, I didn't get the chance to tell you. We broke up. You cheated on me."

"Wow, I'm an asshole."

"Yeah. You are. Although in my mind, I walked in on you and that random guy and joined in, but I wasn't going to tell my family that part of the made-up story."

Clark groans. "Fucking tease."

"Drink? I'll replace the one Tommy spilled."

His lips quirk. "Sure. I'll let you buy me one."

"It's open bar."

"Even better. I'll buy you one."

I turn back, and of course, the bartender's at the other end again. "I think we're in the wrong spot. It's like the Bermuda Triangle for service. It took us forever to get this one." I hold up my glass. "What'll you have?"

"Scotch."

Without even thinking, I lean in and catch the scent of beer. Then I look down at his hand where his now almost-empty bottle is. "Pretty sure that's beer."

"Hockey players are smart, huh?"

"Dumb as doornails, really."

"At least you can be self-deprecating."

"Always an admirable trait," I say as serious as I can.

Clark lifts his bottle. "A friend gave this to me earlier when I arrived. Not a huge fan of beer, so I've been nursing it all night."

"Ah, so it's not a total loss that your suit drank more than you."

"Except now I have to pay to dry clean the rental." He

gestures to his wet chest, and I have to fight the urge to run my hand over it.

You're in public, which means kindergarten rules—hands to yourself.

I wish I'd remembered this rule six months ago, because God knows how many times I've jerked off thinking about this guy and that kiss we shared. Talking to him now, it doesn't feel like six months has passed—it's as if we've taken off from where we left it—but at the same time, it feels like I've been fantasizing about him forever.

And now he's here in front of me looking adorably wet and teasing me.

"Send the bill to the B's," I say. "Serves Tommy right for being a dick."

A passing bartender takes pity on us, and we quickly order two scotches.

After we're given new drinks, Clark turns to me. "So, what's hockey like to play? I wanted to talk to you about it that night, but … well, yeah, a lot of things didn't happen that night that I wanted."

The glint in his eye has me wanting to ask him to get out of here and do exactly what Tommy told me to—hook up and walk away—but I'm going to be good. Because I'm worried once wouldn't be enough with Clark. He's been vital in the moving-on process from Ash, and while I think I'm completely over my ex, I'm still not in a position to be with someone. I'll never be ready for that until I'm out, and I can't come out until my career is stable.

Right. Hockey. He asked a question about hockey.

"It's exhausting," I say. "But worth it."

"I bet the money helps."

"Is that another dig at the dry cleaning bill?" I keep my tone light, because I get the sense he's fucking with me. "Tickets to this place were what ... a thousand bucks a head? I think you can afford it."

"I, uh"—he takes a sip of scotch—"was given my ticket."

I cock my head. Tommy and I were given comped tickets too, but that's because Maddox and Damon wanted us to make an appearance as a favor to Matt and his husband. They needed big names attending as a selling point for other big names. It makes me wonder who this guy is to warrant a free invite.

"What do you actually do for a living? Because it's obvious you're not in corporate business."

He mumbles through another sip, as if he doesn't want to tell me.

I can barely hear him. "A rider?" *Do not make a "that sounds promising" joke.*

"*Writer*," he says more clearly.

"Oh, dear God, take my money," I joke. "You poor thing, you're probably starving. I can probably bribe a guy to give you a whole tray of appetizers too."

"I see you've inherited some of your dad's dry wit, but I do all right. I can manage a little dry cleaning."

I reach for some napkins over the bar. "Let's see if we can fix it."

My movements are as reflexive as slashing someone on the ice. I don't mean to do it, and I know I shouldn't, but for some reason, my hand does it anyway. I rub the stain forming on his suit, but it's no use. And then I realize I'm touching his chest. A really nice chest. Now my hand refuses to pull away, as if it knows it's touching greatness.

"S-sorry." I drop my hand as if his suit burns my skin, which is probably even more suspicious to anyone watching than touching him in the first place.

"Don't sweat it. It's not every day I have a hot guy's hands on me." The corners of his mouth tip up ever so slightly.

The quick response is on the tip of my tongue. "That can't be true. You're hot."

Fuck, I shouldn't be doing this.

Why the fuck not? a little voice says. I think it's coming from my dick.

Clark continues to stare blankly at me, as if he's having the same war going on in his head as I am, but when he opens his mouth and I expect him to say we should get out of here, that's not at all what comes out. "Ollie, I need you to know something. More specifically, I need you to know my real name."

"Okaaay." I drag out the word, confused by what his name has to do with anything.

His eyes widen as a hand lands on my shoulder.

"Great, you two have met," my agent, Damon, says next to me.

"Beetle!" Matt Jackson's husband says and crash-tackles Clark into a hug.

Beetle? What type of name is Beetle?

"We were supposed to meet?" I manage to ask.

"Ollie, this is Lennon Hawkins," Damon says. "He's a friend and works for *Sporting Health Magazine*."

My head spins, all the blood drains from my face, and I barely hear anything past Lennon's name.

Lennon. Fucking. Hawkins.

Suddenly, I know why I had issues with those articles. The reason it seemed like they knew my secret is because the person behind them *does.*

"*You?* You wrote those articles about me?"

I'm so pucked.

CHAPTER FOUR

LENNON

My palms sweat. This wasn't how this was supposed to go. I feel like I'm back in high school, surrounded by jocks who wanna pick on the gay kid. Only this time, it's not because I'm gay. It's because I'm—

"A reporter," Ollie says, his jaw tight. "You're a reporter."

"Not the kind you're thinking," Damon says. "He's a decent one."

The flirty guy I've been talking to is replaced with an angry bear of a hockey player. "Decent? Lennon Hawkins thinks I'm a talentless pigeon."

What the fuck? "Whoa, I did not write that."

Ollie pales even more. "R-reporter," he whispers, no doubt realizing someone in the media knows his biggest secret.

I wonder if he's doing what I've been doing ever since he bumped into me—remembering what his mouth tastes like. His strong hands, hard body … *Focus, Lennon!*

"I work for *Sporting Health*," I emphasize. "We're not a tabloid." *I will not out you* I want to say but can't with Damon and Noah here.

Ollie shakes his head, abandons his drink, and walks away before I get a chance to explain. Damon calls after him, but Ollie's massive body doesn't slow down.

I've been preparing for this meeting ever since my editor reassigned me to hockey after I started writing articles about Ollie. The past six months have been a whirlwind, and I never meant for this to happen. I wrote the first article on a whim, because I found myself going home every night and watching old clips of Ollie's games. He has so much fucking talent it'd make any sports fanatic cry to see how amazing he is on the ice. But that's the thing; no one was seeing it, because Tommy Novak's star shines too bright.

My articles on him got a lot of hits, more than any article the regular hockey guy had written recently, so as easy as that, Harry gave me the Eastern Conference to cover while Kevin got moved aside. He's still covering the Western Conference, but he's about as happy with the move as I was. I had little say in being transferred from baseball and football. That's how my industry works. Shit pay, unstable jobs, and cutthroat coworkers who'll steal your job if you drop the proverbial ball. Not that I meant to be cutthroat. I wrote an article, saved it in the work cloud thinking I could maybe pitch it to my editor or shop it around to other magazines for freelance pay, and then the next day, I had a phone call from Harry asking why I'd never expressed my interest in covering hockey before.

Because I'd never had a hockey player's tongue down my throat before.

Now my editor has sent me to follow the Dragons' journey to the playoffs.

I'd totally blame this run-in on fate being an asshole—I was never supposed to see Ollie again—but I can't really do that. I'm the one who wrote that article because I couldn't help stalking him and his career.

If anything, I should call myself an asshole for putting us both in this situation.

I thought I'd have a few more days before I'd need to explain, though. I was ready to meet him at the arena and tell him the deal and reassure him. In private. Running into him here, and then the way his face lit up when he saw me, I couldn't bring myself to do it. Not right away. I wanted that spark, that connection we had six months ago, to last a little bit longer.

Now, I can't do anything but watch him leave. A part of me says to run after him, but angry jocks were a nightmare to navigate back in high school and college, and I think it's scarred me from ever trying to rationalize with a raging meathead.

"You think Ollie's a talentless pigeon?" Damon asks.

My gaze breaks away from Ollie's retreating ass and meets the gaze of another raging meathead, albeit a retired jock.

"You wrote that? Not cool," Noah says. "Wait, what's a pigeon?"

Damon continues to glare at me. "Someone who isn't good enough to score goals on his own and takes advantage of their teammate's skill."

"I did not say that," I argue.

I never said he was talentless. If anything, he has enough talent to be huge. While his stats are impressive, he could be one of the biggest contenders in the league.

"If we want to get technical, I said a trade would be beneficial for him so he could get out of Boston because his talent was being overshadowed by Novak. I thought hockey players had thick skin?"

Damon sighs. "Nah, just thick skulls. I'll go talk to him."

Noah remains with a knowing look on his face. "You didn't tell him who you were, did you?"

I adjust my glasses, which don't need adjusting, and don't answer. I usually wear contacts, but I ran out and haven't had a chance to order more since coming to New York, so I'm all self-conscious about being my nerdy self again.

"You'd think you would've learned your lesson after me," Noah says. "I would've kicked your ass if Damon let me."

When I met Noah in a bar, I hit on him and tried to get a scoop about his now husband. It backfired, but it's how we became friends.

"I won't print anything he said," I reassure Noah.

"I know that, but Ollie won't. He's probably freaking out right now. What did he say to make him run out of here?"

I sip my drink. "Nothing, really." Except, you know, outed himself to me and didn't know I was a reporter. "Hockey is exhausting is probably the worst thing he said. No one would care about that."

Noah's eyes narrow, and I wonder if he knows I'm lying.

"How're things in Chicago?" I ask, changing the subject.

Noah knows it but placates me anyway. "Windy."

"I miss it already."

I could be in New York for a few months if the Dragons make the playoffs. They're only one win away from cinching their spot, and if they manage to do it, I'll be following them to each of their games. I think my boss is hoping for a Cinderella ending—the underdog story of the year. However, from my research, I've learned the Dragons are known for cracking under pressure, so I'm not entirely sure my stay in New York will be long.

"While you're here, I can hook you up with Matt's brother," Noah says. "He'll be able to get you into clubs and all that shit. I'd do it myself, but Matt and I are going on a much-needed vacation next week."

"Sounds great." Totally lying. I'd rather stab my eyes out with a pen. I'm not the clubbing type. Nothing is a faster boner killer for guys than me doing the robot.

"Where are you staying?" Noah asks.

"The cheapest hotel the magazine could find. It's above a Chinese restaurant, somehow smells like Indian food, and it still costs a fortune."

We have a budget for travel expenses, but I'm still paying out of pocket. The only other option was to stay in Jersey, and I didn't want to do that commute.

"You should come stay at our place. Save the magazine some money. I doubt Jet would mind having a roommate while we're gone."

"You do realize I could be here until the end of the hockey playoffs, right? That's three months."

He grabs my shoulder. "After what you did for us, we owe you."

Did for them? All I did was keep my word that I wouldn't print anything about his and Matt's personal problems. I don't want to be that kind of reporter.

"Are you sure?" I ask.

"Come by whenever."

"Thanks. I might take you up on that. I'm paid up until the end of the week, but after that, I'm all yours."

"Done," Noah says. "And one last question. You're not going to torment Ollie, are you? I haven't seen a guy run away from someone faster."

"No. I'll apologize for not telling him who I was. Hopefully, start over."

"Are you going to apologize for writing all that pigeon stuff? You say you didn't mean it offensively, but it's pretty clear he took offense."

"I still maintain my article was favorable."

"You're so fucked," Noah says. "You haven't been around professional athletes much, have you?"

Well, no, I haven't. I'm usually in the press box at games and in the pit at press conferences. Mass interviews, mass answers, and nothing personal. I'm never given the opportunity to ask a question. There are bigger magazines and outlets that get priority. Like *Sports Illustrated* and *Fox Sports*.

"Just because you're married to one doesn't make you an expert," I say.

"I've spent time with Matt's entire team. Trust me, there are more egos and diva attitudes in the NFL than on *RuPaul's Drag Race*. Have fun with that." He walks away, but I call after him.

"Hockey players aren't like football players though."

I screwed up, and I need to explain, but Ollie will take it okay, right?

All I get is a laugh in return.

Shit.

Noah may have a point. As I wait by the player's entry at the Dragons arena, I get more glares than smiles. It's no doubt because of my press pass. Or maybe they're wondering why I'm not with the rest of the "vultures" who are here to report on the morning skate. The team plays Toronto tomorrow night, and if they win, they're going to the playoffs, which will be the first time they've made it in the past five years.

I'm supposed to write an article today on who looks hungry on the ice, who's going to kill it, and who's going to choke.

The only way I'll be able to write the article is if Ollie doesn't kill *me*. And with the way he stalls in his tracks with a murderous glare as he sees me, I think killing me might be high on his list of priorities.

"Can we talk?" I ask.

"I don't talk to reporters." Even though he looks forlorn, he pushes past me with angry steps.

I chase after him, the slick floor beneath my feet making squeaky noises from my dress shoes. "Are you sure that's how you want to play it?"

Shit, that came out as a threat.

Way to go, Lennon.

Ollie spins on his heel, and his meaty hand grabs my upper arm. He pushes me down the corridor, his grip getting tighter with each step.

My stomach does a stupid fluttery thing at his touch—even if it is rough. "You do realize I'm the one who wanted to talk, right? You don't have to drag me. Not that I mind the manhandling ..."

Wrong thing to say.

He shoves me into the room where press conferences are held after games and closes the door behind him. In his defense, he probably didn't use a lot of force to push me, but he needs to be more careful with those guns of his.

His gear bag drops to the ground, and he stalks toward me.

Ollie's intimidating with his size and large biceps, his short-sleeved T-shirt showing those sexy-as-fuck arms covered in tats. I want to run my tongue over them while my hands weave through his ash-blond hair, which always looks wet. With sweat, with gel, I don't know, but I also don't care, because damn, he's hot.

What is wrong with me? He looks like he wants to kill me, and here I am wondering what he tastes like?

"What do you want?" he asks through gritted teeth.

"Right now?" I croak. Does he know I'm thinking about licking him?

"Money? Paying me the courtesy of warning me before publicly outing me? What? Why are you here?"

Right. No thinking about licking the hockey god.

"I'm covering the Dragons for the playoffs." I'm proud any sound comes out at all.

An undignified grunt falls from Ollie's mouth. "Of course, you are."

"And I want to let you know I won't say anything. Or print anything. About any of it. I want to support gay men in sports. Not ruin them."

He looks confused for a second. "So, you're not here for money?"

My eyes narrow. "Don't you think if I was going to bribe you I would've done it by now?"

Ollie shrugs. "Maybe you ran out of money or lost your job or are desperate, I don't know. All I know is a piece of shit article is written about me, and then I'm traded, and this uppity, pompous reporter won't leave me or my career alone. Then it turns out that reporter is *you*. You've been making money off me for months, so maybe you're getting greedy now."

He has a right to be pissed, but that still doesn't stop irrationality making me mouth off over my articles.

"My articles are not shit. They've all said you have potential."

"You said I was hiding behind Tommy. And you're the one person outside my family, Ash, and Tommy who knows I'm …"

The guy I met six months ago didn't hesitate in saying he's gay. This guy? He's the angry jock I expected him to be when I found out who he was, so I don't know why I'm disappointed.

"Can you even say the word?" I say and then tell myself to shut up. Taunting him isn't a good idea.

His demeanor might be casual, but the vein in his forehead and the quick pulse in his thick neck says he's freaking out on the inside. "Gay, gay, gay, gay, gay. You should know from when we met I have no issues saying it or accepting it. It's the world who has an issue with who I am, not me."

"And I want to ease your mind. I don't want to make my career that way, and I'm not about to out someone. It's up to them when they take that step."

He doesn't lose his cold composure. "Good to know you won't sell out to get ahead."

"Why are you still pissed? I don't have to keep quiet about anything, but I am." God, that came out wrong too.

Learn how to talk to an angry hot guy, Lennon, for fuck's sake.

"Just don't understand why they'd put someone on the play-offs who doesn't know shit about hockey."

I pull back. "What did I write that was so wrong?" Does he know how much time I spent writing about him?

I thought he'd be more pissed about the possibility of being outed than about a few online posts saying he has the potential to be a star but was being squashed playing for Boston. "I never said you were talentless."

"*Strömberg would thrive if he was in the encouraging environment he requires to grow into a player who doesn't need to hide behind a sniper.*"

I try not to smile, but it breaks free. "You memorized my article?"

"We're done here." He stalks toward the exit, and I can't help being entranced by the way his bulky frame crosses the room. Hockey players tend to have this amazing ability to be graceful even though they're over two hundred pounds and mow people down for a living.

With one more glare thrown my way, he picks up his bag and leaves, the door shutting with a resounding click.

"Could've gone worse," I reassure myself.

I knew he wasn't going to be happy when he found out who I was, but I fear it has killed any chance I had to ever see the Ollie I met six months ago.

CHAPTER FIVE

OLLIE

When I hit the corridor, I take a deep breath. It doesn't help me calm down. Storming into the locker room, I throw my bag in my cubby with more force than probably necessary. I don't know if there's a way to undress aggressively, but I'm mastering it.

"Whoa, who fucked your sister?" Bjorn asks. He's a D-man and the size of a grizzly.

"What?" I snap.

"Only time I've been that pissed off is when I found out the captain of the football team in high school was sticking it to my sister."

I start gearing up, and my tension eases a little at Bjorn's unintentional distraction. "What'd you do to the poor guy?"

"Hockey player versus football player? The guy doesn't have any teeth."

"Ironically, like a lot of hockey players."

"Exactly," Bjorn says. "So, who fucked your sister?"

I huff. "Don't have a sister. Only brothers. And I don't care who fucks them."

"Then what's up your ass?"

Nice wording, Bjorn. Bet he wouldn't be saying that if he knew the truth, because he wouldn't want to know the answer. Cocks. Lots and lots of cocks. Okay, so one cock. And not anymore since the guy it was attached to walked out on me, but that's not the point.

"Journalists." I pull on my shin guards and tighten them a little too hard, because distraction time is over, and I'm still mad.

"Aww, is the pressure too much?"

The reminder that I was on a team that actually made the play-offs last year is on the tip of my tongue, but that won't go over well. It'll also only be a reminder that they traded me.

"I can handle the pressure," I say. What I can't handle is the only guy I've been interested in since Ash is Lennon Hawkins. When that first article came out, I hated that this guy who didn't even know me could see right through me.

Finding out "Clark" is the one who really wrote it crushed me, because it suddenly wasn't some random guy who had a hunch I was hiding something. It was a guy who *knew* it to be true, but he ran the article anyway.

At least he didn't out you.

I have to keep reminding myself of that, because I should be thankful, not pissed.

"It's that Hawkins guy I can't handle," I say.

"Because he's a fag? Didn't picture you for one of those phobes."

I drop one of my skates and have to scramble to pick it back up to pretend his words didn't affect me. Or confuse the fuck out of me. He accuses me of being a homophobe while using a slur? It's not the first time derogatory terms have been thrown around a locker room. Won't be the last. But it's in the casual way he says it—with no anger or malice, like the world is supposed to talk like that without repercussions, that gets to me.

"He called me a pigeon," I say, trying to squash the part of me that was raised by a strong opinionated woman who'd rip into anyone who talked like that—locker room or not.

"Ouch. But look on the bright side: he didn't fuck your sister."

"I said I don't have a—"

Bjorn's gone before I get the sentence out—geared up and stalking out the locker room.

I shake my head. Tommy wonders why I haven't clicked with my teammates yet. I've been here for months but haven't made friends. I've been thrown in the deep end, and I feel like the new kid at school. My game is suffering because of it; I know that. Maybe Tommy makes a point when he says I don't trust anyone on the team because I can't be one hundred percent honest with them.

I've faced off with many of these guys in the past, but that's business. And skating with them, I do feel the connection there sometimes—like we get each other—but then the next minute, I'll expect someone to be where I want them to be on the ice, and they're somewhere completely different. I don't know how to be me and build trust with these people or how to force teamwork that's not flowing.

We're lucky we have a shot at the playoffs at all with some of the mistakes we've made.

Kessler, the right-winger on my line, turns to me. "Ignore Bjorn. He doesn't have that thing in his brain that stops him from spouting shit."

"Or using colorful language, obviously." I continue to get ready but avoid eye contact while I wait for Kessler's reaction. Let's see if we can be oh for two on the gay-friendly scale.

"Uh … yeah. I promise not all of us are dicks."

I nod. "Good to know."

"But you'd know that if you came out for a drink with us every now and then. Just sayin'."

"I was just thinking the same thing," I say.

Kessler smiles. "We should get out there."

I finish gearing up and grab my hockey stick and helmet. "Did Coach say what we were doing today?"

"Penalty drills."

I groan.

"My sentiments exactly," Kessler says, and I follow him down the chute and out to the rink.

As soon as my skates hit the ice and I start warming up, I feel eyes burning into me. Without needing to search the press area, I know Lennon's tracking me with his gaze, but when I turn to scowl at him, he's talking to the guy beside him.

Must be wishful thinking then ...

I tell my conscience to fuck off.

The more I think about the benefit, the angrier I get and the more aggressive I become. Clark was this perfect guy, and it's disappointing to find out the reality is a lot less appealing. Not that he looks any less appealing. He's like a poison apple from all those fairy tales. Pretty on the outside but can destroy me if I take a bite.

The team's been on the ice for about an hour when Kessler passes me the puck, and I charge past the blue line, but Bjorn is right there.

He slashes my ankle, but the coaches miss it. Which pisses me off even more. They don't miss me illegally body-checking him though.

A loud whistle blows.

Of course.

"Strömberg! You're already a man down and you're pulling this shit? Get your head out of your ass and in the game."

"Yes, Coach," I say, breathlessly.

"You fucked your line."

Sounds fun. I keep that tidbit to myself.

Coach throws his hands up and yells, "Change it up."

I skate my way to the bench, and this time when my eyes lock with Lennon, he's staring right at me. It's impossible to decipher his expression. It almost looks sympathetic, but that can't be right. I can already see the article about Ollie Strömberg crumbling under the pressure and making stupid mistakes in practice.

I'm already on edge without him being here making it worse, yet I still find myself drawn to him.

Ugh.

"Strömberg!"

Fuck, I zoned out, and I realize more than a few minutes have passed. I jump over the rail and get back into the drill, but my head's not in it. If I'm honest with myself, my head hasn't been in the game since the trade.

I'm in a rut, and I don't know how to pull myself out of it.

In the middle of a play, music blasts through the speakers of the arena with Pat Benatar's "Hit Me with Your Best Shot." It's followed by a round of expletives that echo around the rink.

We all stop on the ice and stare up at the DJ booth.

At my last meeting with Damon, he asked if I knew of any jobs available at the arena. Matt Jackson's brother needed work, and it happened to work out that our game DJ had resigned, so I put Jet's name forward. He got the job, but listening to him scrambling to turn the music off while swearing his heart out in a thick drawl, I'm beginning to wonder how he made it through the interview.

It's the last straw for the coaches, and they give up. "You're skating like newborn foals out there. You think that's gonna get us to the playoffs?"

"He's great with the pep talk, ain't he?" Kessler says beside me.

"Can baby horses even skate?" I ask, and Kessler tries to hide a laugh.

"Get off my ice," Coach says. "And Strömberg, come to my office when you're showered."

A chorus of "Oooh" and "Someone's in trouble" rumbles through the arena until Coach yells at everyone to cut the shit.

All I can think is I'm about to be sent back down to the AHL.

I perch on the edge of the seat in Coach's office—as much as my big frame allows me to anyway.

"Is there anything going on that we need to discuss? A problem with anyone on the team …" Coach starts.

I sit up straighter. "What? No. Nothing like that's going on."

He leans back in his chair. "Something's gotten in your head. I thought when you first came to us that the trade might've messed you up a bit, but there's something still missing out there."

Where to start. It's the trade, it's my sexuality, it's wondering if giving up my relationship with Ash was worth it, it's Lennon's articles, it's … everything.

"We fought hard to get you, because you're one of the best wingers in the league. Or, you could be if you'd drop your hesitance out there. Boston didn't want to let you go. We knew how desperate they were for Malik, and we wanted the best in return."

"Should've tried for Novak, then," I mumble.

"So, you're saying your stats are only because of Tommy Novak?"

"No," I say way too quickly. Admitting that would be like saying Lennon's article made good points. "Tommy and I made a great team is all, and I still don't know any of the guys here yet, but I promise to make more of an effort. Kessler said something about hanging out or whatever. I'll push harder, I'll—"

Coach holds up his hand. "Your position's not in danger. I asked you in here to see if there's anything I can do to help if something's going on, because you're not the same kid on the ice here that you were in Boston."

He's right, and I know I need to up my game.

"I'll find a way to do better."

Coach nods. "Go on, get out of here."

Defeated and pissed off—at myself mostly, but my brain still wants to blame Lennon for some reason—I leave his office only to be assaulted by more swearing through the arena speakers.

Sounds like Jet's having as a good a day as I am.

Instead of heading for the exit, I take the stairs up to where the DJ booth is, because having someone like Jet and his brother on my side will be a good thing in the long run.

Jet was on stage at the benefit, but the difference in his appearance as he opens the door is astounding. The guy on stage wore tight, ripped jeans, heavy guyliner, and an old T-shirt. His shaggy hair was slicked in the front but messy in the back, like a mini Russel Brand, but right now, it's loose and wild around his face and neck, there's no makeup, and he's in black slacks and a Dragons sweater vest. After seeing him glammed up, he kinda looks ridiculous.

"Hey. Jet, right?"

He stares at me, wide-eyed and flustered.

"You're ... you're Oll—" Recognition dawns on his face. "Thank fuck. I thought management was on their way up here to rip me a new one."

I stifle a laugh as I step past him. On the dashboard of his equipment is a bright red light labeled *mic*. I point to the button and switch it off.

Jet's face falls, and his skin turns ashen. "Oh fuck, I'm so fired."

"Don't worry, in Gordie Howe's own words, 'Hockey players are bilingual. They know English and profanity.' It's nothing no one here hasn't heard a million times before, and the offices are generally empty at this time. But, uh, you might not want to do that during the game tomorrow."

Jet slumps and falls back into his chair. "I'm in way over my head."

"You know, when I asked Damon if you knew how to DJ, he gave me the impression you did."

"I'm a musician. Apparently, Damon doesn't know the difference. But I need this job. I can't go back to being a server or I run the serious risk of breaking plates over rude assholes' heads."

"Damon warned me you can be blunt."

He also said I'd like this guy, and I think he's right.

"If it makes you feel any better, I know what you mean," I say. "I bussed tables throughout high school." I make my way over to the computer and pull up a spare chair. "I guess we should start with the basics."

"Do you know how to do this, or will it be like the blind leading the blind?"

"First year playing for Providence, I took a hard fall and got a concussion. Each game, I snuck into the DJ booth to watch. I was supposed to stay away for at least two weeks, but something you need to know about me is I live and breathe hockey. The arena DJ let me play with the controls."

I was also half-convinced at the time my career was over, so I might have been melodramatic in needing to learn a new skill. I won't mention that aloud though.

"If you help me fake my way through my first game tomorrow, I'll blow you."

I try to cover my uncomfortableness with an easy smile. "There's that being blunt thing again."

Jet winks. "Don't worry. I freak my brother's teammates out with that too. Messing with straight guys is fun."

The way he eyes me, I sense he's testing me in some way, or maybe I'm being paranoid.

"Right. And you're, like, a baby. Way too young for me."

He cocks his head. "Interesting. I assumed you would've been more concerned that I had way too much penis for you …"

It's my turn to break into laughter. "Your reputation precedes itself, *JJ*."

"Ugh. You've been talking to my brother, haven't you?"

"He might've called to thank me for getting you a job here."

Matt warned me not to call Jet JJ, but Jet offered to blow me to fuck with me. I'd say we're even.

"Do you know *anything* about DJing a hockey game?" I ask.

He stares at me blankly.

"Anything at all?"

"Well, I know this button"—he points to the red switch I flipped off—"turns on the mic to the arena."

"Play transitions, motivating the home crowd with song choice, dissing the opposing team—"

"I have to pay attention to the *game*?"

I don't know whether to laugh or cry, and the way he smirks, I get the feeling he's still messing with me.

Today's going to be a long day.

X

I try to drown out the noise of the crowd, but they can smell victory. All I can smell is sweat. Any hockey player who waxes poetic about the smell of the ice is lying his ass off. By the third period, the air is filled with the stench of pads soaked in perspiration.

As I take to the ice for a line change, my skates hit the ice with a satisfying thump before I take off at lightning speed.

We may all be exhausted and running on fumes, but this is my favorite part of the game. The fight to stay in this drives me.

We're one up, and there's a minute left on the clock.

But I know better than to start celebrating early, because everything can change in the blink of an eye.

As if thinking that jinxes the team, Logan—one of our D-men —takes a stupid penalty. Fucking idiot.

Toronto takes the power play as their opening, and flashbacks of practice have me on edge and cursing expletives that hockey players are known for.

The gasps of the crowd are ignored, and my only focus is on preventing the five Toronto players storming us from getting past the blue line.

That lasts about one point six seconds. I'm mowed down by a D-man, Kessler's thrown against the boards, and I see our chance at the playoffs melt away faster than the ice under my blades.

The lamp lights up, and my heart leaps in two different directions—into my throat and to the pit of my stomach.

It's all tied up now, and our time is running out.

The home fans protest while the Toronto players celebrate. The anger of the crowd falls into a void when Toronto gets the puck again.

Winning this is still an option, but we're too busy trying not to lose this thing to come up with offensive strategies. We're still one man down and overworking defense.

My teammates' defeat is what the Dragons are known for. The team is utterly dejected, exhausted, and cracking under the pressure. I hate that it's happening this late in the game. We *had* it.

I skate my damn legs off with nothing but determination on turning this around. While the others are trying to clear the puck out of our zone, I'm busy trying to get the puck back in our possession.

In my head, the interception happens flawlessly and in slow time. It'll be on highlight reels for years to come with a heroic soundtrack behind it. In reality, it's a messy dive for the puck, and I'm lucky I stay upright on my skates. But the important part is I pull it off.

Everyone in the arena gets to their feet, and the noise becomes deafening, but I can mostly tune it out.

I fly down the ice with Canada on my heels and cross the blue line.

The anticipation building in the crowd is palpable in my veins. This is what I live for.

But when I turn to pass the puck, Kessler and Martinez aren't where they're supposed to be. If Tommy was on the ice with me, it would've been a done deal. I have no choice but to take a shot on goal, and my heart deflates even more when it lands right into the goalie's glove.

The period ends with a loud buzzer, and this shit is going into overtime.

I need a fucking drink. Or a blowjob.

Coach claps my back as we head down the chute into the locker room. "Good hustle."

That's all the words of inspiration we get. The rest of the break is filled with different renditions of "What the fuck happened out there?"

As bitter as I am and can't stop thinking this wouldn't have happened had I been playing for Boston, I need to stop thinking about my old team. This is my team now, and this is our fight.

"This isn't the end," I murmur more to myself than anyone else.

Kessler holds his glove out for a fist pump. "Let's get out there and finish this thing."

When we head back to the bench, my eyes catch on the giant screen. The camera's focused on me, but I don't recognize myself at first. All I see is a bloodthirsty hockey player.

It still surprises me sometimes that this is my life. Everything I've sacrificed, everything my family believes I've missed out on, comes down to this and the way this game gives me a high nothing else ever has.

With only five extra minutes to lock this down, both teams scramble to get one in the net. Kessler and I are eager for our turn, and as Coach calls for a line change, we both hit the ice and take charge.

Kessler, in an aggressive—but totally legal—move, strips Toronto of the puck and plows down any D-man who gets in his way as his skates propel him across the ice. I keep up, and for the first time since joining the team, I feel truly in sync with a teammate. Kessler's footwork is mesmerizing, his puck handling skills are something to admire, and as we approach, Kessler dekes the goalie and sets up the perfect play for me to put one in the net.

It's not lost on me that it's usually the other way around. I'm used to being a playmaker, setting them up for my teammates to score, but tonight is my night, and this is my chance to prove myself to certain journalists that I have the talent to be here.

Kessler passes to me, I slap a wrist shot into the left back corner of the net, the puck sails past the goalie, the lamp lights up, and we take home the victory.

We just won the whole fucking game.

CHAPTER SIX

LENNON

I spend most of the press conference ogling a triumphant and relaxed Ollie. I can only imagine the type of high he's on right now after scoring the winning goal. His smile has the ability to break hearts and light up the goddamn room, and if I could, I'd write an entire article on how pretty he is when he's not scowling.

Somehow, I don't think Ollie or my editor would be okay with that.

I type out the game recap, send it off to my editor, and then make my way out of the stadium to meet Jet and head home. We're almost the last ones to leave the building by the time I've finished.

"Everyone's gone to a bar a few blocks away if you're up for it," he says.

"Like … with the team?"

"Yeah. They're in the playoffs. *Everyone* is going."

I adjust my laptop bag on my shoulder. "You go on. I'll catch a cab home."

"Nuh-uh. I might've pretended to give you a choice right now, but it was an empty gesture. We're going."

"Why?" I'm not a joiner. Never have been. Might have something to do with never being asked to join when I was a kid. I got used to being on my own.

"Because it's a bar full of meatheads. You need to be my gay buffer in case they try to suck me in with their hetero-ness."

I sigh. "One drink."

"Three."

"Two?"

"Four."

I purse my lips. "I don't think you realize how this negotiating thing goes."

"Okay, fine. We'll stay for five drinks." Jet holds my hand and drags me down the street, and my lazy feet stumble after him.

When Noah told me Jet was Matt's little brother, I expected a mini, younger, broody Matt. Turns out, he's an adorable twink with attention deficit disorder.

The sports bar is crammed to the max and smells like fried food, beer, and bad decisions. The bar area has a line as long as the entire NHL roster, and there's barely room to move, but Jet holds my hand again and pulls me farther into the club.

The setup is not like a normal nightclub but not an average sports bar either.

Loud and happy cheers roar through the small space, and it's all coming from the back where the team is. Half of them already have their ties either loosened or off, post-game suit jackets are hanging over chairs or on the floor, and they're rowdier than your average sober man.

My gaze spots Ollie as soon as we get closer, and I can't help wondering if it's the win or the alcohol that's lighting up his face like that. Or maybe it's that he's not looking at me.

While the suit he wears is no tux like the night of the benefit, he looks just as hot. Fuck it, he looks hot in everything, even the casual jeans and T-shirt he wore the first night I met him.

He's still mad at you, I remind myself.

Ollie's teammates surround him, handing him a fresh drink as soon as he's finished with the one in his hand.

Before we can reach the players, we hit a wall of women hoping to vie for a hockey player's attention. We can't seem to get around them, so we stand awkwardly waiting for them to move.

Jet leans into me. "I feel like my eyes are too young to see this much skin. I'm impressionable, damn it."

"If they were guys, you wouldn't be complaining."

"Fucking duh."

We push our way through, still holding hands so we don't lose each other, and we finally make it to where the rest of the Dragons' staff and team are.

Ollie catches sight of me, and he immediately frowns. Then he glances at Jet's and my hands together, and the glare deepens.

I use my free hand to give him a casual two-finger salute, and he cocks his head as if he can't tell if I'm genuinely waving hello or mocking him. It's hard for me to tell, so he has no hope.

Jet leads me in the opposite direction than Ollie, to two women sitting on couches along the back wall. I recognize one as the team's PR and media person.

"Ava, right?" I say loudly and shake her hand when she offers it.

"Lennon Hawkins. *Sporting Health Magazine,*" she says.

"Impressive."

"I read your articles about one of my players."

I try not to roll my eyes. "I think my reputation is getting blown way out of proportion. Let me guess. That player would be Ollie Strömberg."

"Ollie and Lennon have Taylor Swift levels of bad blood," Jet says.

"What would you know about it?" I ask.

"Noah told me. And you're both idiots."

"Most men are," the other woman says and introduces herself as Camille—the GM's assistant. After we shake hands, I turn back to Jet.

"What do you mean, we're both idiots? Ollie's the one who's mad at me because he can't handle criticism."

Before he can answer, a loud crash of glass hitting the floor sounds from the players' table, and there are screams from some girls and laughter from the guys.

"You're not going to report on all this, are you?" Ava gestures to the messy state the team is already in.

I throw my hands up in defeat. "Off the record. Promise. I'm only here because of my roommate."

Jet raises his hand. "That would be me. He wanted to go home, but I convinced him to stay for at least five drinks."

"Two."

"Okay, seven."

I'm learning really fast that negotiating with Jet is pointless. "Guess we better get started on them then."

The burn of staring follows me to the line at the bar, and I know exactly where it's coming from. Ollie's gaze is locked on me, as if trying to kill me with the Force. I'm tempted to fake choke, but I don't want to make a fool of myself when no one will understand what I'm doing. This crowd doesn't seem like the *Star Wars* type.

A teammate gives him another drink, but he still doesn't take his eyes off me even as he sips the dark liquid. The man of the hour, the hero of the night, doesn't have to wait in line for drinks like us nerds.

He finally breaks our stare off when a girl in a short tank top and even shorter skirt approaches him. The smile that finds his face makes me hate her. He smiled like that at me only a few nights ago, before he knew who I was, and now I've never hated being Lennon Hawkins more. Which is saying something considering it sucked being me as a teenager.

Why does this guy get to me? Because he reminds me of all those asshole jocks who I couldn't help but want in high school and college? Because for a split second, I thought I had a chance?

He puts his arm around the puck bunny, and her face glows as if she won the freaking lottery.

Wrong tree, precious.

The girl on Ollie's arm steps even closer to him, and I grit my teeth. Someone pushes me from behind, and I realize there's a gap at the bar in front of me.

I mindlessly order two glasses of scotch and make my way back to Jet. Ava and Camille excuse themselves to go to the bathroom, and Jet stares at me with young, hopeful eyes as he reaches for the second drink.

"Shit … how old are you again?" I ask.

"Twenty-one."

I eye him warily.

"Ish."

I hesitate but relent. "Don't tell your brother. Matt could snap me in half with one hand."

"I'm a grown-up."

"You know who never has to point out they're an adult? *Actual* adults."

Jet playfully shoves me, and I laugh, but it dies when my eyes meet Ollie's across the room.

Geez, there he goes glaring at me again.

"Okay, seriously, what happened between you two? It can't only be some articles," Jet says. "You won't stop staring at each other."

"I think he's trying to kill me with his mind."

"I'll tell him telepathic assassin is off the list of possible careers for him if the hockey thing doesn't work out."

"Did he say something about hockey not working out?" I ask, taken aback.

Jet pinches my arm. "Put Reporter Lennon away and be Friend Lennon."

"I'm not his friend. *Clearly.* But I was curious because he has talent most people would kill for. I know my articles got to him, but if he let me explain it to him instead of trying to jump down my throat—"

Jet looks down at his drink. "I Googled last night after Noah told me the story. Read your article. The first one. You want the honest truth?" When he meets my eyes again, I get the feeling I'm about to walk into a trap.

That doesn't stop me from defending myself. "I said he needed to get out from under Tommy, and look at tonight—he killed it."

"You also referred to Tommy as a star and implied that Ollie was only good because of him. And I've heard talk around the arena. They say Ollie's not the same on the ice without Tommy, so he's getting it from the media and his teammates. Tonight was either a fluke or he's finally gotten over the doubt." Jet leans in closer. "The doubt that started with *your* article."

I hang my head. "That wasn't my intention. At all." I wanted his star to shine brighter.

"I could see you two being friends if you could manage to get along."

"How do you even know him?"

"He got me the job at the arena and helped me cover up the whole not knowing how to DJ thing. Apart from my bandmates, I haven't met many people since moving to New York, but you can't be my friends if you don't get along. I refuse to be in the middle of two guys unless it's in the fun way. Ooh, damn, a blond sandwich with you and Ollie would be hot."

I raise my eyebrow.

He ignores it and moves on. The ADD is strong with this one. "Okay, so this is what's going to happen. Because I'm Ollie's friend, I'm gonna go say hi and congratulate him on how awesome he was tonight. Are you going to grow some balls and come with me or hide over here like a child too scared about monsters in his closet?"

"Your mouth's going to get you into trouble one day."

"I'm betting on it."

The closer we step toward Ollie, the less composed he appears. His eyes are glassy, he sways a little, and as he finishes off a drink, another teammate replaces it with a new one.

Jet and I have only been here for fifteen minutes, max, and in that time, I've seen Ollie take two new drinks from someone like he's on some sort of mission.

When we get close, Ollie steps around his puck bunny friend. "Hey, Jude."

Great. Let's start with The Beatles jokes. "Original," I murmur.

"Let me guess what tomorrow's headline's gonna be." His words are slightly slurred, but not too bad, and his Boston accent is a little thicker. "Big Idiot Goofball Falls on His Pretty Face and Should Be Traded Again Because He Sucks and is a Hack But He Managed to Pull One Out His Ass in the End."

Even though he's being an ass, I can't help but find him entertaining. "That's way too long for a headline. And good to know you think of yourself as pretty."

He looks as if he doesn't know if I'm mocking him or not.

"Not that you'll believe me, but my article will say you saved the whole team. Congratulations on making the playoffs." See, at least one of us can be mature.

Ollie blinks at me, and his shaggy, unstyled hair falls into his eyes. It's the only time I've seen his hair unruly and not slicked back. I think I like it even better than the wet look.

No. Stop liking Ollie things. He's no different than the others.

"You were awesome," Jet says, pulling Ollie's attention away from me.

Oh sure, he'll shake Jet's hand and give him a smile. "Thanks, man. You totally didn't suck as game DJ either. Even if some of your song choices ... were, uh ... inventive."

"You were listening? I woulda thought you'd be too busy kicking ass and taking names."

Ollie laughs, and I hate that I like the deep rumble as it vibrates through the loud club. "I caught snippets."

"My personal favorite was Bieber's 'Love Yourself' when Toronto started a fight," I say.

Ollie smiles in my direction, but then his face drops as if he realized he's not allowed to like anything that comes out my mouth.

"Everyone knows that song is code for go fuck yourself," Jet says. "I found it appropriate."

"Yo, Strömberg! Over here," Ollie's line mate Kessler yells out.

Ollie stumbles away from us, seemingly forgetting the girl who was patiently waiting behind him.

Someone else hands Ollie another drink, and he gets caught

up talking to them. He's well and truly on his way to being buzzed.

Jet leads us back to the less crowded side of the bar where Camille and Ava are with fresh drinks. "That wasn't so hard, was it?" he asks me.

"No. But can we leave yet?"

"We just got here. Go get another drink."

If I wasn't living with the guy, I'd be tempted to ditch him right about now, so instead, I head to the bar and wonder exactly how I've become Jet's puppet. I'll have to ask Matt and Noah how they ever say no to him.

Despite my protests, as the night wears on, we actually have fun. I drink a few more, and the PR rep and I end up having a lot in common. We both went to Saratoga and both minored in sports management although she graduated a few years before I was even a freshman. She majored in communications, whereas I majored in journalism.

Throughout our chat, my gaze keeps finding Ollie, and he's getting sloppier by the minute. I know he's stupid drunk when he looks over at me and he *smiles.*

Then he looks at the girl who's been following him around like a puppy, and he sways as he tries to concentrate on what she's saying. It almost looks as if she's speaking alien with the way his forehead scrunches.

Ollie sways a bit more, and I realize he's more than stupid drunk. His official level of drunkenness is probably around three-quarters of the way to shitfaced. That's only a few steps below "I can't remember my address" and right on the verge of asking profound questions like "Do penguins have nipples?"

His *friend* grabs him by the hand, and he follows her out of the bar after wolf whistles and back slaps from his team.

Ugh. The sickly feeling coming from my gut can't be jealousy. I don't have that right. But as I watch them leave together, there's no doubt something inside me doesn't like it.

I finish off my fifth drink and send Jet a telepathic *please can we get out of here now?* And I've either gained superpowers I'm unaware of or my face gives me away, because Jet nods at me.

"Was that number five?"

"Yup."

He relents and stands. "Okay, I did promise him I'd let him go home after that."

"I feel like I should be offended you're running out of here as soon as possible," Ava says. "Am I that boring?"

"No, hon"—I lean in and kiss her cheek—"you made my night tolerable." While a certain hockey player made it almost unbearable.

"Not your scene?" she asks.

"Not really."

Jet and I make our way outside, but as I go to ask which way the subway is to get back to Noah's place, I see Ollie's lips on that girl's mouth.

They're by the curb, just kissing away like Ollie does this all the time.

So much for being gay, gay, gay, gay, gay as he pointed out the other day to me in the pressroom. The lengths some of these closeted guys will go to …

I swallow my irrational disappointment and go to leave when Jet pulls me back.

"Quick—look like you're wasted," he says.

"Uh, do what now?"

"Just do it." He grabs the back of my neck and pushes my head down, forcing me to hunch over.

"What the fuck?" I try to shake him off me, but for a smaller guy, he's surprisingly strong.

"We're saving him from the jersey chaser."

"In hockey, they're puck bunnies." I try to push him off me again. "And by the look of him, he doesn't need saving."

"Friends don't let friends do stupid drunken things. You'd know this if you had any friends."

Touché. Apart from Noah, I don't really have anyone. I relax under Jet's hand and follow his lead.

CHAPTER SEVEN

OLLIE

This feels … wrong. So wrong. And not because I'm kissing a woman, but because my lips are tingly. And numb.

Like my fingers.

And my ears.

Wait … can I normally feel my ears? Can *anyone?*

I wonder if this is as weird for her as it is for me, because there's no spark. It's not horrible, but I'm counting the seconds for her to pull back because pushing her off me would be rude … right? Or maybe I like leaning on her because I don't have to think about standing upright.

She breaks the kiss, and yep, definitely using her to remain standing. We both stumble and then laugh.

"I really hope you don't take offense to this, but …" She averts her shiny gaze away from me. "That felt like kissing my brother."

"You kiss your *brother?*" I wonder what she'd say if she knew I'd rather kiss her brother.

She lets out a little giggle and slaps my shoulder, and I try not to lose my balance again. "No. You know what I mean."

"Sorry," I slur. It kinda comes out as *Shlorry*. "I'm, like, all kinds of drunk."

Ash always used to warn me about leading puck bunnies on, but until tonight, I've never hung around them long enough for them to get the wrong idea. A hello and a selfie for social media is usually the extent of it. Never done the kissing thing. That's definitely new.

"Ollie, I need a hand," an urgent voice says beside us.

I turn, slightly dazed. Jet stands there, trying to hold up Lennon-fucking-Hawkins who's hunched over and holding onto his stomach. "Wha... huh?" I ask.

"Lennon got super drunk and doesn't feel well. I can't hold him up on my own." Jet glances at the girl and then back at me. "Sorry to interrupt, but I need your help."

Reflexively, albeit slower and more wobbly than usual, I'm by his side and helping hold him up. Momentarily, I forget I'm mad at him. He grips me tight, and I hate that it feels good. *He* feels good against me. Just like kissing him in the stairwell of the Honey Bee did months ago.

"You should take the cab and get your friend home," what's her face says.

There's a cab? My head snaps to the yellow car waiting by the sidewalk.

"Thanks," Jet says to the woman who I should know her name but don't, "but we've got him from here. You take this one, and we'll get the next one."

"Are you sure—"

Jet turns on his Southern charm. "Now, what kinda gentlemen would we be if we left a pretty girl on the street in the middle of the night?" It does the trick, and she gets into the cab with a sweet smile aimed in Jet's direction.

Phew.

When the cab's gone and around the corner, Lennon stands full height, knocking me backward.

I stumble and almost fall, but they're both there to hold me up. I throw my arms around their shoulders, and one of them smells delicious. Like spiced vanilla. I think it's Lennon, but I can't be sure, so I lean in Jet's direction for elimination purposes because he's safer. Less Lennon-y.

"Whoa there, big guy," Jet says.

"I'm fline. Uh ... *fline*." Ugh, why can't I say *fine.*

"Yeah, you look it," Lennon says.

My head lolls in his direction. "Aren't you the drunk one here?"

He shakes his head. "Not even close."

"You looked like you needed help," Jet says.

"She looked like she was trying to eat your face," Lennon adds. "And I know how pretty you think it is. Thought you might've wanted to keep it that way."

I don't mean to laugh, and my head tells me not to, but I'm starting to think my body isn't attached to my brain right now.

"Brain don't feel drunk. Body not listening." That makes sense ... doesn't it?

"Okay, caveman," Jet says, "how about we get you a cab?"

"I dunno even how it happened," I slur some more. "I didn't buy any drinks."

Lennon chuckles. "You, Mr. Big Shot, had people buying you drinks all night."

"Oh, right. Because I'm fucking awesome."

Lennon pats my back. "Humility is an admirable trait. Just sayin'."

"But did you see that *goal*? That shit is why I fucking do this. Ash always said it was a meaningless game—there are bigger things in life and other bullshit, bullshit, bullshit."

"Who's Ash?" Jet asks.

"A shithead," I answer.

"Thanks for the clarification," Jet says sarcastically.

A cab appears from nowhere, and they help me into the back seat.

"What's your address?" Lennon asks. He has one hand on the door and stares down at me with an expression that's either pissed off or amused. It's weird he can pull off both at the same time and look hot while he does it.

I blink at him, my mind empty. "Umm …"

"That's what I thought." Lennon pushes me into the middle seat and gets in next to me while Jet runs around the cab and boxes me in on the other side.

"It's not my fault I don't know my address yet. I know how to get there." I look around, but everything's kinda blurry. "Yeah, bang a left." I point. "I think …"

Jet rattles off an address, and when the cab starts moving, my stomach churns. That can't be good.

"You've been here for months," Lennon says.

"Numbered streets are hard." The words are mumbled, but Lennon still finds them amusing.

"Tell me 'bout it," Jet says. "Took me forever to work it out."

The car turns a corner, and the alcohol threatens to make a reappearance. Urngh. I close my eyes and throw my head back on the seat.

Jet and Lennon talk, but I don't take in what they say—something about giants not being able to hold their alcohol—and the next thing I know, I'm being shaken awake.

"Come on, big guy," Jet says. "You're twice our size and a bitch to carry."

My eyes slowly crack open, and I'm hanging halfway out the cab.

"Maybe we should drag him," Lennon says.

"There you go being all nice again."

"Hey, I'm always nice."

"I can walk." I can totally walk.

My legs tell me that I'm lying. Seriously, I didn't drink *that* much, did I? When I fall out of the cab, Lennon and Jet pull me up by my arms and help me to the steps leading up to an expensive-looking brownstone.

I groan. "Fuck. Stairs."

Jet and Lennon laugh as they help me tackle them.

As soon as we cross the threshold one hundred years later, I mutter, "Thanks. And not for the stairs. But, like … you know … things."

"Things?" Jet asks, his tone mocking.

"Thanks for saving me from that chick."

"Woulda thought a straight guy like you would've been pissed," Lennon says.

God, his knowing attitude is annoying. "Fuck off, you know I'm gay." And apparently my mouth has no filter now.

"Well, I didn't know," Jet says, "but I suspected because you totally checked me out when we met."

I straighten up. "No, I didn't." I look at Lennon. "I swear I didn't."

Lennon shrugs as if it's no big deal, and that pisses me off. Can't he care even a little bit?

"I was looking at your tats," I say to Jet.

"Sure you were," Jet says. "That's what all the straight boys say when they wanna go gay."

Thumping in my brain rhythmically pounds, and I think it's the alcohol, but then Lennon grumbles as if he can hear the pounding too.

"Do they seriously ever stop?" he asks.

"Who?" I'm confused.

"Matt and Noah," Jet says. "And no, they don't. But they leave for Fiji in a few days for a *long* vacation."

Is he saying they're doing what I think they're doing? "Wait … they're …"

Jet slams the front door hard. "That should alert them to our presence." The sex noises don't stop. "Shoulda known they wouldn't have cared."

"I think it's sweet. In a perverted way," I say.

Lennon huffs a small laugh. "I think I like drunk Ollie."

"Bullshit. You hate me."

"Think you've got that the wrong way around there, buddy." He slaps my shoulder.

"Mmm, true. You don't hate me. You think I'm shit at hockey."

"Oh, for fuck's sake. You're great at hockey. The best. We should give you the number ninety-nine jersey and tell Gretzky to move over. There's a new legend in town."

"Gretzky's number's retired. But you'd know that if you knew anything about hockey. Which you don't. Which is why I hate your ass."

"Wait … you hate me or hate my ass?" Lennon appears more amused than offended.

"Your ass. I want to hate you but can't."

"What's wrong with my ass?" His smile pisses me off.

"It's a great ass," I mumble.

"He has a point. It's a really nice ass," Jet says.

Ah shit. Stupid mouth. "For the love of Gretzky, this is why I don't drink. Like ever. Mouth. Stop. Talking."

"Who knew all you needed to bust open that closet door was alcohol," Jet says.

"I'm not closeted," I argue. "I mean … not really. Just, you know … to the NHL. My family and friends back home know. Ooh, the great and powerful Tommy Novak knows. That counts." Neither of them says anything, and I realize I'm rambling. "Oh my God, shut up," I say to myself.

Jet grabs my arm. "How about we tackle these stairs, you can sleep it off, and we'll talk when you're sober."

"More stairs?" I ask, my voice coming out as a whine.

"One more set," Jet says.

"Ugh, you sound like my trainer. When I get to the top, are you going to tell me one more set again? That asshole does it to me every time."

"Just the one. I promise," Jet says.

"He says that too!"

Lennon laughs, and I find myself smiling back at him.

Damn it.

Mad, Ollie. You're supposed to be mad.

Ash always used to complain that I don't get hangovers. The worst I generally get is a headache. Today is one of the few times in my life I wish I wasn't like that. The stupid shit I said and did isn't distorted or blurry or something I could easily forget.

I wince when I remember being passed drink after drink, and I took them no questions asked. Then I remember the girl, the obvious come-ons that I ignored to keep gazing at Lennon across the bar, wishing he could be anyone else but … *him*. A journalist who calls me on hiding shit. Because that's why I'm truly pissed, isn't it? It's not that he thinks I'm talentless, which is bullshit. I know he doesn't think that. I used that girl last night to distract me from gravitating toward Lennon, and then I walked her out anyway when I wasn't interested. God, I'm an idiot. And an asshole.

If it weren't for Lennon and Jet, I might not have gotten away from her so easily without blurting out I'm gay …

Oh, fuck. I told Jet I'm gay.

I tell myself not to panic, because it's Jet. He's Matt Jackson's little brother. He'd know what kind of position I'm in.

Doesn't help settle my stomach, though.

The sun streams into Lennon's bedroom, where they dumped me because it was the closest room off the stairs and they were exhausted from hauling my ass up them.

I try to psych myself up to go out there and face the fallout from last night, but a note on the bedside table catches my eye. It sits on an open laptop with an arrow pointing to the screen. It reads: *Truce? Click here—L.*

I hit the space bar, and the computer comes back to life from power-saving mode, opening to Lennon's article that was posted this morning by his magazine.

For the first time in my history of nonexistent hangovers, I might actually be sick.

Strömberg Trade Saves Dragons.

While we won't see an end of speculation over the success of Strömberg's trade until the end of the playoffs, it could have been all over last night with the Dragons' epic battle to take Toronto down.

The Dragons have had a rocky season, beginning strong but suffering losses due to injuries, trades, and obvious tension on the ice.

Last night's game was brutal, ending in a desperate fight to stay alive. In the last second of the last minute in an overtime period, Ollie Strömberg skated like his life depended on it.

Having been traded from Boston earlier this season, he had the need to prove himself to his new team. Without the overshadowing Novak figure dimming his light, Strömberg proved his rising stardom worthy.

My heart beats erratically the entire time I read—which takes longer than usual thanks to the whole squinting-at-the-bright-light-of-the-laptop thing.

He still doesn't get it, but he's right about one thing. My teammates are not on the same wavelength. Last night's game never should've gone into overtime, and even though we're taught not to play the blame game, all of us question what went wrong and when.

It could be internally debated all morning without coming up with an answer.

I can't delay having to go outside this room and face both Lennon and Jet no matter how much I want to, so I find my clothes on the floor and recoil when I remember both Jet and Lennon undressing me down to my boxers while I was dead weight. Even my dick couldn't get excited about them taking my clothes off because I was too drunk, but it definitely doesn't have that problem now at the memory.

I palm my cock to try to squash my growing erection. Stupid dick getting excited over Lennon, and it's not like it's the first time it's happened in the past six months.

I try to tell myself this morning's hard-on is over Jet, but my brain and my body know I'm lying. Jet's objectively hot, but the thought of going there? I shudder. I like my men old enough to drink.

It's because you haven't had sex in a year, I remind myself. Yep, let's go with that excuse.

While I get dressed and wait for my cock to deflate, I can't help snooping around Lennon's room. The furniture's rich intricacies and meticulous matching design is old New York meets modern. From the slate feature wall behind the bed to the heavy wooden vanity and drawers, everything looks like it cost a shit ton money. The only thing giving any indication of Lennon's personality is the pile of clothes hanging out of a suitcase.

I know how that is—traveling from city to city and living out of a bag.

While I contemplate how much trouble I'd get in if I went through Lennon's things—curiosity about the guy is a bitch—yelling from the hallway catches my attention.

"What in the ever lovin' fuck's goin' on in here?" The Southern accent is deeper than Jet's. Sounds like Matt.

"Whoa," another voice says. "You two are fucking?"

When I open the door to see what's going on, I immediately regret it. Across the hall, where Matt and Noah stand in the open doorway, Jet and Lennon climb out of bed wearing nothing but boxer briefs. They scramble for their clothes, but I can't stop staring at Lennon's long and lean form. He's toned enough to have a little bit of definition in his abs and pecs.

More memories from last night haunt me. Jet and Lennon holding hands in the bar, the way they stuck by each other's side all night, and then when I said Lennon has a nice ass …

Jet agreed about Lennon's ass, and the more I think about it, I remember it being flirty and a hell of a lot smoother than when I'd said it.

They … hooked up? Why do I hate that idea so much I want to punch something?

CHAPTER EIGHT

Ollie's entire face hardens, and his gaze flicks from a barely dressed Jet to me and back again.

"Ollie?" Matt asks.

Ollie startles and averts his gaze from us to Matt. "Uh … hey." He does this weird half wave that makes him both adorable and awkward—reminding me of the guy I kissed in Boston. I hate that I'm not the one bringing that out in him.

Jet finishes throwing on some sweats while I find my shirt.

"Lennon and I ain't fucking, so put your big brother claws away," Jet says. "Mr. Hot Shot forward of the New York Dragons needed a place to crash because he got so wasted he couldn't remember his address. And I dunno if you guys are aware, but straight guys ain't too keen on sharing a bed with a gay dude."

Although I can't be sure, because I can't see from this angle, I swear Jet winks at Ollie, because Ollie's mouth drops open to say something that never comes.

"Besides," Jet says, turning back around to face us, "even if we were fucking, you two wouldn't get a say, because I'm twenty fucking years old."

"And showing off your maturity level right now," Matt says.

"You both need to cut the big brother shit."

"What did I do?" Noah asks incredulously.

"Please. You're worse than this one." Jet points to Matt. "I'm still convinced you've set Lennon as some sort of spy."

I snort. "Because I'd be *so* good at that."

"So, it's just a coincidence that since he's been here your friends don't turn up every couple of days to say 'hi?' Subtlety really isn't your strong suit, guys."

"We're just lookin' out for you," Matt mumbles.

"Yeah, uh … well," Ollie interrupts, "as fun as this is—learning my family's not the only dysfunctional one—umm … I'm gonna go …"

"Stay if you want," Matt says. "I was about to go for my morning run and bring back breakfast."

Ollie stares at me, and then his gaze flicks to Jet. "Nah, thanks. I'm good."

"You remember where you live now?" Jet asks, and for once Ollie's scowl isn't directed at me.

"Yeah. Thirty-one East Twenty-first Street."

"Fucking numbered streets," Matt says.

"Thank you!" Ollie says. "Apparently that wasn't a good enough excuse last night. But, uh"—he glances at me again—"I'm gonna …" He tips his head in the direction of the stairs and then makes a break for it.

"Shit," I mutter. "Ollie, wait up."

I run after him as fast as I can, but I almost fall down the stairs. He reaches the sidewalk by the time I finally find my feet and catch up to him. I'm barefoot, don't have my glasses or contacts in so I can't see shit, and I have no idea what to say when I get in front of him, because I haven't thought it through.

He spins to face me so fast I have to take a step back.

"What?" he barks.

Yeah, what? Why did I chase him out here?

"Did you read my new article?" *You're such a loser.*

Ollie's glare doesn't let up. "Yeah."

Uh, okay.

"All it did was prove you still don't know how you fucked up with the others."

"Huh?"

He shakes his head. "They all implied I'm hiding something, and this one you're like *Hey, look at the superstar! He's a hero. Pay extra attention to him.*"

It takes a minute to understand what he's saying, but when I do … "Wait, you think I've been hinting at"—my gaze darts around the street, making sure it's safe to talk candidly—"you know what?"

"Well, what else could you mean by needing an encouraging environment to be the best player I can be, and—"

"Exactly that!" I shout and then shake my head with a humorless laugh. "This whole time, you've been thinking I've been subtly taking digs at your sexuality? I thought you were pissed because I crushed your precious ego."

He huffs and glances away. "Okay, well, maybe it was a little of that, but, well, yeah. I don't like how you made some excellent points that made me feel more shame and guilt over being closeted than anything my family has ever said to me."

Ouch. I'm suddenly seeing it from his perspective, and it's even worse than I thought. I only spent half an evening with his family, but it was easy to see how they make him feel about having to hide.

"I'm so sorry, Ollie. It was never my intention to pressure you into thinking you had to come out or—"

"I wondered how it was possible for some no-name journalist to know so much about me and see deeper than just hockey. I hated it because it made me uneasy. I lost the most important person in my life, and then here comes this article that had the power to make everything I'd worked for go away and make losing Ash completely useless. Turns out it's because the person who wrote it spent dinner with me and my crazy family."

I take a deep breath and try to keep calm, because even though I now see why he's so pissed off, I don't think he's really thought it through. Either that or he's too blinded by the pressure he's under. "You can be pissed at me all you want, because I get it now, but I also wanna say something without you getting pissed off more."

"Doesn't matter anyway."

I chase after him when he starts walking again. "What doesn't matter?"

"Save your breath."

I step in front of him so he can't take off again. "Hear me out, and then you can keep sulking, but I'm wondering if you're the only person who sees my articles that way because of your self-guilt. I said you were hiding behind Tommy because of your skills. I wrote those articles with no hidden agenda, and I was honestly only referring to hockey. If you interpreted it differently, that's on you. Not me. I promised you six months ago I wouldn't say anything to anyone, and I meant it. I didn't even tell Jet I already knew last night when he found out."

Ollie stumbles backward. "You didn't? But … why? I mean, he knows now, so—"

I shrug. "It's your thing. Your life."

"But you're a journalist."

"We're not all vultures. If I'd stumbled across you in a bathroom six months ago and you were shooting up drugs or strapping a knee injury or doing anything else that would actually affect your career, then yeah, I would've exploited the shit out of you."

Ollie snorts.

"The articles I've written? They were only about hockey. You might want to look at your guilty conscience before you continue to hate me."

Ollie mutters, "I don't hate you. For some reason … whenever I'm around you … Fuck, why is this so hard? I'm all edgy and I can't think. I suck at this whole … thing."

"Communicating thing?"

"*Apologizing.* And then on top of that, you slept with Jet, and for some reason, that makes me even more ragey, and—"

"Whoa, hell no. I mean, well, yeah, we slept together, but nothing happened. I like my men old enough to drink." Not to mention I like them bigger than me, muscly, and well, the opposite of Jet.

Ollie laughs hard.

"What?" I ask.

"I said the same thing about Jet."

"Nothing happened," I say again, even though it really shouldn't matter either way.

Ollie moves closer and lowers his voice. "Good."

My breath catches in my throat, and it snaps Ollie out of whatever's going on in his train of thought.

"Fucking hell." He steps back again. "You make me forget who I'm supposed to be in public."

"I don't know if that's a good thing or a bad thing."

"At this point in my life? It's definitely bad."

Right.

"Can we please start over?" I ask.

"Like, start over start over?"

"Start over as friends. I promise if it gets to you so much, I won't write a single article about you. Not even if you score the winning goal of the Stanley Cup. I'll describe you as that hockey player with the hair, some muscles, and the missing teeth. That could be a number of you."

"Hey, I still have all my teeth." Ollie smiles. "Except a few back ones. And okay, this one"—he points to his right canine tooth—"is an implant. But the rest are entirely my own."

"Even with that in the description, it could still be any of you."

"True." He runs a hand through his hair and blows out a loud breath. "We can start again."

I step forward and hold out my hand for him. "Hi, I'm Lennon, but you can call me Clark."

Ollie shakes my hand. "I'm Ollie, and you can call me Ollie."

"I'm a sports journalist who sometimes writes obliviously asshole-y things."

"I'm a hockey player with a fragile ego."

"Friends?"

Our hands are still joined, awkwardly moving up and down as if we're still shaking when we're not.

He swallows so hard his Adam's apple bounces. "A hockey player and a sports journalist walk into a bar... Nope, doesn't sound right."

"We're not all vultures," I remind him again but can't fault him. Some of my coworkers wouldn't even hesitate to sell Ollie's story.

His hazel eyes glimmer as he murmurs, "Okay. Friends."

The Dragons sail through the first round of the playoffs thanks to

Ollie's scoring streak continuing. It's like something clicked during that last Toronto game, and he's been on fire ever since.

His gorgeous smile can't be wiped off his unfairly handsome face during the press conferences after the games. It really does suck how hot the man is. And now that he's not scowling at me every five seconds, it's distracting, which means my post-game articles are a little thinner than they should be.

Oops.

In the middle of the last press conference, as an act of faith or perhaps an olive branch for our new formed friendship, Ollie gets Ava's attention and whispers something in her ear. The next thing I know, she's calling upon me to ask a question.

I blink as everyone in the room turns to me.

I really should be more prepared than I am. There are questions I always have ready just in case but having never been called upon, even when I used to yell out with all my energy, I never expect to use them. Most of the time, someone's asking the questions I have written down anyway. It's come to a point where I don't even try to ask anymore because while *Sporting Health* is reputable, it's not big.

Now here's my chance, and Ollie's giving it to me. Suddenly, all my questions seem lame.

My heart beats erratically. "Beating Pittsburgh in five games, what is the team's plan for the break until your next series?"

The question is vague, but it's better that than the permanent one on my list which is to ask management why they think no man has come out in the sport. Asking that would be like slapping Ollie in the face right now.

The coaches say some shit about them studying their upcoming opponents and training, but the whole room knows the team's first stop is to get utterly hammered tonight. Tomorrow, they'll be dealing with watching tape and practicing while nursing hangovers.

When the press conference winds down, I send my article off and make my way to wait outside the staff entrance for Jet. After five minutes, I check my phone and realize he'd messaged me during the press conference.

A band had to pull out of a gig at Club Soho so Fallout is covering, which means Jet's already gone.

I push off the wall just as the door swings open, and Ollie charges out with his gear bag over his shoulder. He stops short when he sees me, and it's hard to tell what he looks better in: hockey pads, a suit, or just his underwear.

I try not to picture his muscled and tattooed body while Jet and I helped him undress the night of the Toronto game. He was drunk so it feels like an invasion of privacy to jerk off to the memory. Not that I'd do that ... daily ...

Nope, not me.

"Lost?" Ollie asks and his lips quirk. "Or waiting for me?"

Find words. Any words. "Jet, actually." I clear my throat. "But he got called to a gig at Club Soho. You heading out with the team?"

Ollie adjusts his bag and stares into the empty parking lot. "Guess they all left without me."

"Did you want ... I mean, if you're not catching up with them ..." What am I doing?

"Did I want to what?"

"Uh, I was gonna go check out Jet's show. If you wanted to come. With me, I mean." *Where's a wall when you need to bang your head against one?*

"Will there be food? I'm starving."

I laugh. "Of course, you are. And yes, I think they serve food there."

"What type of club is it?" His question, innocent enough, is not about the food.

"It's not a gay bar. Although Jet said when Fallout plays, the crowd seems to be mixed with both het and gay couples. It's safe enough that people won't assume anything if you're spotted there. You know, unless you pull a Matt Jackson and blow someone. Or get blown."

Ollie chuckles. "I'll try to keep my mouth and dick to myself."

"Damn. There goes that fun idea." *Don't flirt with him, you idiot.*

He shakes his head, but his smile remains. "We going or what?"

"You mind if we stop by my place first? I wanna dump"—I hold up my laptop bag—"this."

"Sure. Can I leave my crap there too? I'll pick it up later."

"No problem."

The trip home is only a small detour, but by the time we get to Club Soho, Ollie has me on edge. All he's done is sit next to me in a cab. Part of me wishes he didn't get to shower after the game, because a hockey player after three periods is no rose. Maybe the stench of man sweat would turn me off him.

Who am I kidding? I'm *me*. That'd probably be worse.

I have a weird kink about locker rooms that I'm sure a psychologist would love to analyze, but I prefer to keep my jock fantasies on the down low.

"Whoa, long line," Ollie says when we reach Club Soho.

I lift my chin. "Watch this." Jet told me he'd put my name at the door, but as I swagger—for some reason I think I'm cool enough to pull off a swagger right now—toward the bouncer, my confidence wavers. What if Jet forgot and I say my name and he doesn't let us in? What if—

"Holy shit, Ollie Strömberg?" the bouncer says.

I sigh.

Ollie turns to me and lifts his chin to me this time. "No, watch this." He holds his hand out for the bouncer to shake. "Hey, man, how's it going?"

The bouncer asks him for an autograph on the back of his name sheet, and then we're let inside no questions asked.

"I was totally on that list, you know."

Ollie grins. "Sure, you were."

Can't I be cool once in my life?

CHAPTER NINE

While this is not an actual date, it totally feels like one. I assume. I've never had a date because Ash and I went from childhood friends to living together in about five minutes flat.

I buy us drinks while Lennon swoops in to grab an emptying table as we walk in. Jet's already on stage doing his thing, and I convince myself that getting the drinks is what friends do.

Which is what we are now. Apparently.

Because I'm a dumbass.

I can't be friends with Lennon Hawkins.

He reaches for his scotch as I go to hand it over, and our fingers brush against each other. The glass slips out of my hand, but his is right there to catch it.

Yup, being friends with him is going to damn near kill me.

I distract myself by taking my seat and turning my attention to Jet on stage. His natural presence is indescribable, but whatever it is about him that makes him charismatic, it's amplified when he's singing. He's gonna make it big one day.

Lennon leans in, his breath warm next to my ear. "He's impressive, huh?"

I nod, my mouth too dry to make words work.

A couple near the front of the stage catch my eye. They're off to the side, practically being hidden by a massive speaker, but I still notice them.

It's two guys, both with meticulously slicked hair and trendy clothes. One has his back against the taller guy's front, and the one in front is leaning back enough for their mouths to come together.

To do that here, in public, the pang of jealousy hits me like when I see Matt and Noah in the tabloids together.

I must stare longingly a little too long, because Lennon leans in again.

"This might not be a gay bar, but at least it's a safe space. We can go if you're uncomf—"

"Will you dance with me?" The question flies out of me without much thought.

This place is obviously accepting, and I've never been somewhere it was safe to touch another guy without ridicule or risk of being recognized.

Ash used to try to get me to go out to these kinds of places, but I never had the guts. Lennon got me here without even trying. And now I'm asking him to dance when I shouldn't be.

Lennon laughs. "As fun as dancing sounds, that would be a no. Like, hell no."

I turn my head to speak in his ear. "Should my ego be offended again?"

He shakes his head. "Not at all. You should be flattered I won't subject you to my dancing. I'm, like, the worst, and I just got you to respect me again, so I'm not gonna screw that up by showing you my shocking moves."

As disappointed as I am, it's probably for the best anyway. They might be accepting here, but the bouncer did recognize me. Anyone else could.

At that thought, I shuffle my stool farther away from Lennon and paranoia sets in. The switch flips that easy.

It was a constant problem in my relationship with Ash. He's an affectionate guy and comfortable in his skin. The only place outside of our home where he could show that affection was at our parents' houses.

I'd like to not think about appearances in public and how I'm "supposed" to act, but it's always in the back of my mind. In all the time I was with Ash, I didn't like having to control my actions and be careful all the time but thought it was necessary. Now, all I can think is how much I hate it and don't want to have to do it anymore.

CHAPTER TEN

LENNON

I feel sorry for Ollie as he takes to the ice to face off his old team. Game one of Boston versus New York is a disaster for the Dragons and ends in a fucking shutout.

By the time I finish my notes to write up later and make it to the team's hotel bar, where they're drowning their sorrows, I can't find Ollie anywhere. I don't know why I've come looking for him in the first place other than to say sorry about the game—something he probably doesn't want to hear anyway. The excuse to search him out seems thin now I'm here.

Deciding to abort my mission, I turn on my heel, but on the way back through the lobby, I run into Tommy.

"Hey, reporter dude."

"Hockey dude."

Tommy seems amused that I won't take his shit. "Looking for Strömberg?"

"Umm …"

His lips quirk, and he quickly glances around. "What, you don't think he tells me everything? I had to listen to him whine over your stupid articles for weeks before he was traded. Then after the benefit? All I can say is I'm lucky to still have my balls."

"I … uh …" What am I supposed to say to that?

"But I also know you have some sort of truce or whatever. He's in room nineteen oh three if you want him."

I do want him, but probably not in the way he means, and my confusion must show.

"If you want to see him," Tommy clarifies.

"Right … uh … okay, thanks." I nervously push my glasses back up my nose. "It was nothing. I was going to give my commiserations on the loss."

"He might want to hear that from you. Definitely wasn't interested in hearing it from me." His smugness isn't lost on me.

"Well, with you grinning like that, I can't really blame him."

"Have you guys been spending more time together than he let on? You sound just like him." With a laugh, he wanders into the bar, no doubt planning to give Ollie's teammates hell.

I stand still, debating whether or not to go up to Ollie's room. It's to give sympathy, nothing important, and if he has a roommate, it could get awkward.

Ollie doesn't seem like the type of closet case to pretend he doesn't know any queer guys, but that might be different if one turns up outside his hotel room.

The smart thing would be to leave—go back to my own hotel a block away. But even though I tested at a higher than average intelligence as a child, I never said I did smart things.

I take the elevators up to the nineteenth floor and hesitate again outside his room. Straining to listen, I put one ear against the door to try to hear how many voices are in there, but I can't hear anything. Either he's alone or the walls are too thick. Or he and his roommate are asleep. Although, I doubt that.

Before I get the chance to pull away, Ollie opens the door

without warning, and I fall into his impressively large chest. He's already out of his suit and only wearing sweats and a tight T-shirt, and I can feel every hard muscle against my face.

"There's an interesting way to greet me."

I pull back, but my gaze gets stuck on something. Is that ... I narrow my eyes and assess the small bump underneath his shirt. A pierced nipple?

Ollie clears his throat.

My gaze flicks up to his. "Sorry. I ... I—" *I cannot find words.*

"You ..."

"I came to say sorry about the loss."

Ollie cocks his head. "Was it your fault we sucked out there? Or did you write another article about me and you've come to give me a heads-up?"

"No, you jackass. I didn't write another article. I'm being a friend here, because according to Jet, I have no idea how to be one, and friends commiserate or congratulate their friends when they win or lose a game."

He folds his arms across his chest that's stupid and hard. "And you couldn't have sent a text?"

"Still don't have your number."

"Jet does."

"I'm not Jet's keeper."

Instead of slinging more quips, Ollie smiles and steps back. "Coming in?"

"Were you on your way out? It's cool if you were." Despite my words, I enter the hotel room.

"Petrov left his hotel keycard next to his bed. He just left for the night, and I was gonna try to catch him because I didn't want to be woken at *fuck you* o'clock to let his drunk ass in here, but he'll be long gone by now thanks to this little detour." He waves a hand between us.

"Not my fault. You could've left me standing out here like a moron."

"Could have if you weren't pressed against me."

Is that ... flirting?

"Touché. Why aren't you down at the bar with the rest of the guys, drowning your sorrows in alcohol?"

"I'd prefer not to be hungover for tomorrow. Coach is gonna ride our asses."

"Sounds fun. Your coach is hot for an older guy."

Ollie snorts. "Well, there's that, but also I think we can both agree me and alcohol should never mix."

"I dunno. I kind of like it when you're drunk."

Fuck, am I flirting back?

Rules. Boundaries. Remember them.

"Because, you know ... you're nicer to me when you are."

Ollie takes the bait. "Your know-it-all, mouthy attitude isn't as annoying when I have no inhibitions."

"Hey, you never complained about my mouth the last time we were in Boston."

Oh God, why did I bring that up?

Ollie laughs, deep and rich. "True."

An iPad catches my eye on his bed, and I can't see what hockey game's playing on the screen, but I'd bet my left nut he's watching tonight's.

"Why are you torturing yourself?" I point at the bed.

"It's not torturing. It's *working*. My job doesn't end just because we're off the ice."

"Then why are your teammates down at the bar and you're not?"

Ollie runs a hand through his ashy hair. "Because they don't have as much to prove as I do?"

There I go again, underestimating what Ollie has to go through. I saw a little of it with Matt, but I only met him and Noah at the brighter end of the tunnel. Ollie's still in complete darkness, hoping to make it out the other side.

With a sigh, I pull my laptop out and dump my bag on the floor. "You mind if I watch too then? I need to finish up my article anyway."

"Go for it. I think I've seen the same play about six times now and still can't make sense of it."

As I climb on the bed, I pull my laptop in my lap and leave his tablet propped up in the middle. "The one where Joseph and Novak passed the puck so many times it ended up in Crosby's possession without anyone noticing? That was insane."

"I think it's official. Tommy has replaced me." Ollie slumps down next to me.

"It was a fluke," I lie. The truth is, Boston's form was on point, but Ollie doesn't need me psyching him out even more.

He pulls his tablet into his lap, and I have to inch a little closer to see the screen better. I try to focus on the game and not the giant hunk of man meat beside me.

"We played like shit tonight, and I'm trying to figure out where the hell it all went wrong."

I open up the document with all my notes from the game. "You know, I don't think it was your team's fault. There wasn't really anything wrong with how you played. Boston just played better."

"Maybe," he murmurs, but he's studying the screen as if it holds all the answers.

"Here." I pass him my notes. "If you can make sense out of what I wrote down in my shorthand typing, you'll see I'm right.

Your problems weren't technical. It was that their goalie was on fire, and they got a few lucky calls. It happens."

"So, you're saying they're just better than us? That doesn't make me feel any better."

I laugh. "No. They had a better night. That's all."

I can't be sure, but I swear I see the moment he believes me. He turns back to the game but doesn't appear as invested as he was twenty seconds ago.

When the game comes to a close, Ollie's shoulders sink. "I was kinda hoping it would end differently being played back."

I finish typing out my article and send it off without self-proofing. My editor will be pissed, but I should've already gotten it to him half an hour ago.

When I close my laptop and put it back in my bag, I go to stand, but Ollie's voice stops me.

"You want to watch a movie or something?"

"A movie?" The bedside clock reads well past midnight, and I should go back to my hotel and get some sleep. Do I move to do that though? Of course not, because I always do questionable things around Ollie, starting with offering to be his fake boyfriend for a family dinner. "What about your roommate?"

"I'm allowed to have gay friends, Lennon." His eyes seem uncertain, as if he doesn't quite believe himself. "Or, I dunno, tell him you're writing another article."

This is walking a fine line, and I get the feeling if I stay shit's gonna get messy, and we've just started getting along.

"I could stay for a movie." Apparently, my mouth decides to send a big *fuck you* to the warnings running through my head. "What've you got?"

He taps away on his screen and pulls up a selection.

"Should've pegged you for an action, *no brains needed*, type of guy," I say.

"Fine then." He taps some more and pulls up a different folder filled with titles like *Donnie Darko*, *Sin City*, and *Get Out.*

"Ugh. Way too far the other way," I complain.

"Are you the Goldilocks of movies? Here, look for whatever you want." He passes me his tablet.

I scroll through the genres in his movie file, clicking on a few things but going back to the main folder seconds later. Ollie makes impatient noises, which makes me even pickier. He's kind of hot when he's snarky.

When I scroll down farther, a folder catches my eye. It's labeled in capital letters: PORN. "Good to know you don't even try to hide your stash."

I jokingly go to click on it, but he must think I'm actually gonna do it. A large hand wraps around my wrist, his grip firm but not painful, and I laugh.

"Calm down. As interested as I am to open it, it's kind of like Pandora's box. There could be clown porn in there or something, and then you're not the one who'd be scarred for life."

"Clown porn?" he asks while practically choking.

"There's some really weird shit out there."

He lets go of my hand. "What I want to know is what you've been looking up if you landed on clown porn."

"It started out looking at guys in drag, and it went downhill from there."

Ollie pulls back as if contemplating that. "Drag queens, huh? Is that your thing?"

"Oh, we are so not getting into this." And I'm so not confessing the drag thing was out of curiosity. My true fantasy is jocks. Exactly like him. Not going to tell him that either. "You won't let me see your collection, so you get nothing from me."

He thinks about it for a moment before turning to me. "Well, now I want you to look. I feel like I need to defend my porn choices."

Is he seriously suggesting I watch his porn? With him … like … right there?

The smug challenge in his eyes almost has me pushing the button, but the slight blush on his cheeks makes me think he's bluffing. God, I want to know what he's into …

No! Bad Lennon.

That would only add to the conflicting feelings I already have for Ollie.

"I refuse to kink shame, so it's safer if I can't see what's possible to judge." I clear my throat and look at the screen again. "Don't you worry about, you know, one of your teammates stumbling across this?"

"I have a passcode, and I'm not really in the habit of leaving expensive things like iPads lying around the place."

"Expensive? Isn't this junk change to you?" I hold up his tablet.

Ollie shrugs. "We never had a lot of money growing up. I mean, we weren't poor or anything—far from it—but five boys in one household costs a shit ton without the extra bells and whistles like toys and gadgets. Then in my first year playing for Providence, I was on shitty pay. It gradually became more and more, so it kinda feels like I still don't have money even though I do. I dunno, it's hard to explain, but yeah, growing up the way I did, I know not to leave my shit lying around the place. For more reasons than just privacy."

"Makes sense."

The icon mocks us as we stare at it, and then each other, and then away. God, we're pathetic.

I click on the folder labeled Classics just so we can get away from temptation. My entire face lights up. "Wait. You think *Thor* is a *classic*? Where are the real ones like *Cool Hand Luke* and *The Princess Bride*? This is even more disturbing than your porn choices."

"Hey, you never saw my porn choices."

"I'm still going with clown porn."

"I promise no clown porn. I think the most adventurous thing on there is, like, group stuff."

My cock shamefully perks up at that as if it has its own ears and is listening in. I shift to try to make it less obvious, and I think Ollie knows what he's doing to me, because he grins.

The safest, most boner-killing movie catches my attention. "Okay, we're watching this one."

Ollie groans. "*Dirty Dancing*? What the hell?"

"Need I remind you this is your tablet and your movie collection?"

"Fucking Ash. He had the worst taste in movies."

"Sure, try to blame the ex."

"So much for not falling asleep," Ollie says. "Are you really going to make me watch this?"

"Yup."

We settle in to watch the movie, lying next to each other with the tablet between us, and even though I'm keenly aware of how close his body is, can feel his body heat, and have to concentrate hard on the movie that's supposed to suppress my boner, it turns out Ollie makes an excellent point. If you don't want to fall asleep —don't watch *Dirty Dancing*.

A rough hand grazes my cheek, and I lean into it. I think I might also moan.

Ollie's chuckle brings me out of my daze, and I slowly open my eyes and realize …

Shit, I fell asleep.

I startle awake and turn my head toward Ollie, who's staring at me with a small smile. His hand still lingers on my cheek, and I don't understand what's happening.

"What's going on?" I croak.

"As cute as you are when you're sleeping, you promised me you'd keep me awake until my roommate came back."

I bolt upright, looking frantically around the empty hotel room. "Roommate?"

Ollie laughs. "It's okay. I messaged Kessler, and he said Petrov took off with some puck bunny. He probably won't be back tonight at all."

"Then why are you waking me?" I grumble and settle back onto the pillow.

"Because you're in my bed."

Surely, the sleep deprivation and half-passed-out state I'm in is imagining the sexy growl in his voice.

"My bed is, like, an hour away," I complain and close my eyes again.

"Isn't it down the block in the next hotel over?" Ollie asks.

"If you make me get up and crawl my ass in that direction, it'll take an hour to get there."

"Fine. Stay. But just … I don't want to be a dick about this, but can you, umm … set an alarm, and—"

My eyes widen when reality sets in. "Shit. Meathead can't have gay journalist sneaking out of his room in the morning. What was I thinking?"

Ollie grabs my wrist as I try to make an escape from the bed. "You think I'm a meathead?"

"If the skate fits."

"I don't know how to feel about that."

I sigh. "I don't mean it in the brainless jock kind of way. I mean, I joke about you being brainless, but we both know you're not. You're actually quite articulate."

"That totally feels like you're calling me a smart dumb person."

"Hey, you think I'm a bloodsucking journalist when I've proved I'm anything but."

He nods. "Yeah, okay, I'll give you that. And it's true you probably shouldn't be in here, but I want you. Uh, here, I mean. I want you to stay, but I … umm …"

There's the awkward guy I met six months ago.

The hand on my wrist relaxes, but his thumb makes circles on my palm that send a shiver through me. "If you keep sleeping next to me, I'm probably gonna do something I shouldn't."

I blink at him a few times, still a little out of it. Do something he shouldn't. Like *me*? He should do me.

"Fuck, totally do something you shouldn't" falls out of my mouth.

"Wait, wha—" He doesn't get his whole sentence out before I'm moving in close and capturing the mouth I kissed all those months ago.

Can I blame the sleepy haze on why I'm throwing myself at this man who up until not that long ago hated me? Maybe.

But, damn, how many times have I fantasized about these lips since the first time this happened? His playoff beard scrapes my skin, not quite long enough yet to be soft, but his mouth is hot and messy and all consuming.

He sucks in a breath, but a strong hand cups the back of my head, holding my face to his.

Everything clicks into place as if making out with Ollie Strömberg is the only thing that makes sense in the world, while at the same time, everything wrong with the situation tarnishes it around the edges.

Hooking up with a hockey player: bad idea.

Closeted hockey player hooking up with a journalist in his hotel room where his entire team is staying: terrible idea.

Running my hand down said hockey player's hard chest and glorious muscles: fucking brilliant idea. Or stupid, because I know we have to stop it. But right now, I'm going with brilliant.

Ollie grabs me around my waist and pulls me on top of him. His tablet gets thrown to the floor, hitting it with a thud. If it were mine, I'd be worried about it breaking, but Ollie doesn't give a damn. He only kisses me harder and pushes his tongue into my mouth.

It reminds me of the kiss we shared six months ago, only this is way hotter. And more horizontal.

Horizontal is good.

Another brilliant idea.

Ollie's hand slips between us, and his fingers make their way under my shirt.

I shamelessly grind over the hardness in his pants, and his free hand goes to my ass.

Breaking our lips apart, Ollie breathes heavy. "Damn, I've been thinking about this for six months."

Wait, what? I pull back and stare down at him. "Even when you found out who I was?"

"Especially then. I think my cock thought I despised it with how many hate jerk-off sessions I had thinking about you."

"Aww, that's the sweetest thing anyone's ever said to me." My sarcasm might be real, but the image of Ollie getting off to the thought of me makes me both pause and want to rip his clothes off.

"Kiss me again." Ollie leans up to take my mouth. He doesn't quite reach because I bring my hand up and put my fingers over his lips.

"What are we doing? We can't do this."

"Can we … not think about that right now?" To emphasize his point, Ollie rolls his hips beneath me.

"Fuck. Best argument ever. Let our future selves deal with this shit." I move my hand and kiss him again, and I find myself in a heavy make-out session as if we were teenagers.

Ollie doesn't try to take it further, just keeps teasing me with his perfect lips and probing tongue.

Needing more skin, I sit up, straddling him. My hands bunch in his T-shirt and push the hem up toward his throat. "Goddamn it," I whisper, and Ollie smiles.

His body is insane. Muscles on muscles and decorated in tattoos across his chest that stop just above his pecs.

Mi Vida. My fingers trail over the words written across his chest, but he grabs my wrist to stop me.

I want to ask what they mean and why he's suddenly staring at me with widened eyes, but a dark bruise catches my eye on his side. "The hit you took in third?"

"I've had worse. It's fine."

"Damn, that's hot."

Ollie chuckles. "Me being injured is hot?"

It plays right into my jock fantasy, but I won't be bringing that up any time soon. "Uh-huh."

"I'll try to get beaten up on the ice more often. Maybe become an enforcer."

I shake my head. "Nah, you've got more talent than that."

He stares up at me with nothing but appreciation in his soft gaze. I don't know if it's from the compliment or my hand skimming over his skin and giving him goose bumps.

My hand trails over his pierced nipple, and he shudders beneath me. "This wasn't in the night you got super drunk," I say.

"Playoffs. Need it in or we'll lose."

Ugh, hockey players and their superstitions.

"Worked tonight then," I say dryly.

In the blink of an eye and with the strength of a hockey player, he rolls us over so I'm pinned underneath him.

"If this is supposed to be some sort of punishment for mouthing off, I have to say you suck at it." My finger, still hovering on his nipple under his shirt, trails down his hard chest. "Isn't that like … I dunno, a safety concern? You guys are so violent."

"Eh, I put tape over it, and then we wear so much protective gear we can't feel anything anyway."

"Still. It'd be a shame to lose a nipple." Especially ones as pretty as his. I don't say this out loud though. Who tells a person they have pretty nipples?

Ollie laughs. "Would it now?"

His hazel eyes lock with mine, and the air between us becomes serious. Ollie's face slowly falls. When his mouth comes down on mine, it's soft and no longer urgent or exploring. It feels like a promise we both know he can't keep.

His fingers make slow work of my buttoned shirt, and then they trail down my chest. They continue their sweet assault to my stomach and then lower to my pants.

"Your belt buckle is in the way," he whispers against my mouth.

"That's not my belt buckle."

Ollie groans and collapses on top of me, burying his face in my neck. "Who knew you'd be a tease?"

"I'm full of surprises."

His hand cups my cock over my suit pants, and I try not to yell out when his grip tightens, but a grunt escapes.

"Full of lots of *big* surprises." He strokes my cock so slowly, and I let out a whimper. "Damn," he whispers. "I want this inside me."

That building anticipation, the soaring to higher heights, and that feeling you get while chasing an orgasm plummets, and his words sober me.

My eyes fly open and meet his half-hooded, lust-filled ones. "I'm a bottom."

His hand stops moving on my aching dick, and I can practically see the moment his need crashes too. He sits up, straddling my lap, much like how I was on him only a few minutes ago. "So am I."

We stare at each other at an impasse, neither of us knowing where to go from here.

"Blowjobs?" Ollie whines, and I laugh.

"How are you a bottom?"

He narrows his eyes. "Are you about to get stereotypical on me?"

"Well, shit. Yeah, I guess I was. I just … you look like a top."

"And what exactly does a top look like?"

"Domineering."

Ollie snorts. "Ash had been out for four years before we got together. He already knew what he liked and didn't like, so …"

"So, you got the short end of the stick? So to speak."

He barks out a laugh. "I'm not discussing Ash's stick with you, but I will say if you ever met him, you'd think he's the opposite of domineering."

"Wait, does that mean Ash was the first guy you were with?"

Ollie cocks his head. "Ash is the *only* guy I've been with. I thought you would've known that."

"But …" I think about all this time that's gone past since we met. "No one?"

Ollie leans over me. "No one's even come close to tempting me since I met this pain in the ass reporter a few months ago."

"Not even when you hated me?" My voice is small.

"I've never hated you. Far from it. I've wanted you every day since we met."

He kisses me again, slow and tender, his tongue massaging mine, and I try to savor it. Just because he's admitted he wants me, that doesn't mean it can happen.

I've been down this road with closeted guys before, and I can't do it again.

But when he lowers himself on top of me fully, a little voice in the back of my head begs, "Maybe just for a little while?"

I'm about to surrender when—

Bang, bang, bang. "Strömberg. Open up." The thick, Russian accent must belong to—

"Petrov's back." Ollie scrambles off me.

"Shit." I get up as fast as I can and start putting on my shoes that are beside the bed.

Petrov bangs on the door again. "Wake up. I forgot key and need to piss."

"Just a sec," Ollie calls out.

"Fuck, what do we do?" I whisper.

Our interview excuse won't fly when we're both half-undressed, breathing hard with flushed cheeks.

There's a knock on the door again. Now I'm struggling with the small-ass buttons on my shirt. I give up about halfway done and stand to throw my laptop bag over my shoulder.

Ollie steps forward and whispers, "He needs to use the bathroom, so hide and sneak out while he's in there."

"Hide?" I hiss. "Where?"

More banging. "Ollie!"

"Shit." Ollie grabs my arm in a rough way like he did that day we met at the arena. Still don't mind the manhandling.

Not the time, Lennon.

He shoves me behind the door as he opens it, and I hold my breath.

"What the fuck took you so long?" Petrov asks and charges with his big-ass feet pounding on the carpet toward the bathroom.

Once the bathroom door's shut, I make a break for it, and Ollie steps into the hall with me.

He glances left and right down the hallway and opens his mouth to say something, but nothing comes out.

I fake a smile because I know what's coming. "Don't worry about it. Didn't happen."

Apparently, making out with me has rendered him speechless. I wish I could say that's a common occurrence with me, but this would be a first. The sucky thing is it has nothing to do with my skills.

"It … that … I mean, that was too close," he finally says.

"I know."

The toilet in the room flushes, and Ollie's head twists faster than the girl's from that old movie *The Exorcist.*

"Good luck in game two." I turn on my heel and hightail it down the corridor to the elevators, all the while wondering how the hell I'm supposed to forget tonight ever happened.

CHAPTER ELEVEN

OLLIE

Getting that night with Lennon in my hotel room out of my head is next to impossible, and every time I think about his lips or how amazingly hard his cock felt under my hand, I can't help wanting more. I imagine kissing his naked skin, having him inside me, and wonder what he looks like when he comes. None of that can be turned into reality, so like it always has, hockey helps me block out the real world.

Games two and three, we pull off wins. Barely. Both times are a struggle, but we manage. Game four is a fucking mess, and game five isn't any better.

"What happened to us out there?" Petrov asks as we make it back to our hotel room for the night.

We'll be in New York for game six, and if we make it to game seven, we'll be in Boston next week. I'm not getting my hopes up we'll be back.

"We're getting progressively worse," I say.

Petrov loosens his tie and takes it over his head, throwing it like he doesn't care where it lands. "I'm going out. Going to find hot chick and wham, bam, thank you ma'am her like I did after game one."

I try not to laugh. "Petrov, who taught you that saying?"

"Bjorn."

Ah. Figures.

Petrov is quick to get dressed and leave, remembering his keycard to get back in this time.

The superstition thing isn't so bad during the regular season, but when the Stanley Cup is at stake, some of us take it a little too far. Nearly all of us have our routines and little quirks.

Redoing what happened the night of game one isn't an option for me though. No matter how much I want it to be.

Since that night, I've only seen Lennon in a professional capacity, and even though I beg him silently to ask me a question at press conferences, he's only directed his questions at Coach.

Maybe I could go to his hotel under the proviso of being superstitious …

No, don't go over there.

But what if it was to talk and hang out and nothing more?

I shake my head. After last time, I don't think I could just hang out with him. I'm going to be strong.

That doesn't stop my fingers from flying across my phone screen.

You happen to know Lennon's number?

Damn it.

Jet: *Whhhhhhhhy?*

Should've known Jet wouldn't be easy and hand it over no questions asked.

Me: *Because I'm asking. That's why.*

Jet: *Did he write another article you want to ream him for?*

Depends on what type of *reaming* he means.

Me: *I JUST WANNA HANG OUT. IT'S DEPRESSING WHEN WE LOSE, AND ALL MY TEAMMATES ARE BRINGING ME DOWN.*

Or I assume they would be if I were with them.

Jet: *YOU LOST? DAMN.*

Me: *YOU KNOW, JUST BECAUSE WE AREN'T PLAYING IN OUR ARENA, YOU SHOULD AT LEAST FOLLOW THE SERIES ...*

Jet gives me the number, and I've never been more thankful.

Me: *GUILT TRIP FOR THE WIN! THANKS, MAN.*

Now I have to decide if I'm going to use the information or not. I shouldn't, but I'm also not going to try to lie to myself again by saying I won't.

I could text, but that'd give him a chance to not reply. I hit dial on his number instead.

It rings numerous times, and I imagine him staring at his phone debating whether to answer the unfamiliar number. I imagine the adorable concentration line over the frame of his glasses which he gets during press conferences.

Although, he must've got his contacts prescription refilled finally, because he hasn't worn his glasses all week.

I prefer the nerdy glasses.

"Lennon Hawkins." When his voice finally hits my ears, the professional tone does things to my groin.

This is not good.

"Hello?"

Shit, I've been too quiet. "Your reporter voice is hot." Fuck, not what I was supposed to say.

"Thank you?" Lennon sounds unsure, and I don't know if it's because he's being sarcastic or he doesn't know who it is.

"It's, ah, Ollie."

"I know." He's smiling now. I can hear it in his voice. "What's up?"

"Ah ... Petrov's gone out for the night."

"Thanks for the scoop. I'll write it into my article right now."

"Smartass," I grumble and let out a loud breath. "He has this … theory."

"Okaaay."

"That to not suck in game six, we need to do exactly what we did the night after game one."

He's silent for a beat, and I begin to wonder if the call dropped out. Or maybe he dropped the phone. "Umm …"

I know exactly what he's picturing right now. Us, fooling around on my bed, kissing as if we were told the world was going to end, and leading to something we should be thankful got interrupted.

I hesitate before saying, "I'm not saying he has a point, but it'd be kinda fun to see if he did."

Lennon stays silent.

I sigh. "Okay, yeah, not a great idea."

"Ollie …" His tone is soft, but his voice has an edge to it, and I know what's coming.

My eyes fuse shut, and I pinch the bridge of my nose. "I don't know why I called. I wanted to see you, but talking to you right now, I remember why that's a bad idea."

I can't be with him in the way he deserves. It's not like we could go on a date like a real couple or do any of the shit Ash wanted me to while we were together. Pursuing Lennon would make me an asshole, but all I want to do is find out what room he's in and go over there and finish what we started five games ago.

"I think Boston is the issue," Lennon says.

"Huh?"

"Boston," he says as if it's the most obvious thing in the world. "The two times we've kissed was when we were here.

Totally Boston's fault. You don't want me. Boston wants you to want me."

"Boston is a shitty wingman," I complain.

"Yeah. Not the best at picking the ideal guy for you."

"What's wrong with you?"

"Let's just say you're not the first closeted guy to screw with me. I kind of have a penchant for them."

Shit, I'm already an asshole. "It's not my intention to screw with you."

"That's a slight improvement on the others."

"*Others*? How many have there been?"

"Two. Plus multiple crushes."

A pang of jealousy hits me, which is ridiculous. Lennon's been with other guys. That's a given. That doesn't mean I want to hear about it, though.

"It started with Daniel Pirro." He sighs wistfully, and I hate it.

I may not want to hear it, but apparently, we're doing this.

"In high school, I wasn't out, but I've always been one of those guys where it was obvious. I used to say I'm like the Luke Skywalker of gay guys."

"Wow, think highly of yourself, huh?"

Lennon laughs. "No, but the gay is strong with this one. I set gaydars off within a two-mile radius."

"Sounds convenient."

"Except when you're a sixteen-year-old kid."

I wince.

"I don't know if Daniel or maybe his friends saw me checking him out or if they just got a kick out of humiliating me, but one day after school, Daniel—the fucking captain of the football team —corners me outside my AP class."

AP classes? Figures Lennon is smart. I barely graduated. I did enough to pass so Ma and Dad would continue to let me play hockey. I'm not dumb, but I'm not exactly college material.

"I was always the last to leave, so everyone had already gone. I was waiting for him to hit me or tell me to stop staring at him or something. Instead, he asked me out."

My stomach churns. I don't really want to know where this story is going, and I thank God that I had my older brothers to look out for me. I never had to worry about being outed and getting hurt—all my fear has been about my career, even back in high school. I was practically born wearing skates, and it's all I've ever cared about.

"What happened?" I ask.

"I thought he was fucking with me, but when he stared right at me with vulnerable eyes and asked if I was like him, I … well, yeah, I fell for it. I was getting everything I'd fantasized about for months, so I didn't question as hard as I should have. I went home thinking I had an actual chance with a football player."

I fake gag. "Football. Pfft. Hockey is way sexier."

Lennon must be too stuck in his memory, because he doesn't even try to laugh at my attempt at lightening the mood.

"What did he do?" I ask.

"For our date, he was waiting for me outside the movie theater, and when I approached, he smiled. I've replayed that look on his face for so long, trying to find anything sinister in it, but to this day, I still confuse it for a genuine smile. Because as soon as I reached him, he looked over the top of my head. I turned to find the entire football team behind me."

"Oh, fuck. Did they—"

"They didn't do anything," Lennon says. "A few fag-bombs were dropped, threats, and some pushing around. It was scary, and yeah, Daniel joined in, but the manager of the movie theater stepped in before anything worse could happen. He was on a cigarette break."

"Lucky." I hate to think what might've happened to Lennon if the manager hadn't been there.

"I ran home and made the mistake of telling my mom what'd happened."

"How is that a mistake?"

"It made her worry about everything from that point. She wanted to pull me out of the school, but none of the other schools in the area offered the AP classes I was taking. I chose to stay, thinking it'd be like a movie where I'd be constantly looking over my shoulder and worrying about being attacked by the football team, but I don't know whether it was the manager or my mom talking to the school, but they pretty much left me alone other than some taunting and occasionally tripping me in the hall in front of everyone. I got good reflexes after a while. It wasn't ideal, but I've heard of worse. Last I heard, Daniel had come out in college. Doesn't play football anymore though."

"I'm sorry." The words are empty and meaningless.

The fear I have about coming out seems trivial in comparison to how scared sixteen-year-old Lennon would've been outside that movie theater.

"Then come the college years where I meet Dylan."

"Another football player?" I ask.

"Worse. Baseball."

I groan. "You're killing me, smalls."

Lennon laughs, but there's no humor in it. "He asked me out a few times before I said yes. I wasn't going to make the same mistake."

"How long was it until you made the same mistake?"

"Hey, I lasted a good few months," Lennon says proudly.

"Then he turned up at my dorm after the team won their conference."

"Championship winners are just too hard to resist, huh? Is that all I have to do? Win the Stanley Cup? No pressure or anything."

"After tonight's performance by the Dragons, I don't have anything to be concerned about."

"Ooh, ouch. Is that what your article's gonna say tomorrow?"

"Maybe. But your name isn't even mentioned, as promised."

"Besides, I'm not the one who fucked up out there tonight," I say. "Wait, we're totally getting off track. Dylan."

"When I told Mom I was dating a baseball player, she was worried it was going to be another Daniel situation. I assured her Dylan was different."

"Maybe you should've stayed away from guys with a D," I say.

Lennon laughs. "And become straight? No thanks."

It takes a second to realize what I said had come out wrong. "I meant their names. Daniel and Dylan. You know a name that doesn't have a D in it? Ollie."

This makes Lennon laugh more.

"I'm just gonna shut my mouth. You were saying?"

"We had a couple of dates, doing the whole sneaking around thing, because while he was closeted, he wasn't like Daniel. He was at least willing to admit he was gay but had to keep quiet because of his career prospects of making it to the majors."

I recognize a giant similarity between Dylan and me, and I don't like it.

Lennon's tone softens, as if reading my mind. "You're not like Dylan. You already acknowledge me in public, which is more than he did."

"So, did you get over it and dump him?" It'd make me feel a lot better if that were the case. Part of me wishes I had the strength to tell Ash to leave sooner than he did. We both know Ash stayed with me for far too long.

"I wish I was smart enough for that. Because we both had roommates, we didn't have the chance to, you know, do much … uh, physically. We planned for him to come over to my dorm when I knew my roommate had back-to-back classes. We were kissing when my roommate came back for a book he forgot for a class. Dylan hadn't been there long, so we were still fully clothed but going at it up against the wall. When we heard the door click, we quickly separated, but it wasn't fast enough. My roommate's gaze flicked between us, and before either of us could speak or come up with a lie, Dylan punched me in the face and told me he came by to study, not to hook up, and that he wasn't gay."

I suck in a sharp breath. "What the fuck?"

"Oh, that's not even the worst part. The next day, he pretended like he didn't do anything wrong. Knocked on my door, practically let himself in, and threw himself on my bed, completely ignoring the shiner on my face. Said he was 'protecting what we had.' That weekend also happened to be the start of spring break, so when I went home, Mom saw the black eye, and the worrying became worse. She was convinced I was the victim of a hate crime, and then having to explain it was my boyfriend who did it? I understand she has the right to be worried, but I'm not one to hide who I am."

And I am. And that's the entire reason we're on the phone right now instead of face to face.

"Shit, I didn't mean that as some kind of dig at you. I understand why you can't—"

"It's okay," I say. "I completely understand. It sucks, but it's my reality. I chose this when I decided my career was more important than anything else."

Lennon draws in a deep breath I can hear through the phone. "I wish it was easier for you to have both."

"Can I ask you something? Why, after all of that, did you go into sports journalism? Like, shouldn't you hate the industry and everything it stands for?"

Lennon hesitates, and I can practically hear him opening his mouth to say something but changing his mind. When he does finally find his voice, it's small. "Just because I don't have the talent to play the sports I love, that doesn't mean I don't still love them. I've been obsessed ever since I was little. I like analyzing plays and the general atmosphere of a game and am fascinated by team mentality. I guess you were born with the athlete gene, and I was born with the spectator gene."

"I admire you for not holding resentment." I admire a lot about Lennon after what he just told me.

"Oh, don't get me wrong, I resent those assholes from my past. But that resentment also motivates me to make a change in the sporting industry. I want to write more pro-LGBTQ stories. The NHL, MLB, and the NBA still don't have out players on their current rosters. If it weren't for Matt, the NFL wouldn't either. I wasn't lying when I said I want to support gay men in sports."

"And I have all the hope in the world that you'll succeed."

CHAPTER TWELVE

S topping us from going there again is a smart idea. My cock disagrees, but with the way Ollie reacts to my past, even he can't admit that he won't hurt me. The best thing to do in this situation is walk away before becoming invested.

With my track record, I can't risk it.

Maybe third time's a charm.

Wishful thinking.

Not to mention if we were to start something real, I'd be putting more than my heart on the line. Female reporters who've gotten involved with athletes tend to not stick around in the industry for long. Whether they're honest about it from the beginning—something Ollie and I could never do because he's closeted —or if they're found out, they become targets, labeled as jersey chasers, and then their articles are ridiculed for being biased.

My jock issues aren't the only thing holding me back.

So, yes, even if I'm kicking my own ass for turning Ollie down, I did the right thing.

In the coming days, the Dragons are plagued by illness, injury, and stupid penalties. They lose the same way they started the series—with a fucking shutout.

They leave the arena with their heads hanging low but their hopes high. This is the furthest the Dragons have been in five years, and they show potential for next year.

During the press conference, Ollie's not even present. The team captain and the head coach are the only people giving interviews. They do the usual thank-yous, praise their team for getting as far as they did, and spout bullshit about an optimistic future for the team. By the time I've written up the gist of my article and made my way out of the arena, I can't find Jet or Ollie anywhere.

Not that I want to see Ollie. Last time I sought him out to give my condolences, we ended up lip-locked and grinding against one another.

I wait by the players' entrance and get out my phone. There's no message from Jet, so I text him asking if he's already left.

Leaning against the wall, I tap out some more notes on my phone to add to the article before I send it off to my editor. Every time the door clicks open, I perk up, only to be disappointed when it's never Ollie who steps through.

No, I'm waiting for Jet. Not him.

Keep telling yourself that.

Some of the players look at me weird, like I'm some sort of puck bunny, but most of them keep walking.

Jet texts back saying he left for a date as soon as the game was over, and apparently, it's going so well I shouldn't go home until later. Like, a lot later.

Great.

I'm about to give up and think Ollie's gone too, but as I push off the wall, I run into two people who have familiar faces.

Oh, sweet Neil Patrick Harris, this is not good.

"Clark," Ollie's mom singsongs. Ollie's parents' matching smiles are a little unnerving.

My heart pounds. "Uh … hi, Mr. and Mrs. Strömberg. Didn't expect to see you here." Or ever, for that matter.

"Ollie didn't tell you we were coming?" she asks. "We wouldn't have missed it. We had faith it'd turn out better, obviously, but we were here just in case."

I nod, not knowing what else to do. "W-why … I mean …" Why are they being nice to me? Last time I'd checked, Ollie had said he told them I cheated on him.

"Why what, dear?" Ollie's mom says.

"Umm …"

The door clicks open again, and a towering presence appears behind me.

"Ma. Dad," Ollie says. I swear I hear him curse under his breath. "Hey, can you give me and Le—Clark a minute?"

They give us a peculiar look, but then his dad points toward the parking garage. "We'll be in the car."

Ollie smiles, but it looks fake. "Thanks."

He pulls away from where his teammates are still pouring out of the stadium.

"I have a confession to make" is the first thing out of his mouth. "I lied" is the second.

"Lied? About what?"

"About telling them you cheated on me. I … I, uh … oh, God, this is bad." He takes a deep breath. "I didn't tell them we broke up. They still think we're together."

I step back. "Why? I mean, how? What?"

"Our stupid plan worked. Ma hasn't bugged me about coming out in six months. She's told me if I want to keep you, I'll have to face it eventually, but she's stopped with all the pro-LGBTQ crap and hasn't mentioned that video of Adam Rippon interviewing his own mom in ages."

"Oh, the one where they talk about him deciding to come out before the Olympics?"

"Yeah, that one. Ma can recite that interview word for word, but it's been *months*. It's the longest break I've gotten from all her idealist talk."

"That's great." It's a little sad he had to lie about having a boyfriend to get them to back off, but the important thing is they are. "It's your life. You can tell them whatever, but what has this got to do with me? Other than they still think I'm Clark?"

"I told them you were out of town on business, which is why you couldn't be here tonight. I didn't think … I never thought you'd run into each other."

"I was waiting for Jet, but he's already gone home. Well, technically, he's gone on a date and told me not to come home if I can help it."

Ollie stares off into the parking lot. "I want to ask you something."

My gaze flicks up to his. "What is it?"

"A favor, of sorts. But we both win."

"Listening."

"Come home with me tonight. Spend some time with my parents as Clark, and then crash in my room. I'd offer you my spare room, but Ma and Dad are in there."

"In your room?"

That's the worst idea I've ever really, really, *really* wanted to do.

"I'll take the floor," Ollie says. "I just … if you don't come back with us, Ma and Dad will probably ask questions, and you said yourself you need to not be home right now. Win-win?"

I bite the inside of my cheek. Going home with him would be stupid. Really stupid. But with his parents in the room right next to us, I doubt we'd be in the mood to maul each other. Maybe. Nothing says boner killer like the chance of parentals overhearing. And it will get me out of listening to Matt and Noah's little brother getting plowed.

Even though I know it's a bad idea to dangle temptation in front of both of us, I find myself saying, "Okay. I'm in."

As soon as I agree to it and Ollie's face lights up, I know it's a mistake and I'm one hundred percent screwed.

No way am I going to stay off him tonight.

The sweet torture of being pretend boyfriends starts as soon as we arrive at Ollie's surprisingly modest apartment. The open plan shows a small living room and kitchen with two bedrooms side by side opposite the front door and a bathroom-slash-laundry off the kitchen.

Taking in the hardwood floors and crown molding though, I'm certain the quaintness still costs more than my entire monthly income.

Once in the confines of his apartment and out of the public eye, Ollie turns on Mr. Boyfriend, and fuck, I love it. From the way he wraps his arm around my back to the way he offers me a bottle of water from his fridge without asking and hands it off like I've been here before and done this a thousand times … it paints a nice picture that we can't have.

As we take seats on the couch and Ollie puts on *SportsCenter*, the rest of us grumble.

"Don't do this to yourself," I say and turn to his parents. "Is masochism an Ollie trait or a Strömberg trait?"

"Definitely an Ollie trait," his mom says. "Nic and Vic too. It seemed to skip over Leo and Max."

"But Leo and Max are stubborn as all hell," his dad says.

"Now *that's* a Strömberg trait," Ollie says. "All of you guys are the worst." He looks at me. "That trait skipped me. Obviously."

"*Obviously,*" I mock.

"What about your family?" his mom asks.

"Uh, well, I have a younger sister who's still in college. She's known to be stubborn. Mom and Dad are kind of set in their way of thinking. I'm delightful."

"So delightful," Ollie says dryly.

"Where did you grow up?" she asks.

Ah, the ultimate meeting the parents pastime: grilling the boyfriend.

"Upstate New York."

"What was that like?" Ollie asks. He's pressed against me, his arm lying across the back of the couch behind me, and I swear he moves closer as he asks. Is he using this as an excuse to touch me when we agreed we weren't going to do that? Because I want to hate him for taking advantage but can't, because I like it too much.

My hand lands on his thigh, and I cock my head. "Shouldn't you know? I talk to you about it all the time."

His eyes widen, either in surprise at my hand on his leg and that I'm milking this situation for all it's worth like he is or he's pissed as hell that I just threw him in the deep end. "Right. But you know I always tune you out."

I pinch his leg, which only makes him laugh.

"Ollie said you had to work tonight?" his dad asks.

"I did." And shit, I still do. I'm surprised my phone isn't

blowing up from my editor waiting for the article so he can fix it and go to bed.

Harry's up most of the night anyway—God knows we hear about his insomnia constantly—but he gets grumpy when we turn our shit in late.

Ollie's arm drops to my shoulder, and a gentle hand runs down my arm. My breath hitches, and fuck, this charade could be the death of me. It's barely gotten started, but it doesn't take much for me to get going when I think of Ollie.

His touch is sensory overload. The scent of his cologne gets stuck in my nose, the warmth of his chest right near my head makes my face heat, and when I swallow, I swear I can still taste him from last week.

Then I realize he's talking to me. "Huh?"

He tries to hide his amusement, but it doesn't work. "Did you need to finish off a report or something? For work? You can use the bedroom."

"Thanks. I shouldn't take long."

The excuse is what I need to peel myself away from Ollie, but when I get up, his eyes go to my crotch, and if the small grin he tries to hide has anything to say, he's proud of his work. Except now I get to try to balance my laptop on my hard-on. That's gonna be fun.

What's going to be even more fun is trying to pick the correct bedroom. A boyfriend who's been here before would know which one Ollie uses. There are two doors, side by side, both equally possible to be Ollie's bedroom. Do I play eeny, meeny, miny, moe?

A throat clears behind me, and when I turn, Ollie stretches his arms over his head and subtly points to the door on the right. Smooth.

And as soon as I make my way over to it and close the door

behind me, Ollie's mom's muffled voice says, "He's a keeper. Cute as a button."

"Walls are pretty thin, Ma."

Probably doesn't help Ollie's apartment is bare. The room is simple. Bed, bedside drawers, and a dresser in the corner. Noise must bounce around the emptiness.

I finish off my bittersweet article and upload it to the work cloud. Normally, I'd ask Harry what the plan is now. The Dragons' season is over, and while technically I've been following the whole conference, my focus has definitely been on this team to pull off the win. Now they haven't, I could be sent back to Chicago or assigned to follow a different team. Maybe Kevin will take back the playoffs seeing as it's getting near the end.

Which would mean leaving New York.

I'm still staring at the empty space in my email when Ollie enters the bedroom.

"'Rents are going to bed."

"Oh, okay." I call out, "Goodnight."

In reply, there is a low "Such a sweet boy."

Ollie laughs. "She loves you."

"So I heard, but—"

I can't finish my train of thought because Ollie starts stripping out of his suit. He eyes me the entire time, never looking down at his buttons as he undoes them expertly. His fingers work his clothes, and I remember what it was like to have those fingers on me. His large hands gripping my ass as I ground on top of his dick.

"You're so not playing fair." My voice is whisper-quiet so his parents can't hear.

Once he's down to his boxer briefs, he pulls back the covers and climbs into bed next to me. "We're boyfriends. It's nothing you haven't seen before." Then the bastard winks.

"Don't think for one second you can use our situation to your advantage." I'm only half-serious.

His smile drops a little but not completely. "Not at all. No touching." Ollie lies back, pulling the blanket over his waist but not up to cover this chest. His beautiful, hard, tattooed chest.

"Didn't you say you'd sleep on the floor?"

He runs a hand down his delectable pecs to his abs. "Are you really gonna make me sleep on the cold ground? I totally will if you ask me to."

I sigh. "No."

I close my laptop and put it back in my laptop bag. Then I even the score a little. I don't have as much finesse or tact as Ollie and drop my clothes to the floor without the scorching eye-fucking he gave me while he stripped. Still, payback seems to be working with how much his eyes roam over me. I want to taunt him about seeing something he likes, but we're already playing with matches. I don't want to start an inferno.

I climb back into bed next to him, and turn on my side to face him, pretending like I'm not hardening in my briefs with every second I stare at his bare chest.

I need a distraction. "What're your plans now?" I ask. Nothing like reminding him he just lost the Cup to bring the mood down.

Ollie's eyes turn from heated to sad. "Dunno. There's not really anything in New York for me. I'll probably go back to Boston and do the family thing. You? You still gonna follow the playoffs?"

"If my boss wants me on it, yeah, but I might be heading back to Chicago. My assignment when Harry sent me here was kind of vague. It was to cover the entire conference, but he wanted me to follow you guys specifically. Probably because of all the articles I wrote about you."

Ollie's lips tug downward.

"I'm hoping to go back to football again when it comes around, but I don't know what my editor has planned for me. He was convinced you guys were going to take it out this year, so I could really be sent anywhere now you're out."

"Just another disappointed person." Ollie sighs. "Chicago, huh?" His tone is hard to dissect. "So, really, this could be one of the last times we see each other?"

"Until next season, probably. I don't know what upcoming projects Harry wants me on, but he's been impressed with my coverage of hockey even if *some* people think I don't know what I'm talking about."

Ollie turns his head to face me. "I was wrong."

I gasp. "Sorry, what was that? Can I, like, dictate that to my phone somehow?"

"Shut up. I. Was. Wrong. You're a great reporter, Lennon."

I point to my chest. "Clark. Shit, you're so bad with names, dude."

Ollie shoves me so I roll onto my back. "Go to sleep already."

Go to sleep next to Ollie while sporting a major boner? Not going to happen. Still, we lie there in the darkness, both of us not sleeping. I can tell because Ollie's breaths are uneven, and even that somehow turns me on.

God, I want to reach down and take my aching dick into my hand. Or maybe push Ollie's head down there. That'd work too.

"So, this is what it's like to die from blue balls," Ollie grumbles. "I'm gonna start calling you Blue, because it's always your fault."

I burst into laughter so loud I'm sure his parents can hear me. Ollie's hand clamps over my mouth.

"I really don't want the folks to think I'm getting laid in here."

"If someone laughs that hard during sex, you're doing it

wrong," I say against his hand before he removes it. "This was such a bad idea."

"Horrible idea," he agrees. "But I have a proposition for you."

I cock an eyebrow in the dark and then realize he probably can't make that out. "Another one?"

"We agreed we can't hook up, right?"

"Right."

"But jerking off is totally a solo act, right?"

"Right."

"So, if we jerk off together without touching one another ..."

Terrible. Horrible. Stupid, stupid, stupid idea, but that's not gonna stop me. No way. "I love technicalities."

In one swift move, I reach under the blanket and pull my underwear off. Ollie does the same, and then he reaches over to turn the bedside light on and throws lube and tissues on the bed.

"I'd say something about you preparing for this, but you didn't know I was coming over."

"I haven't had sex in over a year. Where else do you think I'd keep supplies for getting myself off?"

"I'd feel sorry for you if it wasn't about the same amount of time for me."

"Why the fuck have you not had sex for a year?"

"Really want to get into that right now?" I ask, holding up the lube.

"We're so coming back to this later."

I'll have to come up with another way to distract him from asking that again, because no way in hell am I admitting that since meeting him no one else has even interested me. And before that, I was already in a slump.

As I squirt lube into my hand, I feel his stare on me, and I become a little self-conscious. "If we're supposed to pretend like the other one of us isn't here, you're gonna have to stop looking at me like that."

"Like what?" he asks, innocently.

"Like you want to tear me apart."

"I'd much prefer you tear me apart."

I snort. Ollie's a bottom. Still can't get over it. It's not like I haven't topped before, but when I have, I've been too self-conscious about making it good for them, and I can never last long. Bottoming, I can let myself go.

Ollie kicks off the blankets, and miles of mouthwatering muscles lay two feet from me, and I can't tear my eyes away. If I thought he felt big while we rubbed against each other last week, it's nothing to seeing how awesomely huge and pretty his dick is. I don't even know if it's possible to have a pretty dick, but Ollie does. Thick, veiny, and uncut.

"If we're supposed to pretend like the other one of us isn't here, you're gonna have to stop looking at my cock," he mimics but in a much higher voice. I want to dispute that's not at all how I sound, but that doesn't come out of my mouth.

"I can't help it," I blurt instead.

"Shame we can't hook up then."

We can't. We really can't.

"I mean, really, if we're looking at each other, it's the equivalent of watching porn," I say, trying to rationalize my blatant worshiping of his cock.

"Yay, more technicalities," Ollie says, as I watch him lazily stroke his long, hard, gorgeous length.

"So long as I don't have to break out the clown makeup for you, it'll be fine."

He laughs, but it doesn't last long as he watches me grip the base of my shaft and squeeze a little too hard. It's not going to take long to send me over the edge, and this is supposed to be about getting off, but I want to make it last.

Ollie breathes heavy beside me, his teeth gritted, and if I had to guess, he's trying to hold back from moaning too loudly. His strokes slowly increase in pace, and a pearly drop of precum drips down the side.

I want to lick it. God, I want to lick him. All over.

I shudder and start a punishing pace on my cock. Tightening my ass muscles, I thrust up into my hand over and over again, never once taking my eyes off Ollie.

"I wanna touch you so bad," Ollie whispers. "I won't, but fuck, I want to." Ollie lifts his legs and moves his lube-slicked hand down to his balls and farther down while the other one takes over pumping his cock.

"Wait, are you—" I make the mistake of giving him eye contact.

His eyelids are hooded, his mouth parted slightly. The look of lust is almost enough to have me coming.

"Am I what?" he taunts. "Playing with my ass? Is that what you wanted to ask?"

I nod.

"Flip around and see for yourself."

I hesitate.

"Just like watching porn, remember?" he reminds me.

As soon as I maneuver myself on the bed and get full sight of Ollie two fingers deep inside his own ass, I can't hold back anymore.

The grunt that escapes me as I shoot all over myself has me biting my knuckles on my free hand to prevent it from turning into a shout.

Ollie's large fingers disappear all the way inside him and stay lodged in there, no doubt pressing against his prostate. He strokes his cock faster until ropes of cum land on his impressive abs. Some reaches his tats, and I had no idea how hot cum-covered tattoos could be. We both sink against the mattress.

"Best live porn ever," Ollie says.

"Fuck yes."

CHAPTER THIRTEEN

Lennon might be going back to Chicago. Yet another sucky thing about losing last night, although, that's not the worst of it. The worst is that I thought I was getting somewhere. This year wasn't my first playoffs, but it's the first year I imagined winning it and holding that cup over my head and believed it was a possibility. Recently the fantasy also included me coming out and telling the world that being gay doesn't affect playing hockey. Idealistic, maybe, and complete bullshit that I need to win the Stanley Cup before feeling worthy, but that's how it is.

Lennon's relaxed face sleeping next to me gives me the kind of optimism I want to hold onto—something I never really had with Ash.

I don't know if I can endure another season just hoping to make it to the Cup game, and the thought of making it all that way and losing again … that'd make it two years. Two years where I'd have to continue to live like this. Three if we don't make it the next year. Four after that.

It's as if I can hear Lennon's voice in my head: *Hey, look at that, the hockey player can do math.*

My point is, it's a lot to put the fate of your life in the hands of a hockey game outcome.

Not that I can really complain about my life. I'm on a multi-million-dollar contract that has two years left. I have future security with the money I've already made. Yet, for the first time ever, I want what Ma and Dad have been spouting for years.

Hockey has always been enough for me until now.

I want to take to the ice as an openly gay player. Win some games, go home exhausted, tired, sometimes bruised, and with any hope, I'd be met by a gorgeous guy—who, at the moment admittedly looks a hell of a lot like Lennon in my head—welcoming me home with a kiss ... and okay, maybe a blowjob, but I don't think I should put *that* on my official list of goals or anything.

I've put my life on hold for six years playing hockey, lost someone I truly loved and cared about, but it's the guy next to me who gives me the courage to want to do this. And not by promising me a future or telling me I have to, but by simply understanding where I'm coming from and accepting that I need to do this in my own time. With my parents, with Ash, it has always felt like they can't give me support until I'm out. Like I'm living my life the wrong way. Lennon ... he may want to protect himself from me hurting him, but he gives me his support anyway. He's technically in sports too, so he understands in a way the others don't.

I never knew empathy could turn me on, but there you go.

The smell of bacon comes from my kitchen, and I know Ma's been up since mom o'clock cooking me a consolation breakfast for losing our chance at the Cup last night.

She used to do the same thing when I was in the juniors and I'd lose the championship.

If my nose is accurate, there's only a few minutes until the food will be ready, and I'll have to pull myself away from Lennon. We're not even touching, but his presence is warmer than the blanket we share, and being next to him feels like waking up on a lazy winter day, cozied under heat with no reason to get out of bed all day.

I don't want that feeling to go away, but I know it will as soon as we get up.

There's a knock on the door and a high-pitched singing voice. "Can't sleep the day away."

I groan. "I'm twelve years old again."

Lennon chuckles but doesn't open his eyes.

"We're depressed in here," I call out to Ma. "We lost."

"You lost," Lennon mumbles. "My team's still in it."

I gasp. "Who's your team?"

"Chicago. Duh."

"Where's the loyalty? You were born in New York."

Lennon smiles through a yawn as he rolls onto his side to face me. "I predict it now. Chicago versus Boston for the Cup."

"No way. Chicago has to beat Vegas, and they've dominated all season."

"How much do you want to wager?"

"Totally wanna say blowjob, but I'm guessing that's not allowed."

Lennon climbs out of bed, finding his clothes on the floor. "I was thinking like a hundred bucks."

"Whoa, don't break the bank there."

He dresses and looks for the rest of his things, not giving me eye contact as he says, "Like you said that night of the benefit, I'm a starving artist and can't afford to feed myself. A hundred bucks is a hundred bucks."

"What's a hundred bucks?" Ma's voice comes from the now open doorway.

"Invasion of privacy, Ma. You can't come barging in here—"

She throws up her hands. "I gave you plenty of warning, and besides, I heard you talking in here. What's a hundred bucks? And did I hear something about starving? Food's on the table."

"My boyfriend thinks it's gonna be Chicago and Boston in the finals."

"No way," Ma says. "Vegas and New Jersey."

"Vegas and Boston," I say.

"San Jose and Detroit!" Ollie's dad calls out.

"I'll take that bet," Ma calls back.

"Did he miss both of them get knocked out last round?" Lennon asks.

"He only ever follows my games," I say. "He'd rather be watching football."

"I understand that," Lennon says.

I flip him the bird but glance at my mother as I do. "Can, ah, I get some privacy to find my clothes, Ma?"

"Nothing I haven't seen before, but fine. Hurry up before breakfast gets cold."

Ma closes the door behind her, and Lennon stares over at me.

"When are you going to tell them the truth about me?" he whispers.

I shrug. "At our engagement party?"

Lennon shakes his head. "Don't even."

"Fine. The announcement of the birth of our first child."

He's still unimpressed.

"I'll tell them when they need to know. Right now, they think I'm happy, and I'm fine with letting them think that."

"The longer you leave it, the harder it'll be. I'm okay with doing this for you, but I still think you should tell them."

As I finish getting dressed, Lennon's phone rings. I leave him to it and go out into my dining room and take a seat opposite my dad at the table. Ma's already piled up the plates, and the empty seat next to me has a stack of food in front of it. No way in hell will Lennon eat all of that. Ma's used to feeding athletes with insane metabolisms. Even Max, who's the least sporty of us, is still ripped thanks to the twins giving him free personal training.

Lennon's low murmurs drift through the apartment.

"Now that your season's over, you'll be able to make it home for Grandma's eightieth," Ma says.

I shovel food in my mouth. "I'll probably come home for the off-season anyway."

When I look up, Lennon's standing in the doorway to my room, staring at his phone in his hand.

"What's up?"

His gaze flits between me and his phone again, and he bites his bottom lip. "Looks like I'll be joining you in Boston." He lifts his phone. "That was work."

He's still following the playoffs? I try to hide my excitement, but I'm sure the wide smile on my face gives it away.

"Great. You two can stay with us," Ma says, "and Clark can meet the rest of the fam at Grandma's birthday party."

Lennon's eyes widen, and so do mine. He lifts his head and mouths "Tell them."

All I can do is shake my head. "Thanks, Ma, but I think Clark's work will put him up in a hotel."

His shoulders slump. I can only assume from relief of dodging having to stay with my family.

"Thanks for the offer, Mrs. Strömberg, but I'm all set."

"Well, you at least have to come meet everyone. The entire family will be excited to meet Ollie's boyfriend. Trying to get any information out of him about you is like pulling teeth."

I silently beg Lennon to do this one thing for me. It's a big ask, and I know this is unfair to him. If he says no, I won't push, but it'll be one day. Just one. With my entire family.

Shit, I wouldn't wish that on anyone.

He can either read my mind or sense my desperation because he smiles at my mother. "I wouldn't miss it."

CHAPTER FOURTEEN

While I pack my stuff, Jet bounces on my bed like an excited child. "I knew there was more to you and Ollie than y'all were letting on."

He's been in a fit of laughter ever since I told him my predicament. From meeting Ollie in a bathroom months ago to agreeing to keep up this ridiculous charade for Ollie's family.

"Are you guys fucking now?"

I glare at him. "Your mouth's seriously gonna get you in trouble one day."

He finally stops bouncing and his face drops. "Why does everyone keep telling me that?"

"Because one day, when you're big and famous, you're gonna say the wrong thing to the wrong reporter, or celebrity, or random person, and then you're gonna be in the tabloids for all the wrong reasons."

"No such thing as bad publicity."

I raise my eyebrow. "Do you think your brother would agree with that?"

Matt's story going public got him kicked out of the NFL.

"Good point," Jet says. "But probably won't matter anyway. The whole fame thing probably isn't gonna happen for me."

My hands freeze, holding a balled-up shirt that I was about to throw into my suitcase. "Do you really believe that or are you fishing for a compliment?"

Jet looks away, a wave of shaggy brown hair falling across his forehead. "We have a meeting with a record label next week, but—"

"What?" I exclaim. "Jet, that's awesome. Why didn't you say anything?"

"Because I don't know if it's a good fit for us. The guy who came to the club to meet with us said they'd need to change a lot for us to be marketable. They want to change my name, change the band's name, change our image, pick one genre for the first album instead of the eclectic shit we play."

"Who's the record label?"

"Joystar Records. You heard of them?"

I shake my head. "Nah, but that doesn't mean anything. And it sounds like they're already invested if they've already made plans for you. This could be your big break."

I wish I could take a photo of his face right now, because it's the only time in the past month or so of knowing him that he appears serious. "Maybe. We'll see. Benji and Freya are excited this label wants them too. Their last lead singer ditched them for a solo contract."

"You're going to rock it, and then when you get super famous, I can tell the world I once shared a bed with a rock star and lived with him for a little bit too."

"Until then, I guess all you can say is you've shared a bed with a hockey god …"

"Nothing happened." Not really, anyway.

"Nothing happened with us either," Jet points out, "but that wasn't going to stop you from saying it. Which leads me to believe something did happen between you and Ollie, and now you're trying to cover it up."

Get this kid a detective badge.

"Whatever," I mutter intelligibly, which only makes him laugh. I throw the last bit of my clothes into my suitcase and zip it up. "I think I'm all set."

Jet climbs off my bed. "Wait, I need to know. Are you into each other now?"

I hang my head. "This is like freaking high school."

"You know, Matt and Noah started in a fake relationship."

"I do know. The reason they're so nice to me is because I didn't splash that information all over the internet."

"Just sayin'. They started the same way, and now they're married."

I grimace. "Ollie and I didn't start that way. It totally started with an accidental proposition in a bathroom in a gay bar."

Jet's entire face lights up. "So, there *is* something between you two. I knew it."

I groan, but then a knock sounds from the front door. "Thank God."

Jet and I head downstairs together, but he's all excitable. Seriously, if there were human equivalents of dogs, Jet would be a chocolate lab puppy with his rich brown hair and crazy energy.

When I greet Ollie, Jet's still bouncing behind me.

"You two are so gonna get married."

Ollie looks confused for only a second before he dismisses it as if he's already used to Jet's randomness.

"Goodbye, Jet," I say. "Tell Noah and Matt when they get back tomorrow that I'll be back in a few days."

Jet mockingly salutes us and sends us off with a "Have fun.

Shotgun best man at your wedding. I don't care which one of you."

"What was that all about?" Ollie asks as we descend the steps leading to the street.

An awaiting cab rests at the curb.

"Nothing," I say as I open the back door and ask the driver to pop the trunk for my suitcase.

"Didn't sound like nothing."

"He thinks because Matt and Noah started in a fake relationship that you and I will get married."

"But we started in a bathroom."

"That's what I said. Then he teased me about there being something real between us, but whatever."

Ollie steps close. Like *so close I can count your teeth* type close. "Would that be the *worst* thing in the world?"

"Probably," I rasp.

He seems to enjoy my awkwardness. "Fair enough."

My eyes narrow. "You're going to make Boston hell for me, aren't you?"

Ollie fakes offense. "Pretending to be my boyfriend wouldn't be as bad as the fiery pits of hell. Now you're being dramatic."

I cock my head.

"But in all seriousness, I totally am. It's gonna be fun."

"I'm starting to think I should've asked for some sort of compensation for this favor."

He waggles his eyebrows. "We can discuss that later."

"Laying it on pretty thick there."

"Sure am. I'm allowed to now because you're my boyfriend."

"Fake boyfriend."

"Semantics. Ready?" He gestures for me to get in the car first.

I slide over, and as he settles a few inches away from me, it feels as though he's touching me when he isn't. I get a sense this is what it'd be like to be with him for real. He has a way of getting so close I can feel him everywhere, but he doesn't touch. That's too risky.

It works at driving me crazy. Phantom touching, is that a thing? I know amputees sometimes have phantom limbs, where a missing leg makes them feel an itch they'll never be able to scratch.

Sitting next to Ollie this close without touching makes my dick think it'll never be touched again.

It's like the worst foreplay ever. All buildup with no release coming … pun intended.

I make myself laugh, and Ollie stares at me out the corner of his eye. I wave him off.

"You're going to stay with your parents while you're there?"

He hesitates. "Uh, yeah, about that …"

I purse my lips. "What?"

Ollie glances at the cabbie, and then back at me and speaks low. "Well, my parents live in Milton, about half an hour out of the city. It's not exactly too far that they wouldn't expect us to not see one another while you're in town. I was kinda thinking, maybe, I'd crash in the city after game two."

I'm going to be seeing Ollie and his family more than at his grandmother's birthday.

"Yup. Definitely should've asked for compensation," I mumble, but it's forced. The idea of seeing Ollie more and having excuses to touch him? Yeah, I'm not complaining too hard.

CHAPTER FIFTEEN

OLLIE

The anticipation might be killing me. Lennon should be here any minute, and I haven't seen him since we parted ways at the airport yesterday. He took a cab into the city and checked into his hotel and then attended the game last night.

I was fully prepared to go to the game with him and show my support for Tommy and my old team while I was at it, but as Ma said, "It's only game one, and I know that boy of yours has a cute butt and Tommy is practically family, but it's been months since you've been with *actual* family. You're with us tonight."

No matter how many times I complained that if I were still in the playoffs I wouldn't have been here at all this weekend, she still wouldn't let me go.

"Shoulda played better then," she said simply.

"Brutal, Ma. Real fuckin' brutal," I'd replied.

As soon as the doorbell rings, I'm on my feet and rushing for the door.

"Someone's eager," Dad says from his armchair. Seeing as we had family time last night, Dad and I are watching the replay of last night's game in the living room while Ma runs around trying to get ready for today's party.

We offered to help, much to Ma's dismay. By the time I'd messed up the third thing she asked of me, she told me to get out of her kitchen or lose some fingers. Dad too.

"I have to give him plenty of warning on how to deal with you lot. Hence why I asked him to come early."

"Preparation is always important in all areas of life, son." Did my dad just make a gay sex joke? There is such a thing as over-compensating, and my parents like to reiterate they're one hundred percent okay with my sexuality. As if pushing me to come out isn't enough of a hint.

I shudder. "I am not touching that one with a ten-foot pole."

Dad laughs.

Lennon stands at the door with his messenger bag over his shoulder and wearing those glasses.

Oh, holy Gretzky, those glasses.

"Hey," he says and then looks at me weird. Probably because I'm blocking the doorway like a moron.

"Come in," I croak and step aside.

As soon as he's inside, I can't resist touching him. My hand reaches for his, and he flinches and stares at our intertwined fingers. When his narrowed gaze travels up to my face, I shrug and lead him into the living room. We have to make this look real after all.

"Clark," Ma says, rushing into the room. She hugs him, but I still refuse to let go of his hand.

"Good to see you again, Mrs. Strömberg." He looks at Dad. "Mr. Strömberg."

"You too." Dad stands from his seat to shake his hand.

"Okay, we're going up to my room." I start leading Lennon away.

"You know the rules in this house," Ma says. "No boys allowed in your room."

When my mouth drops open, Ma giggles. "You should see your face." She's laughing so hard she slaps her knee.

"Don't mind this one," Dad says to Lennon. "Small things amuse small minds."

"That's why I married you," Ma says.

Lennon laughs. I remain horrified. My parents are on point today.

"Okay, we're going now." I take Lennon up the stairs and then to the second, smaller set leading to the attic.

I think I deserve some sort of prize for not pouncing on him the minute we cross over the threshold.

"What are we doing up here?" he asks. "Want to show me your childhood bedroom or something?"

"You think I got to live in this mansion being the baby?"

"Youngest children are always the most spoiled. My sister's a brat."

I smile. "In this family, the oldest gets the best room."

"Fair enough." Lennon dumps his bag and glances around the space, and I can no longer take it.

When he spins on his heel, he stumbles back, because I move closer, and I'm guessing he isn't expecting it. I reach out to steady him, and my arms go around his back.

Lennon's breath catches as I close the distance and move us backward until his back hits the door.

"What are we doing?" he whispers.

I like that he says *we* instead of *you*. He's in this as much as I am.

"I was thinking we might need to practice."

Lennon runs his tongue over his bottom lip. "Practice what?"

"Touching." I swallow the imaginary gravel in my throat.

"Kissing." My hand reaches for his cheek. "Other stuff to make us look like real boyfriends."

"Other stuff? Are you telling me your family is expecting us to put on a porn show for them or something to prove our relationship? Because that's all kinds of fucked up."

I chuckle. "Can I lie and say they're expecting it? I don't care if you think they're fucked up if I get to do this."

I lean in and press my lips to his, but he's too busy laughing to be invested in the kiss. I fix that by pushing my tongue into his mouth. His laughter turns into a moan as his tongue meets mine.

The kiss goes from zero to sixty within seconds, and he steps forward, trying to get closer, but with no distance between us already, all he does is grind his hardening cock against mine.

"Oh, God," he murmurs. "You really don't play fair."

"Playing fair isn't fun."

We kiss again, losing ourselves in a void between real and fake, but if I'm honest with myself, nothing has ever been fake with Lennon—not even that dinner at the Honey Bee. I might not have realized it at the time, but that dinner was a turning point. It gave me hope about moving on. From Ash, from the closet walls that are getting smaller and smaller every day to the point I don't know how much longer I'll be able to endure the claustrophobia.

I wish we had time to take this further, but I know any minute Ma will be calling us down, and my extended family will begin attacking … I mean, arriving.

"We should probably stop," I say, breathless.

"Shouldn't start what you can't finish, Mr. Hockey Star." He pushes against me, forcing me backward toward the bed. "I thought we were practicing."

I fall onto the mattress on my back, and he climbs on top of me, his legs going on either side of my hips.

"Practice makes perfect." I cup his head to bring his lips back to mine again.

I can't remember kissing ever being as good as it is with Lennon. He sparks something deep inside me: a need, a primal urge. I remain optimistic and believe we can be whole without tearing each other down.

I internally scoff at that, considering what he does for a living and how we started. I thought he was tearing me down when he was trying to lift me up.

Lennon's hand trails down my chest, lifting my shirt. His fingertips press against my abs, and he groans into my mouth.

"You have a thing with my abs, don't you?"

He sits up, the impressive and disproportionate bulge front and center, tenting his jeans. My mouth waters.

"I have a thing about your muscles," he says. "And your tats." He lifts my shirt farther, and I partially sit up for him to take it over my head.

His lips land on my shoulder and move toward my pierced nipple. He tongues the barbell and bites down gently, making my hips buck off the bed. I bite my lip to stop from screaming out.

"I think you like that. I'll file that away for later. You know, in case your family asks. Nipple play: check."

"Well, that is the point of this game."

Game. That's exactly what this is.

Sure, keep telling yourself that.

Nope, I have to shut down any notions of this turning into something more. Lennon continues to move south, down to my stomach, but he pauses at my belly button. I lift my head, and my eyes meet his. He opens his mouth to say something, but before any words come out, there's a knock at the door, followed by Ma walking in.

She gasps, Lennon scrambles off me, and I struggle to find

where he threw my shirt.

"Boundaries, Ma. I'm not a teenager anymore."

"Sorry. I, uh, didn't think … well, you know, I didn't think you'd be doing … that. Not now, I mean. There isn't enough time. People are arriving, and—"

"We'll be down in a minute."

Ma, red-faced and embarrassed, leaves, shutting the door behind her. I don't think I've ever seen that woman flustered.

"Well, that's one way to convince them this is real," Lennon says. I get the feeling he's trying not to laugh and rubbing his jaw is a distraction tactic.

My laugh bursts free though. "I can't believe that just happened. Never happened once with …" *Shit, don't mention Ash right now.*

"Didn't you live with him?"

"Uh, yeah, but we were close by, so I guess there was never a time we had to share a roof with my parents."

Lennon reaches into his jeans and adjusts himself. We shouldn't have started messing around, because now we're both going to be suffering for the rest of the afternoon and evening. Even longer if he's going back to the city tonight. I didn't ask him to stay, but I kinda hope he does.

"We should get down there," I say.

He points to his messenger bag. "Should I leave my laptop up here?"

"You brought your laptop? What, you thought you might get juicy gossip at a Strömberg family function and might need to write a story?"

"Not quite. I just don't feel safe leaving it in the hotel overni —uh, while I'm out."

I can't stop the smile forming on my lips. He was hoping he'd stay the night as well.

CHAPTER SIXTEEN

LENNON

If I thought Ollie's immediate family was intense, it's nothing compared to the distant relatives. Their family tree is made up of the most eclectic group of people I've ever met.

His parents both have Swedish and other European genes but sound like they've lived in Boston their whole lives. Ollie's aunt on his dad's side married a Puerto Rican, and so their three boys with their dark hair and olive skin stand out in the crowd of blond Strömbergs. And what the hell is up with them all being boys? Eight cousins, all boys. It's freaky. At least everyone on that side of the family is slightly shorter than the giants that are the Strömberg brothers. I don't feel as vertically challenged around them. Though, they are still all taller than me.

Then there are the wives and girlfriends—like the family needs their own WAGs club. There's about six nieces and nephews between the cousins, they're under five, and I'm not quite sure where or who they belong to.

I stand in the corner of the backyard watching, just hoping I don't get mowed over.

Yup. Hiding from the kids. Let's go with that lie.

"Did you say this was a party for your mom's mom? Why's your dad's sister and her kids here?" I ask Ollie.

"We're all super close." He wraps his arm around me.

I stare across the yard at the different couples and then at Ollie who hasn't even flinched about the whole PDA thing. "Can I ask you something?"

"Shoot."

"So, everyone here knows? About you?"

Ollie's eyes track my gaze to his arm around me and back again. "Yeah, my entire family knows. Each time someone introduces a new girlfriend or whatever, it's kinda not mentioned or talked about, but I trust everyone here. I'm not kidding when I say we're close. We're one of those sickeningly big happy families."

"You sound like a pod person."

Ollie leans in and in a high-pitched voice sings, "Come join us." He sounds like that little girl from the freaky old movie *Poltergeist.* "It's super fun."

I shiver. "Creepy."

"It's not nice to call your boyfriend creepy."

"Oh, sorry. You're super pretty for a creepy guy."

"Better. Although I don't know what being pretty will do to my badass rep."

"Aww, honey, you're not badass unless you're an enforcer, and you skate away from fights on the ice."

A gasp comes from the side door of the house. "Did I hear you say Ollie should become an enforcer?" his mom screeches.

"Oh boy, you're in trouble now." Ollie takes a sip of his beer.

"Did you just call me *boy*?"

Ollie shoots beer out his nose and coughs. "No." Cough. "I said *oh boy*. Like uh-oh." More coughing.

Aww, my spluttering giant. I've missed his awkward side.

His mom finally catches up to us. "Ollie cannot become an enforcer. He has way too much talent and is way too pretty to get messed up."

"There's that fuckin' *pretty* word again. I'm not pretty. I'm wicked badass."

"Of course, you are, baby." I pat his cheek.

Even though I'm being condescending, he has this weird smile on his face as if I just told him he's won the Hottest Man on Earth competition. Which, in all fairness, if it was a thing, he could totally win.

He puts his arm over my shoulder and kind of leans on me, while he moves in and kisses the side of my head.

"What was that for?" I ask.

"If I'm pretty, you're cute."

"I have no problem with being cute."

Ollie's mom butts in once again. "I think you're both cute, but stop hiding over here."

She loops her arm with mine, taking me away from Ollie, while his brother Leo calls out and intercepts him from following us.

Mrs. Strömberg leans in. "I'm going to be honest with you."

"Uh-oh."

She smiles. "It's not bad, hon. I just wanted to say that I didn't think you and Ollie were right for each other."

Ouch. My face must give away the hurt—the thing that's always been in the back of my mind since meeting Ollie. A jock like him wouldn't go for a nerd like me.

Her hand squeezes my arm. "By the look on your face, that's not what you wanted to hear."

No shit.

"I don't mean it in a bad way, and you need to let me finish, okay?"

Sure, sugarcoating *you're not good enough for my son* couldn't possibly be taken in a bad way.

"That day we met you, I thought the pairing was ... odd." She stops walking in the middle of the backyard with the action still going on around us, and even though no one's paying attention, I become self-conscious.

I play with the collar of my shirt.

"Oh, geez, you're an impatient one, aren't ya? I'm trying to say I was *wrong*."

My gaze snaps in her direction.

"You make him happy. It doesn't matter if you're some corporate hotshot, which is so not Ollie's thing, or you're a little on the cute and innocent side." Her gaze turns toward her youngest son. "I haven't seen him smile like that in a long while. Not even while he was with Ash."

Guilt gnaws at me. I'm not corporate, I'm not Ollie's boyfriend, and I'm not even sure he's smiling that way because of me.

I try to fake my reaction and think how a normal boyfriend would react to acceptance by his partner's mother, but I think my smile is as tight as my throat, which feels like it's closing up.

"Ah ... and about Ash." She's the one avoiding eye contact now.

"I don't need to know about Ollie's past." Especially if Ash is everything I'm not.

"And I wouldn't normally make you hear it ..."

A loud cough that sounds a hell of a lot like "Bullshit" comes from the nearby table where Ollie's brother Vic must be eavesdropping.

Ollie's mom ignores him. "The only reason I'm bringing up Ash is, well, he's basically part of this family. He's here for all the important events, and being with Ollie, you're gonna have to meet him eventually."

Is she saying … I grunt. "Does Ollie know he's coming?"

Am I a complete idiot here? Here I am thinking he's using any excuse to get close to me—even asking me to fake it for his entire family—but what if he didn't ask me here for me? Or for him. Am I here to make his ex *jealous*?

"I doubt anyone has told him—nobody wants to be the messenger—but I'm sure he'd suspect. I just thought I'd give you a heads-up."

"Do I need a heads-up?" I don't know if anticipating meeting Ollie's ex is a good thing or a bad thing.

I'm definitely at high risk of overthinking it.

"Ma," Ollie scolds. I don't know how long he's been behind us. "Stop scaring him off." His arm comes around me again, but now I can't stop the internal questions.

I stupidly thought going into this that Ollie might be milking this charade for all it's worth and maybe using it as an excuse to continue fooling around or whatever. Wishful thinking, obviously.

What if he's like every other jock I've wanted?

What if he's using me to remind Ash that he let the best guy in the world go and he hopes to somehow win him back?

Okay, yup. Definitely overthinking this.

"You okay?" Ollie asks.

I force a fake smile. "Thirsty."

Ollie yells as he pulls me through the throng of kids and people toward the ice bucket near the back door. "Out of our way. Thirsty boyfriend needs a drink."

I shake my head. "You're ridiculous."

"Maybe, but I think you like it."

I can't help a genuine smile breaking through, because yeah. I really do. I should stop analyzing and enjoy this … whatever the fuck it is.

"So, what'd she say to make you go pasty white?" He hands me a bottle of water. "Wait, you want something else? There's beer, tonic—"

"Taw-nic." I chuckle. "So cute."

"You're in Beantown now, Clark."

"Water's fine. If your ex is gonna show up, I don't really wanna drink anything harder."

"Ash is coming?"

Is he faking surprise or did he genuinely not know?

"Your mom said he was. Wanted to warn me. Apparently, I'm the only one with the balls to tell you though." My joke is as flat as the line between Ollie's pursed lips.

"I thought he wasn't going to come. I mean, I knew there was a chance, but Max blew off family dinner last night, and I assumed he was going to do the same today, so there's no real reason why Ash would come without him."

"When was the last time you saw him?" I ask quietly.

"Before I moved to New York. Before that, it was a handful of times since we'd broken up." Something about the way he stares at the ground, as if wanting to hide his expressive face away from me, makes me step forward.

I put my finger under his chin and gently pull it up so he's looking into my eyes. "You truly didn't know he was coming?" Because right now, I don't know if he's a really good liar or being truthful. His words are believable, but his body language pings my bullshit radar. Granted, that radar has proven broken in the past.

He looks away with guilt written all over his face.

"Is he why I'm actually here?" The growl in my voice is involuntary.

"What? No. You're here because I want you here." Ollie steps closer. "You're here because I used the excuse of not handling my family to get you here even though I know how to deal with them. I've had years of deflecting."

"So … you asked me to come because …"

He sighs. "Technicalities, Lennon."

Lennon. Not Clark.

"I need an excuse to do this." His fingers trail my cheek, down my neck, and then move behind my head, causing me to shiver. "And this," he whispers, leaning in and kissing my cheek where his fingers just were. His mouth makes the same journey his hand did but stops at the base of my neck, just at the top of my shoulder.

A throat clears behind us.

Ollie slumps and murmurs into my neck. "Of course."

When he steps away, his playful mood is gone, and his arms stiffen around me.

His brother Max stands a few feet away with a guy I can only assume is Ash, if his avoiding eye contact with either of us is any indication.

And Mr. Toppy? A skinny, punk-looking guy who's shorter and thinner than I am. Long dark hair on top of shaved sides, giant ear gauge on his right ear, neck tattoos, but surprisingly only one inked sleeve.

Not only is he the complete opposite of me but also the complete opposite of what I was imagining.

I don't know why, but I thought Ollie's ex would be another sporting type, like most of his brothers. Doesn't make much sense when the odd brother is best friends with the ex.

We stand there in a four-way standoff. Max glaring at us, Ollie tense and getting flustered as his mouth opens and shuts, me checking out the ex, and Ash looking like he wants to be anywhere but here.

Fun times.

Ash raises his hand to run it through his thick hair, and that's when I see it. The lone tattoo on his left arm. *Mi Vida.* The same script, same size as the tattoo on Ollie's chest.

My life.

I looked it up in a moment of weakness after that night in Ollie's hotel room.

The doubt Ollie obliterated not two minutes ago is back, even though this technically changes nothing. I knew he and Ash were serious. You can't have a relationship for four years and not be serious. But matching tattoos? That's practically the same as a wedding band. No, it's actually worse. Wedding bands can come off.

I try to tell myself that maybe the matching tattoos have nothing to do with their relationship at all. Max and Ash are tattoo artists. Maybe it was practice.

Then I remember the way Ollie stiffened when I ran my hand over that tattoo in particular. I don't know if I can handle such a permanent reminder of his ex right there on his chest.

"They've been staring at each other for like five minutes," someone whispers off to our side. I'm not surprised to find Vic and Nic standing there watching us.

Ollie breaks first and forces a smile. "Max." He lifts his chin toward his ex. "Ash. This is …" He stammers, and I can practically see his mind drawing a blank.

Clark. Say Clark.

"Clark," he finally gets out.

And now we're faced with a game of chicken—who's gonna

reach for each other's hand first. Turns out Ollie's ex is the bigger person.

"Good to meet you." His voice is soft while his handshake is strong.

I nod, because if I lie and say it's good to meet him too, they're all gonna know I'm full of shit.

"Have you seen Grandma yet?" Ollie asks Max.

Max is still seething quietly, and I realize he and Ollie have the same *I hope you choke on air* death glare.

"We were going that way now." Ash tries to pull Max away, but Max doesn't budge.

Talk about a sense of not belonging. I have nerdy glasses, no tattoos, and am dressed in a sweater and chinos. That versus the three tatted-up guys surrounding me feels like a game of spot the odd one out—grade school level.

Ash appears calmer and more put together than Max, which is weird. Shouldn't Ash be the one sulking and glaring?

It's Ollie's turn to stand awkwardly, and now, as I glance out into the yard, it's apparent that numerous family members are being nosy but trying to be subtle. We're definitely on display for everyone to see.

I almost feel like I'm intruding on a family moment, because Ash has been a part of it for so long.

"I'm gonna go help with the food," I announce with way too much enthusiasm.

I turn on my heel and get away from them as fast as I can. Cowardly, considering I'm here as a fake boyfriend and probably should've stayed by Ollie's side, but the more I try to fight it, the more I'm realizing I'm into Ollie a hell of a lot more than I should be. I'm invested now.

And isn't that the stupidest thing I've ever done.

This is worse than Daniel and Dylan combined. Because this

time? Physical injuries aren't a worry. Nope. Ollie has the ability to tear my heart out.

I risk a glance back at him before I head inside the house to help his mom in the kitchen, and with the way he and Ash are smiling warmly at each other, the risk of heartache just became significantly higher.

CHAPTER SEVENTEEN

OLLIE

"You look good," Ash says. "Healthy." Then he winces. "Which, of course, you do. You play fucking hockey." He laughs the nervous chuckle that he has, and I find myself smiling.

Ash was there for all the important parts of my life, so it's weird having this giant gap between us now, but that's what happens when relationships break down.

Toward the end, things were ugly. We were fighting constantly. I don't blame him for the ultimatum or the way things happened and hold no grudges, but it's still weird.

Max hasn't lost the constipated look on his face even with Lennon gone.

"Do you need to go to the bathroom?" I ask him, which makes him scowl harder.

"I don't understand how you two can be so … so …"

"So, what?" I ask.

"*Cavalier*." Max throws up his hands. "You guys had years together, and it seems like a waste now."

I have no idea what he means by that, and before I can ask, he storms away, leaving me with Ash.

"What was that all about?" I ask.

Ash shakes his head. "I dunno. He's been acting weird lately."

"Max is always weird."

We share a smile.

"And how have you been?" I manage to ask.

"Really good. I feel like I've gotten my life back, you know?" He winces again. "Sorry, my mouth is saying all kinds of wrong things today."

I laugh, even if it sounds sad. "Yeah, but that's fair."

God, this is hard. I've heard about running into exes and how bad it can be, but I never imagined it would be like this with Ash.

"It's not fair, and I didn't mean it as a dig at you or anything. It's just … if I'd known you were bringing someone, I might've skipped today, because I'll admit seeing you with someone else is really fucking hard, but—"

"Yeah, well, hearing from my brothers that you've been sleeping around wasn't exactly fun for me either."

"I'm not. I mean … I'm not anymore. I'm, umm, well …"

"In a relationship. I know. The guys told me. And that's completely okay, because so am I. That's kinda what happens when you break up with someone, right? You both move on?"

I'm trying to move on and finally feel like I'm in a place to be able to do that.

"Yeah. You're right. And I am." It's not until he reaches up to run his hand through his hair again—a nervous habit he's had since we were kids—that I realize just how much he's moving on.

My blood runs cold. "What the fuck is that?" I point to his ring finger.

"That's what I'm trying to tell you." Ash sucks in a sharp breath. "I'm engaged."

For a minute, my body and my head don't know how to react. It's only been a year since we broke up, and as far as I'm aware, he was still sleeping around six months ago—if my brother's word is anything to go by.

"That's fast," I blurt out, thinking I only say it in my head.

"It is."

I don't know if I have an opinion about it or not. Part of me really hates it, because we were together for four years and marriage was an abstract concept that was a future thing to worry about. For him to dismiss what we had so easily and so fast and decide this new guy has always been the guy for him …

I mean, can I judge that though? I'm here with Lennon, hoping for more. Then again, I'm not fucking marrying the guy.

I think I'm understanding Max's frustration now. "Who is he?"

"No one you know. He started out as a client."

"When?" I ask.

"When what?"

"When did he become your client?"

Ash looks away. "Two years ago."

Anger surges up. "Did—"

"No, I didn't cheat on you, and I knew that would be the first thing you asked. He came into the shop again about six months ago for another tat, and it just … happened."

"That easy, huh?"

Now I'm filled with jealousy for a whole other reason. Lennon and me … we've been anything but easy. Is that what relationships are supposed to be? Easy?

Or are they supposed to be heart fluttering, chest aching, and my body in a constant state of want? Because that's what it's like with Lennon.

"Well, I'm happy for you." Okay, even I can tell my words are fake and my smile is tight, but I don't care.

It's not that I want Ash back or that I'm still in love with him, but why does him moving on so fast sting like a motherfucker?

I want to move on with Lennon, and I want to date him and see him and possibly fall in love with him. But marriage? I'm so many steps removed from that it seems like a foreign concept for me.

Marriage? Vows of forever?

All I want is a proper date. That's where my life is at.

And that's why it never worked with Ash.

"I'm gonna go see if my boyfriend needs help."

Ash steps forward. "Ollie …"

"I'm good," I promise him. "I'm fine. It was just a shock, but congrats. I mean that." Yet my feet scurry away as if I'm lying.

I have no destination in mind, but my gut seems to know, and it's not until I run into Lennon and my mother laughing in the kitchen that I snap out of whatever fucking emotion I'm feeling toward Ash and suddenly realize what I'm doing to Lennon.

Bringing him here.

Forcing him to pretend to be my boyfriend for my family's sake, when in reality, it's for mine.

Because I want him.

I think I want him more than I've ever wanted anything in my life. Including the NHL.

My chest stutters, and I think it's my heart protesting. This is too heavy. It's too much. Ash, my family, my career … Lennon.

This is beyond unfair to him.

When they finally notice my presence, Lennon's beautiful smile drops.

"Are you okay?" he asks. Of course, he asks. Because he's a nice person.

Guilt gnaws at me every time I remember that.

"Yeah …" I croak. "I just need to lie down for a minute." I

rush up the stairs and slam the door by accident but then cringe when I realize the entire backyard would've heard it.

I will not let this get to me. My feet pace back and forth, the floorboards in the attic squeaking under the pressure.

It's not that Ash is moving on. It's not.

Is it?

Fuck, I don't know.

Maybe it's that he gets to have the life we were planning. It wasn't going to be soon, but we'd discussed it. Our parents pushed for it.

Meanwhile, I'm sneaking a sports reporter out of my hotel room and jerking off with him like it's no big deal.

I guess the problem is everyone involved—my family, Ash, me—all of us thought Ash leaving me would be a good thing. That maybe it would be the push I needed to come out.

Nope, all it did was make me want to convince them I'm happy even without him.

Am I happy, though?

I think about hockey, about my life in New York, my new friends, Lennon and Jet, and realize, yeah, I'm happy, but …

Clarity hits with such force, I have to sit on the edge of my bed.

That there is my issue.

I'm happy, but I'm not complete.

CHAPTER EIGHTEEN

LENNON

"Should I …" I gesture to where Ollie disappeared to, but his mom shakes her head.

"He had to run into Ash sooner or later. Maybe give him a few minutes."

"Okay," I say but don't take my eyes off the stairs.

"He'll be fine." Ollie's mom gives me a reassuring smile. "I have a feeling Ash gave him his news."

"What news?"

Her eyes drop and she turns her head to look out the kitchen window. "He met someone and is getting married." The longing in her gaze and her voice is hard to miss.

"You wish it was Ollie he was marrying?" I ask.

She fakes a smile. "No, hon. I want Oliver to be happy. But I do wish he could've found it in himself to do the one thing Ash needed so it could've been him."

I keep my mouth shut. Telling her how misguided that statement is, even if she thinks she's being supportive, won't get me anywhere.

"Then again, if he was truly happy with Ash, and he was the one, my son wouldn't be here with you today, would he?"

"Umm …" Is that a compliment or an insult? I have no idea.

Her warm face and soft tone suggest she means it in a good way, so I pretend that's what she meant. It's probably the only way to make sure my mouth does, in fact, remain shut.

Footsteps sound behind us, but Max is a blur as he practically bolts past us and up the stairs. A knock sounds, and then the low voices from Ollie and Max disappear behind the creak of the door opening and closing.

"I'm going to take these dishes out," Mrs. Strömberg says. "Are you all right to finish up the salad?"

I smile. "Of course."

As she leaves, I contemplate going upstairs to check on Ollie. He just found out his ex is getting married. That's gotta hurt even if he is over him like he says. But Max is up there. I'll leave the brothers to sort their shit first. Max being the most intimidating brother isn't the real reason for not going up there. Nope. Not at all. Okay, maybe a little. Or a lot.

Fine, I'm being a wimp because Max scares me.

When I put the remaining touches on the salad, I take it out into the backyard, where Ollie's parents are herding the crowd like cattle toward the two long tables set up. Well, they're trying to. It looks more like they're trying to herd cats.

Ollie's adorable grandmother sits at the head of the table, and she's so freaking cute. Her gray, almost purply-tinged hair sits curly on her head but is combed in the front as if she can't reach the back anymore, and her rosy cheeks are covered in so much rouge it almost looks like sunburn, but her smile … her smile seems to be contagious, and I can't help returning it. I think it's because Ollie inherited the same cheekbone structure, and her smile reminds me of him.

Damn. This is beyond out of control now.

I'm a few feet away from the table when I hear "Trust me. Clark isn't gonna last. I give it one more month. Tops." It's Vic.

I freeze, completely dumbfounded.

"If you say so," Ash mumbles. "I'm happy he's moving on." Ash's voice cracking gives away his lie. "I'm moving on."

"Don't worry about that, either. His little hissy fit probably shows he's not over you." They're both sitting with their backs to me and still have no idea I'm eavesdropping. "But he can't exactly complain when he's too busy being ashamed of who he is to see what he lost."

I'm about to yell *What the fuck?* and lose my shit because they still don't get it. I don't think anyone in this family does. How has Ollie never sat them down and told them what it's really like for him?

Ash huffs. "Guess it was dumb of me to think maybe, possibly, he'd see the ring and pick up his phone to fix it."

Is he saying …

"You don't want that though," Vic says. "You and Taylor are getting married, right? It's not like if Ollie had changed his mind, you'd break it off and go running back to him. He could promise all he wanted that he'd come out, but how many times did he say that while you were together?"

I glance sideways at the table to see if anyone else is listening. They don't appear to be, but if this afternoon has taught me anything about this family, someone's always listening.

"You're right," Ash says. "I just... Shit, I dunno. I guess his continued denial about the way he's living is more proof he can't face who he is."

Their words play into my fears. That I'm here to make Ash jealous and that Ollie doesn't actually want me. I contemplate running, but it's their warped vision of Ollie's position that keeps my feet rooted to the ground.

I take a deep breath and try to calm down, because it's not my place to say anything. Nope. Not at all. Even if I was Ollie's actual boyfriend, it's not my place.

Don't say anything. Do not … say … any—

I plonk the salad down in front of Vic and Ash. "Is that what you believe?"

Okay, great. Not only is my mouth not listening to me, but it's also yelling. Everyone except the kids turn their heads to face me.

"What's wrong?" Ollie's mom asks from across the table.

I stare at Vic and Ash, and Vic stares right back as if he doesn't know what he's done wrong. How can he not understand?

Ash, at least, seems to know he messed up or he's at least embarrassed, as he hangs his head.

"Is that what you really think? That Ollie is ashamed of who he is? That he can't accept he's gay?" I look at the rest of the people at the table, who all stare back with concerned scrunches in their brows, and holy fuck, this family's genes are crazier than I thought. They're all giving me the same look, and it's uncanny how much they look alike.

"What do you mean?" his mom asks, her confusion matching everyone else's.

Oh, God. They really do believe that.

"Hasn't Ollie ever told you what it's like for him? Hasn't he ever told you about what happens in locker rooms? Let's just say the word fa—" I glance at the kids, who've now turned their attention to me too. "Not nice F-words are thrown around like candy. When the guys screw up on the ice, they're called ladies, and the whole sporting industry thinks anyone who's gay isn't man enough to play sports."

They barely blink at me. No reaction, no realization.

Suddenly, I feel like I'm in one of my nightmares. I'm back in high school being stared at for being the only gay boy in school. Not that I ever was, but I was the only out kid in school thanks to the football team.

While self-consciousness tries to make me run away, my anger builds. "None of you understand, do you?" I turn to Vic. "You're in professional sports. How can you sit there and not empathize with Ollie at all?"

He shrugs. "I don't know any gay guys in MMA."

"How many people train at your gym?" I ask.

Another shrug, like a sulking teenager being sent to the principal's office. "About twenty who could go pro if they work hard enough."

"Chances are you know at least, *at least*, one gay guy in your sport. Why do you think they haven't come out?"

"Nah, if someone was gay, they'd say it. Our gym's inclusive. Like, anyone is welcome, and …" As he says the words, the realization kicks in—that maybe he only sees what he wants to see, and some closet doors are made of fucking steel. I can practically see the moment he finally gets what I'm saying, but for some reason, my mouth feels the need to drive the point home.

"What about your gym screams inclusivity? Pride flags on the walls or is it in some membership rule book under tiny font no one reads? Do you guys have any idea what it's like to have to hold your breath every time someone finds out who you're attracted to in case they react badly? Try having to do that in a work environment where you have to come out to an entire team of testosterone-filled men who fight for a living."

Nic pipes up to defend his brother. "No one's truly that ignorant anymore about that kinda stuff, are they?"

I scoff. "How can *you* be this ignorant?"

They really don't get it, and how Ollie has not blown up at

them after all these years is beyond me. I'm not much for confrontation, but this … I can't. I just can't.

"The world has progressed in so many ways, but in others, it's as bad as it always was. We may have tolerance in most places now, but we're far from acceptance. Are you all really that blind to the world Ollie and I live in? I'm a sports reporter, and I still get told I'm in the wrong journalistic field by assholes at my magazine. They say I should be covering fashion instead. These are people in media—the news source to the entire world. You still wanna sit there and tell me the world is no longer ignorant?"

"Sports reporter?" Ollie's dad asks.

Fuck.

"I thought you were in business," his mom says.

And now I've not only screwed everything with Ollie's family, but with Ollie as well.

"I … I have to leave," I say in a voice much smaller than I've been using, because I let my tongue run away with my thoughts, and now I've screwed everything up.

I turn to go, but Ollie's right there with Max flanking him.

"How long have you been standing there?" I ask. His stoic face gives nothing away.

"Long enough."

Without warning, he steps forward and takes my mouth in a punishing kiss. It's all tongue and no hesitation, and a few grumbles about PDA are murmured throughout the group. When he pulls back, he's … smiling.

"I—I … I'm not in trouble then?" I stammer.

His fingers interlace with mine, and he turns to face his family. "Guys, I want to introduce you to Lennon Hawkins."

Silence. Dead silence.

His mom is the one to break it. "The reporter who hates you?"

Ollie turns to me and whispers quietly. "Sorry. You know how pissed I was when—"

"It's okay." I turn to Mrs. Strömberg. "For the record, I don't hate him. He has an ego you may or may not be aware of, and I may or may not have accidentally crushed it."

There are a few sniggers around the table.

Ollie pins his mother with his hazel eyes. "He's not Clark, he's not my actual boyfriend, but more importantly, he's the only person who's ever stood up for me like that." His gaze finds mine again. "Including myself. And it's only now I'm realizing why that is."

"We always stand up for—" his mom starts, but he cuts her off.

"No. You don't stand up for *me*. You stand up for the notion that everyone has to be accepted for who they are. And that's great. But you ridicule me over the fact I'm not ready for the rest of world to know about me. I don't know when I will be. You guys expect everyone to catch on easily, but I think it's been proven that's not gonna happen. Look at the NFL. Not much has changed since Matt Jackson came out."

I could argue that, because the NFL has improved a lot since Matt came out, but that's not the point of this discussion. Whether the NHL welcomes their first gay player and makes changes isn't the issue. The issue is with Ollie's legitimate right to not want to be that guy.

"Lennon pretended to be my boyfriend six months ago because you guys would not let up about how I'm screwing up my life. I love you guys. I really do. But I need a fucking break from all the pressure you put on me."

"Ollie—"

He cuts his mom off again by turning to his grandmother. "I'm sorry, Grandma. I hope you have a great birthday lunch, but

I have to go before I say anything else I can't take back." His hand on mine is tightening by the second, and his chest heaves. Despite his words to say he's leaving, he either can't make his feet move or he's waiting for someone to stop him.

"Come on," I say. "We'll go cool off. I think we both need a breather." I drag him away, and he follows easily.

We make our way down the side of the house, but when we reach the front yard, he spins on his heel and backs me up, pushing me against the clapboard façade.

"What—" I try to ask, but then his mouth is on mine again. Just as punishing as in front of his family, only this time his hands go wandering too.

I allow myself exactly three seconds of this insanity before pushing him away. "You told them the truth." My words come out all breathy, and I have to clear my throat.

"So?"

"So why are you kissing me? We're not … you know … together."

Ollie cups my face. "Because after that? I don't care if we were lying to them. I want something real. I want …"

The hesitance and doubt must take over, because he can't finish his sentence.

"I want you too," I whisper.

We don't make the mistake of promising anything long-term or even official. We just finally give in to what we've been trying to avoid.

He pushes me against the side of the house again, a little too hard this time.

I grunt.

"Fuck, are you okay?"

"I told you that day when you shoved me into the pressroom that I don't mind being manhandled."

That's enough permission for him. Ollie groans and pushes against me, bending slightly so his hips line up with mine, and I let out an involuntary whimper.

"I need … I need …" His mouth is so close to mine I can feel his breath on my lips. "I need us to disappear."

"Huh?"

"I've wanted you since I met you, even on the days I thought I hated you."

"Aww, sweet." I have to bring out the sarcasm because my skin heats, and I'm terrified I'm blushing at the sentiment.

He ignores me. Instead, he leans in farther and puts his lips to my ear. "Do you know how hard it's been these last few hours to not touch you?"

"You've touched me. They thought we were boyfriends."

He's been holding my hand and doing boyfriendly things like getting me drinks, subtly touching the small of my back, and staying super close. Like crossing personal space boundaries close.

"I'll rephrase," Ollie says with a small smile. "I haven't been able to touch you inappropriately." A hand comes between us and moves over the bulge in my pants. "And then you standing up for me in front of my whole family? Doing something I've never been brave enough to do? I can't wait any longer."

I throw my head back, hitting the side of the house with a thud, but I don't care. When this guy touches me … "Okay, yeah, we need to disappear."

"Attic," he growls.

We make our way to the front door and open it as quietly as possible, but it squeaks and then so do the hardwood floors when our feet step over the threshold. And then the sound of kids screaming and laughing comes from the living room.

We both freeze. Ollie tilts his head back out the front door.

With light steps, we head back outside.

"Don't suppose one of these cars is yours?" Ollie glances out at the sea of cars filling the driveway, front yard, and street.

"I didn't get a rental. I took an Uber."

"Fuck," he hisses.

"Do you ever feel like the universe is trying to cockblock us? Your teammates coming back to the hotel when they shouldn't be, your mom walking in on us, a gaggle of children providing a less than sexy soundtrack in the background …"

"We're doing this. Fuck the universe."

I slump. "Oh, man, why'd you have to go and say that? You're gonna get hit by a bus tomorrow for sure."

"And you think hockey players are superstitious."

"Don't come crying to me when you're splattered all over the windshield of a bus. Just sayin'."

"Well, if my fate is already sealed, I guess you better make the most of me while I'm still here." Ollie glances out at the front yard, and his eyes catch on an old treehouse in the giant tree a few feet from the fence that lines the road.

The glimmer in his eye as he takes my hand should scare me, but all I can feel is excitement.

CHAPTER NINETEEN

Kissing Lennon is even better than scoring on the ice. The second I pull him up through the trapdoor of the treehouse, his mouth is on mine, and his body is pressed against me. Not that there's much room up here for him to be far apart from me.

Lennon lets out a tiny squeak when my hand trails down his back and grasps his ass.

It's like being back in peewee hockey and taking to my skates those first few times. Adrenaline, nerves, the desire to fly without falling … the newness of it all has my hands trembling and my body aching with need.

The treehouse is cramped, and I have to hunch over to even fit in here. The place is dusty, covered in cobwebs and dead leaves, and it's probably not structurally safe anymore, but I don't care.

I need this. My lips break away from his and trail down his cheek, past the light stubble on his neck, and down to his shoulder. The material of his T-shirt is not as tasty as his skin.

"Off," I murmur.

"I dunno. I'm kind of scared of getting tetanus in here or something."

I chuckle. "Fine. I'll just have to find somewhere to put my mouth without removing any clothing."

"Sounds like a fun challenge."

As I get to my knees, my back scrapes the side of the tree-house. "Ouch. There's really no room in here. I remember it being a lot bigger when I was a kid."

Lennon laughs. "I bet."

"This is so not how I imagined this going," I say. I think I've got a splinter in my back.

"You imagined *this*?"

"Not *exactly*, but I was definitely hoping for some of this." My hand moves over his cock, and he shudders with a small moan. "I'd planned on doing it after the game tomorrow night and worm my way into your hotel room." My voice goes all high and innocent. *"It's too late to drive back to my parents' house. I'm tired. I promise I won't jump you as soon as we get there."*

"And then you were going to jump me?" He's breathless now as I continue to rub his cock over his jeans.

"Actually, I was going to be so damn irresistible you wouldn't be able to help yourself and *you'd* jump *me*."

"Brilliant plan," he taunts.

"Flawless."

"You're full of yourself, aren't you?"

"Confident." I reach for the button on his jeans.

The light mood jumps out the crudely cut window, along with all the air—if Lennon's gasp when I unzip him and pull out his cock is anything to go by.

His legs wobble, and he lifts his hand to the low roof to steady himself. His other hand flies to my shoulder and grips tight.

"I've wanted to do this for so long," I whisper, giving him a hard pump.

His cock, long and thick, twitches in my hand.

"I've wanted a jock on his knees in front of me since I was a teenager."

"No pressure," I say and finally, *finally*, we both get our wish as I run my tongue over his slit and then down his shaft.

His musky scent makes my dick ache, and if anyone had asked me what I missed most about sex, I wouldn't have said giving head. Receiving, maybe, but not giving. This, right here, looking up at Lennon's blissed-out face while I take him into my mouth, with his glasses slowly sliding down his thin nose … I'd gladly stay in this position forever, if my back wasn't protesting and my knees weren't killing me.

Blowjob in a treehouse? Not a smart idea.

"God, that's so good." Lennon's voice is gruff, something I've never heard from him before, and the aches in my back disappear. All the pain goes to my groin, my cock leaking from excitement. Or neglect. I'm not sure yet.

Lennon's hard length slides in and out of my mouth with ease, and I wish we didn't have clothes in the way. I want to take him all the way to the back of my throat, breathe him in, play with his balls, but through the tiny hole in his boxer briefs, I only have access to his cock. Granted, it's an amazing cock, but I want more.

Later, a voice says.

I pull off to catch my breath and lick my way down the underside, pressing my tongue against a pulsing vein. More delicious precum pools at the tip, and I can't take it anymore. As I take him in my mouth again, my fingers go to my jeans and hastily unfasten them, taking my own cock out.

One hand strokes myself while the other goes to the base of Lennon's dick. I suck harder, and he begins panting.

"I'm … I'm gonna …"

I don't move away, and as the first spurts of his release hit my tongue, I work my cock faster. He continues to fill me, saliva and cum dribbling out the side of my mouth.

I keep going until Lennon comes down from his high, his dick softening in my mouth as I lap at his cum. His grip on my shoulder loosens, and when he takes a step back, I whine. I want more. I want—

Lennon sinks to the floor, and his hand lands on top of mine, stilling it on my cock. "Let me."

He takes his glasses off and puts them in his shirt pocket. I watch as if he's moving in slow motion. He's not moving fast enough.

I breathe hard, and a begging quality I didn't know I had enters my voice when I say, "I'm so close. I need … I need …"

We have to shuffle on our knees in the small space so Lennon's able to lean down and take my cock in his mouth, but when he does, and I finally have those lips wrapped around me, I can't help moaning so loud everyone on the property could hear me.

He pulls off my cock with a wet pop. "I thought we came in here so no one could hear us."

"Oh my God, I don't care right now. Just put me out of my misery."

"This is torture, is it?" His pink tongue darts out and lightly runs up my shaft from base to tip.

"Fuck you. I didn't tease you."

Lennon smirks. "You're right. How mean of me. Maybe you should show me how you like it by fucking my mouth."

My head falls backward. "How are you real?" It's like Lennon looked into my brain and saw my deepest fantasies and then went *Okay, let's do that.*

With my eyes closed, I feel the heat of his wet mouth moving over me again. I glance down at him, and he nods encouragement.

My first thrusts are small and shallow, testing it out. I didn't know it was possible for someone to call me a pussy with just their eyes, but Lennon pulls it off flawlessly.

If that's how he wants to play it …

I grip the back of his head and my hips thrust harder this time, and Lennon hums around my dick. At first, I think it's in pain, but then we make eye contact again, and his eyes are hooded and filled with lust.

Without a doubt, I'm not going to last long. I was already dancing on the edge before he had his mouth on me.

The small space makes it hard to go all out, but with my hand fisted in his hair, and me kneeling, it doesn't take a whole lot of movement to go to the back of his throat.

It's hot and tight, and his cheeks hollow as he sucks me down.

If I hadn't been so on edge from blowing him already, I'd be embarrassed by how fast I come. As the first spurts hit, Lennon hums a satisfied sound around my cock.

"Fuck," I pant over and over again.

I haven't come so hard in my damn life. My body feels like jelly, my legs going numb beneath me.

Lennon pulls off and leans back on his heels, breathing heavy and staring at me with orgasm goggles. I'm sure it matches my gaze.

"We should probably, uh …" I glance down at his cock, still hanging out the fly of his pants.

He laughs and adjusts himself. "Yeah. Probably."

Lennon lands on his ass beside me, and I roll off my knees

and stretch my legs out, but in the small space, they're still bent and at an awkward angle.

We breathe heavy as we fix our clothing, and as we relax against the wall of the treehouse, I reach into my pocket and pull out a joint.

"Smoke?"

"Is that ..." He looks closer.

"Good ol' Mary Jane? Yup."

Lennon smiles. "Should you be smoking that?"

"Not on the NHL's banned list, and besides, season's over. You gonna report on it if I do?"

He grabs the joint out of my hand. "I can't believe you asked me that, asshole." He holds his hand out for a lighter.

"You said yourself if you found me with drugs—"

"I meant like performance-enhancing shit. *Cheating*." He stares down at the joint. "Okay, so how do I do this?"

"You've never smoked pot before?"

"Why's that so hard to believe?"

"It's a rite of passage. Here ..." I take it back off him and light up, taking a deep breath in as I do. "Mmm," I say as I exhale. "Orgasms and getting high. It's better than birthday cake."

Lennon chuckles. "Share."

"I dunno. I don't wanna corrupt you."

"You dragged me into your childhood treehouse to blow you. I think the corruption has already begun."

I screw up my face. "Totally sounds perverted when you say it that way."

"I'm okay with perverted." He takes a drag from the joint and coughs.

"Oh. Yeah. Guess I should've warned you about that. Max said it was strong."

"I'm cool," he says, his voice croaky. "But, uh, Max gave you this? Why?" He holds it out to me.

I put the joint to my lips and take another deep breath. "Because Ash is a dick." I laugh on the exhale. I don't know why that's funny.

"Are you upset he's getting married?"

My brow furrows. "How'd you know?"

"Your mom. I think your whole family knows already."

"Fuuuuck." I throw my head back on the side of the treehouse and bang it repeatedly. The whole structure shakes, so I force myself to stop even though I don't want to. "I don't know why I'm upset about it," I admit.

"You two had a life together. It makes sense. And it's soon, right? Like, to be that serious with another guy already."

"That's what I said." I sigh. "Max hates the new guy. He's pissed because we've both moved on so fast, and it seems like a waste or whatever. Evidently, I think it was that he was more invested in me and Ash getting married than either of us were."

And that's the funny thing about it all. I don't like that Ash is getting married, but it's not because I wish he was marrying me. In fact, when I think about standing at an altar and promising forever, I thank God I dodged that bullet. I guess that says a lot about Ash's and my relationship.

"Is Max still gonna be an ass about it?" Lennon asks.

"Nah. He actually apologized." I hold up the joint. "His peace offering. Said he wants me to be happy, but it's hard for him. He's gonna try though. And he won't be a dick to you anymore."

"Right. I'll believe that when I see it."

"It's a shitty thing, what Ash and I did to him. We put him right in the middle. He's my brother, but he's Ash's business partner. Doesn't give him a right to be an asshole to you, and he knows that."

Lennon reaches for the joint but hesitates for a moment before taking a hit. When he blows it back out, he turns to me and takes a deep breath as if gathering the courage to say whatever he's thinking. "I think Ash would take you back if you came out."

"What makes you say that?" I ask cautiously. I've thought about that very thing a lot this past year, but I always come back to the same conclusion. We made the right decision to split.

"I overheard him talking to Vic. He said he was kind of hoping finding out he's engaged would make you pick up the phone. I'm guessing he meant to call Damon."

Lennon refuses to look at me, and maybe I should be offended he'd think I'd jump at the chance, especially after just blowing him, but in his defense, I haven't really told him much about Ash's and my relationship.

I take another hit. "Here's the thing about Ash and me. Growing up, I idolized all my brothers and followed them all around like a puppy. But when Ash moved in next door, everything became about him. I'd only follow him, and because he and Max were the same age and in the same class at school, it meant I followed both of them."

Lennon smiles. "That's kind of cute. I can imagine little Ollie following after his first crush."

"Cute's one word for it. Max liked to call it annoying and pathetic, but sure, let's go with cute. Anyway ... so ..." I try to think of a way to explain it, but it's a weird power dynamic I don't quite understand myself. "Have you ever met anyone famous?"

"Hello, random subject change. How strong is this shit?" He reaches for the joint again.

"I have a point. I swear."

"I've met a few athletes I idolized growing up, if that's what you mean," he says on an exhale, his voice all husky and sexy again.

I almost lose my train of thought but shake it free. "Yeah. So, you have expectations of them, right? And then when you meet them and realize they're just human, it's a bit of a letdown? Well, I never expected Ash to look at me in that way. When he came out, I was fourteen, which made me look up to him even more, even though I wasn't one hundred percent sure why, because I hadn't worked it out for myself yet. But when we started dating, I kinda did everything his way because whenever he'd dismiss one of my ideas for dinner or make me watch shitty films, I'd swallow my irritation down and remind myself *I'm with Ash.* The Ash. *Ash* wants *me.*"

"He was controlling?"

I shake my head. "No. Nothing like that. I did it to make him happy." I shift, trying to get more comfortable—in the tiny treehouse or with this conversation, I'm not entirely sure. "You know how relationships are about compromising and communication and—"

"I know shit all about relationships. You forget my longest ones haven't even lasted an entire season before."

"Well, with Ash and me, it always seemed like I'd be the one giving in all the time because it was *Ash.* I had some weird hero worship thing for the guy from when I was a kid. Not to mention we had *nothing* in common. The main thing that connected us was our family and our childhood. Add that to the guilt over being closeted, it made for an uneven relationship. Everything was about him. The one thing I had was keeping us a secret—which is a big fucking deal, I know—but that meant to make up for it, I was giving him everything he ever asked for or wanted. We weren't equals. I loved him, yeah, and it's not even his fault that's how our relationship was, but I still have no desire to go back to that."

Lennon's body relaxes, and I didn't realize how uptight he was while I answered that question until the tension leaves him. He leans in and his hand finds my thigh. "You didn't need to explain that, but I'm glad you did. I've been … curious, because until now I thought the only reason you weren't together was because of your career. That maybe … I mean, you have matching tattoos, for fuck's sake."

"You saw that, huh?" I wrap my arm around his shoulders. "I don't regret the tattoo or what it means. Ash was a huge part of my life. He's part of me. But we had way more problems than my closet door. And even if I were to come out tomorrow, I'm kinda taken with someone else now." Leaning in, I kiss the side of his neck. "Some gorgeous blond Clark Kent lookalike guy I can't get out of my head."

"He sounds hot." His laugh is short and self-deprecating and then he turns serious. "Can I ask you something?"

"You can, but I might not answer."

"Fair enough. I'm, umm …"

I get the feeling whatever it is, it's serious, so I make him take another hit of the joint, which is almost finished.

He nods as if building the courage to say what's on his mind. "Why doesn't your family know how much pressure they put on you?"

Ah, shit. I grab the joint and wish there wasn't only one drag left. Still, I savor it while I try to get my excuse together in my head.

"There are a lot of reasons."

"Have you tried to explain it to them? Because the impression I get is they've never seen your side."

"They haven't. They live in a world where they see the

activists on the streets, the pride parades, the fight for love, and they think that's how it'd be across the board. Hell, Massachusetts was the first state to legalize same-sex marriage, so my brothers and I were brought up on it, if you know what I mean. But none of my family has experienced the bullshit of the industry yet— even Nic, Vic, and Leo, who are in sports. They don't understand it's not that easy. How can I be the asshole who yells at the people who love me so much they want me to have the world? Like I'm ungrateful for their support."

"So, you grit your teeth and let them believe you have an issue with being gay instead of telling them what it's really like for gay men in sports?"

"I tell them," I argue, but it's flat, because I think we both know it's not the truth. "I tried telling them in the beginning. I think I suck at words or maybe at getting them to understand it's not about being a coward but about risking the thing I love most. Like, Nic and Vic are in MMA, where you work your way up. You have your competitors and that's it. I have guys in the AHL eyeing my fucking spot. My teammates are also my competitors. We all want first line, we all want MVP, and we all want to be the one to put the biscuit in the basket. I'm replaceable, and any shit on my career could be career suicide."

Lennon smiles.

"What?" I ask.

"Considering you think you're bad at words, you just explained it pretty well to me."

Ugh. He's right.

"Why can't I talk to them like that?"

"I don't know, but I think you need to find a way. Right now, there's a whole lot of confusion going on in that house. Everyone thinks the only thing getting in your and Ash's way was the closet door. They think the only thing between you and happiness is saying two little words at a tiny press conference. It's about time you set them straight."

"Or not so straight."

Lennon lets out a loaded sigh. "Man, this conversation is too deep for my first time being high."

I laugh harder. "Just wait until the conversation that's coming after our explosions earlier."

Lennon grumbles and rests his head on my shoulder. "I wanna sleep."

"Ha. You're all chill when you're high. I think I like it. But uh, my legs are going numb, my ass is sore, and I think I have a splinter in my back."

With a groan of protest, he moves away from me so we can open the trapdoor again to climb down and face the music.

This has been a good break from the family drama, but Lennon's right. I need to try to explain my situation so they understand.

CHAPTER TWENTY

LENNON

I'm not sure I like being high. First, getting out of the treehouse is fucking hard. Ollie looks up at me as I cling to the top of ladder and cry it's too far to fall and I'll die. In my defense, it looks super high. Like me.

"I can't see shit," I complain.

"Your glasses are in your pocket."

"Oh." That explains it.

"Come on, babe. Jump. I'll catch you."

"Aww, he called me babe. That's cute."

He laughs.

"That was out loud, wasn't it?"

He nods and holds out his massive hands. "Come on. It's only a few feet."

"Looks way more."

Ollie laughs again and climbs the first two rungs of the ladder to bring him closer.

I huff. "Fine. But I hope you're a better goalie than you are a sniper."

"Ouch, Lennon. *Ouch*."

I laugh my ass off as I slide my body into the manhole. Then I laugh more at the word *manhole*. Because apparently pot makes me mature. Super mature.

Maybe I should go backward instead of forward down the ladder, but I can't turn now, and it's small and cramped, and damn, half a joint and everything's blurry.

My foot gets stuck on one of the rungs, but my body's too uncoordinated to stop me from falling.

An unmanly squeak leaves me, and the last thing I see before falling to what I can only assume will be my death is Ollie's smile. I land on top of him with a thud, surprised to find I'm not, in fact, dead. He lets out a grunt.

"Did I hurt your manhole?" I ask.

He bursts out laughing. "High Lennon is fucking funny."

I whine. "I don't like being high. Makes me think I can fly … and rhyme, apparently."

"You're such a lightweight. Are you okay?"

I reach into my shirt pocket and pull out my glasses to slip them on. "Yeah. You? Am I going to have the Dragons suing my ass for breaking their best forward?"

His hand skims down my side and palms my ass. "I won't let anyone near this. I promise."

"My hero," I quip.

"Not a hero. I'm just determined to make it mine."

My breath catches in my throat, and I think Ollie knows what his words are doing to me, because he smiles as if he can read my mind.

I want him to want me like that. I want him to possess me, and fuck me, and wait … he said he doesn't do that. I go to open my mouth to get him to clarify, when—

"Uncle Ollie!" a little voice screams.

I scramble off him and notice the twinge in my foot. My ass lands on the lawn, and I wince as more pain shoots up my leg.

Shit. I think I've twisted my ankle.

"Hi, honey," Ollie coos. "I, uh, fell, and my friend was trying to help me up."

With all the innocence of a child, she doesn't even blink. "Grandma's looking for you."

"Of course, she is," he mutters.

We climb to our feet, and yup, definitely injured something in the fall. I put weight on my foot and hiss at the pain.

"Are you okay?" Ollie asks, wrapping his arm around my waist.

"Ankle."

He bends down to lift my pant leg. "It's swelling."

"That's what he said."

Ollie ignores my joke. "You might've broken it." He turns to his niece. "Can you go get Uncle Vic or Leo? Or your daddy if you can't find the others?"

She scampers off with a nod.

Ollie pulls me closer. "Here, lean on me."

I can't help it. I break into song. "When you're not …something. Soooooommmmmething. I don't knoooooooow the words."

Ollie shakes his head. "I hate to see how much pain you're gonna be in later when you're not high."

"I don't think I'm high anymore. It already hurts."

"You're so high. Come on, let's get you inside the house."

We start hobbling our way to the front door when I gasp.

"How are we going to explain this? We got high and fell out of the treehouse?"

Ollie finds me hilarious, apparently. "Okay, I've decided you should be high all the time. Like always. It's pure entertainment."

"I don't think that's a good idea. My articles won't make sense."

"They don't make sense when you're stone-cold sober either."

I mock offense. "To repeat your words earlier. Ouch, Ollie. *Ouch*."

Ollie kisses the top of my head. "You started it."

I want to stay like this, with Ollie's warmth wrapped around me and his lips close, but as we enter the house, he deposits me on the couch in the living room and pulls away. I try to cling to him, but he pushes me back into the seat.

"I'll be right back. I'm just gonna get you some ice."

"I'll get it," a voice says from the doorway to the kitchen.

I tilt my head back and see Leo's retreating form upside down. "The basketball brother has a nice ass."

When I pull my gaze away and meet Ollie's, he cocks his eyebrow at me.

"But you have a nice face."

Ollie tries to cover another laugh and sits on the coffee table in front of me and brings my leg up so my foot is in his lap.

Slowly, he unties my shoe and gives me an apologetic look as he removes it.

I hiss and squirm even though his touch is soft, and even though I'm in pain, the way he's caring for me and trying to be gentle as he inspects the ankle makes me want to say screw the ankle and climb on top of him on the coffee table.

Not a good idea.

"What happened?" Leo walks back in, ice in hand.

"Fell out of the treehouse because he's high," Ollie says with a laugh. I give him the finger.

"Poor Clark," Leo says, and I imagine he uses the same level of condescension with the kids he coaches.

Ollie and I cock our heads at each other in question. He turns to his brother. "You did hear—"

"Ollie, Ma wants you out back," Vic says as he enters the room.

Ollie doesn't move, just puts the ice Leo hands over onto my ankle. "Yeah, not happening. My b—uh, Lennon needs me."

"Clark will be fine with Leo. Ma. Outside. Now."

Again with the Clark thing when Ollie literally just called me Lennon.

Ollie's jaw hardens. "And I said Lennon needs me. We can sort our shit later."

Ah, so he's not really staying for me. He's avoiding facing his family, and I can't say I blame him. There's been miscommunication between them for so long, I wouldn't even know where to start if I were him.

"Here, let me at least look at his foot," Leo shoves Ollie out of the way.

Instead of going outside, Ollie joins me on the couch and holds my hand. "Leo studied kinesiology in college. He knows shit."

"Doesn't make me a doctor," Leo mumbles, "but it doesn't look broken. Can I touch it?"

I nod.

"If it hurts, squeeze my hand," Ollie says.

As soon as Leo's fingers press into my skin, I yelp and do as Ollie says.

He flinches. "Ah, I said squeeze it, not break it."

"Sorry."

"I'm messing with ya. It doesn't hurt." Ollie grins at me.

Leo moves my ankle, slowly rotating it. "Sore?"

"Yeah, but not a lot."

"Most likely sprained. Keep the ice on it. Twenty on, twenty off. Should be fine in a few days. If not, maybe go see a doctor."

"Thanks," I say and go to place my foot on the ground.

Leo grabs my leg and puts it back up on the coffee table. "And keep it elevated."

"Now you really need to go outside," Vic says to Ollie.

"Nope."

Vic grumbles and heads back through the kitchen to the backdoor.

"She only wants to apologize," Leo says quietly.

"Ma's version of an apology is weighted with guilt," Ollie says. "You think I don't already know what she's going to say? *You never told us we were overstepping.* Which I did, but you guys never listened. Or understood, I guess."

"You never pushed either," his brother says.

"All of you thought it was because I was embarrassed about being gay and not that I truly just wanted you guys to drop it because there's not much I can do if I don't want to risk my job."

Leo leans forward with his elbows resting on his knees. "For what it's worth, we're all sorry. We never …"

He slumps, and if I had to guess, it's because he knows whatever excuse he's about to come out with isn't enough for years of pretending Ollie's opinion on this was wrong, even though he's the only one who actually has a right to an opinion on coming out.

Leo continues. "We never thought about what it's like for you. I mean, not in depth. It's easy to tell you to come out, because to us it's an abstract thing. Which in retrospect is kinda ridiculous when you think about it. I work in locker rooms, and I've heard how teenage boys talk. I guess I figured they grow out of it? We admonish them for slurs, but they probably just get smarter about not saying them around us. And just because I don't have any major issues with my kids, that doesn't mean problems don't exist. So, I'm truly sorry for not trying to understand."

Suddenly, Ollie's using my hand for support instead of the other way around. His grip is tight, and my thumb runs along his skin in small circles, trying to reassure him.

Ollie seems to relax but doesn't look his brother in the eye. "Maybe I should've tried to explain better before now. Before Lennon …" His eyes meet mine, and his face softens. "I thought no one would understand. The few times I tried explaining it to Ash, he thought I was being petty and making a mountain out of a molehill."

The back door bangs against the kitchen counter as it opens, and Max is trailed by the twins. Now I'm in a room with all the Strömberg brothers, trying not to get a hard-on. Because seriously, there's an electric charge when all this Norse beauty is in one room.

"We're sorry," Nic and Vic say at the same time.

"So, this is how Ma is gonna play it?" Ollie asks, unamused. "All of you are sent in to butter me up for her big show? I'm guessing confetti cannons, a big scene in front of the extended family, and embarrassment for all. I'm not in the mood to go through that tonight."

"Okay, I don't want to know what you guys were so busy doing in the treehouse that you didn't hear everyone leaving," Leo says.

Ollie frowns. "Huh?"

"Well, when you stormed out, everyone was kinda quiet."

"Ooh," I cut in. "That's bad in this household."

The brothers all break into simultaneous smiles.

Nic nods in my direction. "He catches on quick."

"Ma asked everyone to leave," Max says. "Well, after they ate, anyway."

"Ma's outside by herself," Vic adds. "She wants to talk to you alone. Dad's dropping Grandma back home, and everyone else is gone. It's just her."

Ollie's face morphs into something that looks a hell of a lot like awe—like he can't believe his mom is finally taking it seriously.

He stands, but he doesn't let go of my hand. "You'll be okay for a bit?"

"Is he kidding? I get to hang out and perv on all his hot brothers."

Ollie laughs. "That was out loud too, babe."

"Oh. Well, shit. They're all twice my size too. And two of them are MMA fighters … I might go find somewhere to hide." When they all continue to stare at me, I realize I'm still talking. "My thoughts are still coming out aloud, aren't they?"

Ollie leans over and kisses the top of my head. "Yeah, but I promise they won't touch you."

"Pot is bad," I say.

The brothers laugh, and when Ollie makes his way out back and I meet their stares, they're still smiling at the nerdy guy who yelled at them earlier and then called them hot.

"Sorry," I say. "For, uh …"

"Calling us on our shit?" Vic asks.

"Someone had to do it," Leo says. "How are we supposed to know we're fucking up if no one tells us?"

"Ollie's lucky to have you, Clark," Max says.

I narrow my eyes. "Lennon."

The twins shake their heads and Nic says, "Oh, if you think for one second we're going to forget you guys totally lied to us for months, you're higher than we thought."

Wait, what? "So, you're saying …"

Max pats me on my shoulder. "Welcome to the family. *Clark*."

CHAPTER TWENTY-ONE

M a is a lot of things:

A strong woman who raised five boys.

A loving wife.

Protective.

Over the top.

Meddling.

Happy.

The woman sitting in front of me isn't any of those things. "I'm so, so, sorry, Oliver." Her voice isn't her own, either. "You hear about what happens to those who aren't brought up in a supportive environment, so we wanted to … I don't know, we always wanted you to know how much you were loved and how much we support you."

"I know, Ma, but sometimes it feels like you can't see past the label. That I can't be anything but gay and hockey holds me back, when the truth is it's my only escape because it doesn't matter who or what I am on that ice, and I'm not ready for that to change."

"I know that now. If it weren't for Clark, I might not have, and now I can't believe you let this go on for so long—let us treat you like that."

"Why do you think I moved to New York?" I joke.

Tears spring from my mother's eyes.

"Aww, Ma. I was traded. You can't ask for that shit to happen."

"I thought I was acing this whole parenting thing."

I hate that I'm feeling guilty right now when her words are all I've wanted to hear for so long.

"This is why I didn't tell you or, at least, dropped it whenever things got too heated. You're not doing a shitty job. I think you were so worried about being unsupportive or doing something homophobic that you went too far the other way and didn't realize that by pressuring me to come out, I became just as isolated. I don't know when I'll come out publicly, and I'm okay with that. You need to be okay with me doing it on my own time."

"It just hurts a parent to see their child struggle, and I know your breakup with Ash was hard on both of you."

"I had to make a choice, and my focus right now is, and always has been, on hockey."

"What about Clark?"

"Why do you keep calling him Clark?"

She smiles. "We agreed as a family that he will always be Clark. Even if you get married and—" Her face drops. "Sorry. It's saying that stuff that you don't like, right?"

"With Ash, yeah, you kinda pushed it on us like it'd be a Band-Aid for our problems. If I do get married—which I'm not even entirely sure that's what I'll ever want—I'd want to be out and do it right. I don't want a secret marriage. Hell, after Ash, I don't even know if I want a secret relationship."

"So, you and Clark aren't even remotely together ..." Even if it's a statement, it's posed as a question.

"Uh …"

"Use your words, Oliver. Keeping your mouth shut is what made you resent me for so long."

I blow out a loud breath. "I don't resent you. I never have. And I shouldn't complain, because any gay kid would be lucky to have this family. But faaaark, I need space sometimes."

She seems to understand even if hurt shines in her eyes. "Guess New York was a good thing after all."

I'm beginning to see it really was. "I hated it at first, and I'm pissed Boston's still in the running for the Cup while I'm sitting on my ass, but being away from everyone for the first time in my life, I think I've grown up a bit."

"Says the boy who just got high with his sex toy in a tree-house," she says.

I screw up my face. "First, eww, please don't ever say *sex toy* ever again, and second, Lennon—"

"Nuh-uh. You started with the lie, so he is forever Clark in this house."

"You guys have seriously weird punishments, but fine. *Clark* and I haven't even had sex, so you're wrong. We're friends." Despite the epic blowjobs.

Ma sighs. "Promise me something."

I tense and automatically assume she's going to start talking about putting Lennon's feelings and needs before my career like she would've said to me any other time, but what she does say surprises me.

"When I'm being overbearing, just tell me."

"We try to," I argue.

"Try harder. Come up with a code word, so I know when I'm pissing you off, because as your mother, I still have the right to butt into your life. That will never change. But I don't want to upset you. Any of you boys. You've been my whole life."

"What about Dad?"

She waves me off. "Eh. He's all right. Like, if there was a zombie apocalypse or something, I wouldn't shoot him in the leg, but you boys would be my first priority."

My mother, the badass zombie hunter … apparently.

"I think we just found our code word. *Zombies*."

"Deal. Now, seeing as we're on this talking and opening-up business, you need to tell me what happened between you and Ash, because I get the feeling you didn't tell me that whole story either."

"Zombies! Zombies!"

"Nice try, but you're only allowed to use it if it's dire, and I think it's about time you told the truth about you and Ash."

With a grunt, I tell Ma about all the other issues we had—the imbalance of give and take in our relationship and the way I sacrificed a lot of little things because Ash had to sacrifice one big thing.

We keep talking even when my brothers come outside and join in. When I ask where Lennon is, they tell me they carried Clark upstairs to bed after he fell asleep on the couch.

I laugh, because Lennon probably loved that.

Dad eventually comes home from dropping Grandma off, and even though it's been an eventful and drama-filled day, it's the first time in years we've felt like the family I grew up with.

There's still the ribbing and the teasing, but there's also an underlying awareness that wasn't there before, and I can't say that it's a bad thing.

And I owe it all to Clark. Err … Lennon.

So, when Lennon passed out, he passed the fuck out. Which is probably why I'm woken up in the middle of the night by a very handsy, wide-awake, and horny reporter. Because he's been asleep for twelve hours, and now he's experiencing some sort of marijuana-induced jet lag.

His fingers trail down my back. When I came to bed, his shirt was on, but now I feel his skin against my chest.

"That's one way to wake me up," I mumble, my mind half-asleep but my dick fully awake.

My hand finds his face in the dark and cups his cheek.

He turns his head and kisses my palm and then my wrist. "I contemplated letting you sleep, but then I thought where's the fun in that? I should make the most of this."

I hear the unspoken words. *This: our little window of time where the rest of the world doesn't exist.*

Our something real is something temporary, and I think we both know that. As much as I'd jump at the chance to try more with Lennon, it'll always come down to asking him to step back into the closet for me, and I won't do that to another person, no matter how good his lips on my neck feel.

Or the way his hand slips into the waistband of my boxers and massages my ass cheek.

All thought is lost when he grinds against me, our hard cocks meeting through the fabric of our boxers.

"You didn't get all the way naked before you pounced on me?" My voice is breathless already. That doesn't bode well for how long I'm gonna last.

"I figured that would've been too creepy. Same goes for waking you up with my mouth wrapped around your dick. Thought it might've been overkill."

I bring his face close to mine as I whisper over his lips. "I give you permission to wake me with either of those things whenever you feel like it."

He doesn't have a chance to respond before I'm claiming his mouth and thrusting my tongue inside.

"Mmm, you taste good," Lennon says.

"It's called brushing your teeth before bed. Maybe you should try it sometime."

He gasps and covers his mouth. "Shit. I'll be right back." Lennon tries to get up, but I don't let him.

"I'm kidding. I don't care." To prove my point, I take his mouth again, tasting him, nipping at his lip, and practically devouring him.

Lennon's hands warm my skin as they travel from my back to my chest and down my stomach, venturing everywhere but where I really want it.

It's not enough. Nowhere near enough.

My body ruts against his, and the room fills with sounds of heavy breathing and the creaking of the old bed.

Breaking our lips apart but refusing to move away, I whisper against his skin. "I want to fuck you."

"I thought …" His head pulls back, looking confused.

"I've been thinking."

Lennon opens his mouth, but I cut him off.

"And before you make a joke about not realizing hockey players could do that, let me finish."

He smirks, because I'm guessing that's exactly what he was going to say.

"I've been thinking I haven't been able to make an informed decision before. I've only ever bottomed by default, and yes, I love it, but I'd be lying if I said I'm not curious."

Lennon's smile gets wider, which I didn't think was possible, but then it drops. "Wait … like right now? What about supplies, and—"

"I've got it covered." I roll over and reach under the bed and pull out my duffel bag. "You know how I said I'd planned to jump you? Boy Scouts are always prepared."

An arm wraps around me from behind, and lips land between my shoulder blades.

"We don't need them yet. I want to play first."

I groan and throw condoms and lube on the bed somewhere while I roll us so I'm on top of him. "I like playing games."

Lennon looks like he's in pain, but the word "Yes" falls from his lips like he wants more, and it confuses me. Then I remember his ankle.

"Fuck." I sit up, my legs trapping his narrow waist. "Your foot."

"It's fine. It's *so* fine. No way will I let it get in the way of doing this. I've wanted this since the night I met you."

"Need to make up for lost time," I say.

"Exactly." Lennon rises up and wraps his arms around me, so I can't move from on top of him. Wet kisses land on my chest, and then his lips move to my pierced nipple. He tongues the barbell, sending a shock of electricity down to my overeager cock.

"Hurry up," I whine.

He smiles around my nipple before biting down.

"Holy mother of fucking Gretzky."

Lennon chuckles. "I think I'm going fast enough. I want to taste all of you." His lips lay more kisses along my skin between him muttering, "Every. Single. Inch."

My mouth wants to protest while my body screams "Hell yeah." It makes an interesting gargled sound come out of me, and that makes Lennon turn smug.

"Someone's impatient."

"Someone likes teasing me," I grumble.

"*Someone* needs a little self-restraint."

"I'm a hockey player. It's my job to be full speed ahead all the time."

"Then it'll do you some good to slow down for once." Lennon's mouth continues to taste me. His hands explore my tattoos and make me shiver.

"I don't wanna slow down." I try to grind against him, but his hands fly to my waist and lock me in place. The only way to get out of his grip might hurt him, and I'd rather be tortured than hurt Lennon.

He stood up to my family, and we're not exactly an unintimidating bunch of people.

I admire him for what he's gone through with those dickheads back in college and high school and he's here giving me a chance anyway, even though there's the serious risk I could turn around and be just like them.

Then don't be, my conscience says.

It can't be that easy, though, can it?

As I stare down at Lennon with his mouth moving over me while his hands hold me firmly in place, the sudden easiness of it all becomes clear.

With my new revelation comes the idea that going slow right now might be worth it. Because I want this feeling of being able to take on the world to last.

Plus, two can play at this game.

Lennon must sense my defeat, because as I lean down to kiss him as slowly as my mouth allows, his hold on my hips softens.

Our tongues tangle, our breaths mix, and the atmosphere has gone from needy and frantic to lasting and tender.

I shuffle lower on his lap slowly and gently push him so he's lying on his back again. Just like his mouth had been exploring, I do the same to him. His virgin skin makes me want to get Max to cover him in tattoos, but there's also a part of me that loves the contrast between our two bodies. I love that he's long and lean, and even though he's smaller than me, he's still taller than average and the perfect size to fit against me.

Lennon lets out a little whine as my tongue moves closer to his belly button. I can feel how hard he is against my chest as I continue my path down.

"Shit. Whose idea was it to go slow?" he complains.

I smile against his skin. "Someone who's a genius." My hand skims up his thigh and lightly brushes over his cock through his boxers.

"I hate myself right now." He writhes beneath me, and I love how fast I've turned the tables on him.

"Have to take my time," I say. "Make sure I'm doing it right."

"The only thing you're doing wrong is not touching me enough. I need … I need more."

"More what?"

"More *everything*."

He reaches for my underwear and pulls them off my hips, using his feet to push them down all the way. My cock springs free and hits my stomach, leaving a warm trail of precum. His underwear goes next, and I pull them down his wiry legs.

The old bed creaks in protest with all the moving around.

I wince. "I've never realized how loud this house is until this weekend."

"You probably never realized because you grew up with four brothers who were no doubt louder than the house."

"True."

"I know how to be quiet," Lennon whispers.

I smirk. "Challenge accepted."

"Uh, I don't recall setting one."

"I'm gonna make you scream," I promise.

When my mouth resumes its exploration, moving over

Lennon's lean muscles but refusing to go where he really wants it, his body starts trembling, and his breathing comes in hard and fast as if he's trying not to make a sound.

I chuckle against his skin. "Is someone trying not to make a noise?"

"I hate you. And me. Can we forget the slow thing already? Shit, if I knew you were going to use it against me, I wouldn't have suggested it." He says that, but the lust in his eyes, his shaky breath, and his body's silent scream for more makes me think he's loving this.

"I think it's perfect punishment for trying to drive me crazy." But who am I kidding? This, being with him and trying to control myself, is driving me just as crazy.

I lean back on my heels and try to hold in my moan of appreciation as Lennon's laid out bare for me on the bed. His cock rests against his abdomen, and the drop of precum on his stomach is too irresistible to pass up. I clean it off with my tongue and hum as if being fed a gourmet meal.

Lennon whines. The sound makes my cock ache, and I'm sure if it could talk, it'd be begging incoherently. Much like Lennon.

I can't hear his whispered words but I catch *please* and *hurry the fuck up*. His fists are scrunched into the bedsheets, his hips trying to buck upward, but I pin them down.

The bed creaks again, and the only reason I'm able to push it out of my mind is that it's the middle of the night and everyone downstairs will be asleep.

"Ollie," Lennon whispers, his voice tortured.

I guess he's learned his lesson about trying to tease the fuck outta me.

Sitting up again, I lift his injured leg and kiss just above his swollen ankle. "Have to keep this elevated, right?"

He smiles and rests his leg over my shoulder while he bends

his other knee, giving me the perfect line of sight of his hole as his hips tilt slightly upward. Lennon's gaze fixes to mine as I lift my hand to my mouth and suck on one of my fingers. He nods, and I don't even think it's a conscious move.

His pupils dilate, and a feral look of need crosses his face as I tease him, massaging his rim. I may've never done this to another person before, but I do know what turns my crank and gets me going.

My other hand finds his cock, slowly pulling on it at a pace that would piss me off. It's enough to feel good but not give any satisfaction.

And yup, there's Lennon's scowl I used to hate. Now it's an incentive to keep going. Only problem is my cock is crying for attention and my hands are full.

"Touch me," I beg.

An evil glint passes across Lennon's face, and I know I've given him back the upper hand.

He reaches for me and wraps his fingers around my cock, copying my slow and torturous strokes.

"Like this?" he asks innocently. His hand is dry, and while my cock is leaking, it's not enough to give the friction I crave.

"I'm starting to understand the hate thing you're talking about," I grumble.

My eyes spot the lube on the bed. Before Lennon has the chance to become impatient, I've basically covered us in half the bottle.

"Slippery," Lennon teases, but all traces of mocking disappear when I switch hands, and two of my lubed fingers breach his tight ring of muscle. "Oh, fuck! Sweet Neil Patrick Harris in a harness."

I can't help laughing. "What?"

His eyes widen. "Oh, nothing."

"No seriously—"

He starts jacking me, distraction working to make whatever question I had fall from my brain, and jerks at a pace I'm convinced is the same speed he wants me to finger him.

I'd give him whatever he wants, but this game he wanted to play is a lot more fun than I thought it would be.

The need to come is almost too overwhelming, but I could watch Lennon go stir-crazy for hours. It's a small price to pay.

He closes his eyes and takes deep breaths as if he's trying to calm himself down, but his hand on my cock doesn't slow. If I don't give into him soon, I'm gonna blow. And when his eyes crack open, and his lips twitch around the edges, I know that's his new game plan.

We start playing a game of chicken, each of us getting close to the edge before the other pulls back.

I grit my teeth, and sweat from trying to stave off my orgasm drips down my forehead. When he senses I'm too close, his hand on me stills, and I let out a silent curse.

I massage his prostate until he's panting and begging for it and then remove my fingers and kiss him roughly until he calms down. Then I do it again.

We push each other to the brink so many times I lose count, and Lennon looks like he could lose consciousness.

I love watching his eyes roll back in his head every time my fingers brush his prostate, and I make sure to see it again and again.

"Okay, you win," he says. "I'm never playing this game with an athlete again." Under his breath, he adds, "Stupid competitive motherfuckers."

"Finally!" My muscles are coiled tight, needing release. Not just wishing for it but *needing* it more than my lungs need air.

In seconds, I'm covered with a condom and more lube and easing inside him. We groan in unison, and my balls draw up tight already. I've never felt this kind of tightness or warmth surrounding my cock, and I can't believe I never pushed to try this before.

Holy hell, I'm in heaven. Ass heaven.

Stars dance across my vision, from pleasure or dehydration I'm not so sure at this point.

"Seriously, this is gonna be over so fucking soon."

"I'm okay with that," Lennon rasps. He throws his head back as his hand goes to his cock, pulling on it harder and faster than I was.

I test out a small thrust and shudder at the ripple of pleasure shooting down my spine. Murmured curse words fall from my mouth.

"Kiss me," Lennon demands, and it's one I have no hesitation giving into.

I slide inside him farther when I lower my mouth to his, bottoming out as our tongues tangle.

Lennon's hand still works his cock, and now I can feel it against my stomach.

"I want you to come on me," I say against his lips.

I get a pained moan in response and take that as a sign I need to start moving again. My hips rock, gaining more movement with each thrust.

The bed creaks under our weight, but I'm too busy tuning into the little sounds coming from Lennon beneath me.

He needs to come soon, because no way am I going to last like this. His ass chokes my dick harder than a vise, but I want Lennon to cross the finish line first.

I just have to hold out a little more.

With Lennon's injured leg still resting over my shoulder, his other leg wraps around my hip, and his tight little hole grips me even tighter.

"Fuck," I cry out. "I can't … with the coming and the holding out and the …" And now I'm rambling.

Even thoughts of hockey don't help.

Lennon stiffens and comes on an inaudible gasp. I would've missed it entirely had ropes of hot, sticky cum not splashed against my stomach and chest. The hand jerking himself slows, and his breathing starts to even out, but it's his completely blissed-out face that pushes me over the edge.

I try to hold myself up, but my orgasm rips away the last of my energy, and I collapse on Lennon a little harder than I'd like.

He grunts, and I manage a "Sorry," but all he does is laugh.

"Yet you're still on top of me."

"Can't. Move."

"I take it you liked your first time dicking someone out?"

"Understatement. When can we do it again?"

Lennon laughs, and it's the best sound in the world. Either that or I'm cum drunk.

Yeah, probably that.

I slowly roll off him and onto my back. "So." I breathe heavily. "Neil Patrick Harris in a harness?"

"*Sweet* Neil Patrick Harris in a harness."

"Care to explain?"

He faces me, his blue eyes shining in the dark. "Sometimes *fuck* doesn't cover it."

CHAPTER TWENTY-TWO

LENNON

It's been a long time since I've woken up wrapped around someone, and if it weren't for Ollie's mom calling out "Breakfast is ready," I'd happily stay here.

Ollie's body is warm and large, and his arms encase me tightly as if he's scared to let me go.

I've had boyfriends in the past, and even if they never lasted long, this is probably what I miss the most. Waking up next to someone who makes me all disgustingly mushy inside.

My body's all floaty, my mind empty—a state only a night of great orgasms can achieve.

That all turns to shit when one of Ollie's brothers knocks on the bedroom door.

"Hurry up. Some of us need coffee thanks to being awake half the night listening to your fuck session."

My eyes widen, and I nudge Ollie. All he does is mumble something I can't understand and rolls over to face the other way.

"Your brothers are here?" I ask.

"Mmm, they were all drinking and stayed the night."

"And you didn't think to tell me that? They heard everything."

"We weren't *that* loud," he says through a yawn.

Only, when we drag our asses out of bed and head downstairs, it's pretty damn clear we were that loud.

All four of Ollie's brothers clap and cheer, and his mom refuses to look either of us in the eye as she flits around the kitchen.

"Really, Ollie," Nic says, "you should've known why the oldest was always put in the attic. The noise from up there travels. It was Ma and Dad's way of making sure we didn't bring a girl home and impregnate her."

I'm sure the pink tinge on Ollie's face matches mine.

Note to self: never, ever, have sex with Ollie in his parents' house ever again.

"Well, it worked, didn't it? No teen pregnancies in this house," their mom says and starts putting plates on the table. "But at least you two know for next time."

"Although to be fair, in your own words, Ma, I won't be getting anyone pregnant up there." Ollie's able to laugh off his embarrassment, but I'm not as easy.

"Well, I'd love to stay for breakfast, but I'm going to go drown myself," I say and try to run away.

Only, I run straight into Ollie's dad. "Pfft. No need to run off. There's really no secrets between us now."

Ollie's brothers snicker.

"I'm so sorry," Ollie whispers to me.

Either they've all had their fun or they've taken pity on me, but they drop it after that.

Everyone seems looser this morning than the tension-filled disaster I missed out on while I was asleep all afternoon.

Even Ollie appears more relaxed. He smiles at me in a way I've only ever wished to be smiled at. Like, we're actually a couple.

When we're not. I mean, not *really*. I have no idea what's going on in Ollie's head.

He basically passed out last night as soon as we'd cleaned ourselves up, and it's not like we've had a chance to talk this morning.

After breakfast, Ollie turns to me. "I was gonna go see Tommy today before the game if you wanna come? Or do you have to get back to the city?"

"I've got everything I need for tonight's game, so I'm easy." I wince when everyone laughs. "Walked right into that one, didn't I?"

"You're gonna be so much fun to have around, Clarky," Max says.

Even if I'm mortified, the mockery is different to the type I suffered through in high school, and I know they accept me, which is something I wasn't so sure would happen. Especially from Max, who I thought would never be okay with me being with his brother instead of Ash.

"I could've gone back to my hotel room," I say as we pull into the driveway of a cute house somewhere in suburbialand outside the city.

"I wanted you to come. And Tommy knows about us anyway."

It's slow going on my behalf as we get out of Ollie's parents' car he's borrowed and make our way up the stone path toward the house, which has a giant wraparound porch filled with kids' toys.

"This house isn't exactly what I was expecting for a hockey legend with ten seasons under his belt," I say.

Ollie smiles. "This is their everyday home—the one they live in most. There's also the apartment in the city for game nights and the holiday house on the Cape."

"Yeah, that sounds more like what I was expecting. I guess I've always figured Tommy to be the flashy type not …" I stare at the renovated colonial house, which is beautiful, yes, but it's … normal.

"Tommy's ego on the ice might be huge, but in reality, he's just a guy supporting his family. The difference between hockey-season and off-season Tommy is astounding. I can't wait for you to witness it."

He grimaces, and I assume it's because he realizes what he's said. After the season, I'll most likely be back in Chicago. We won't be hanging out and doing whatever we're doing.

As we approach the house, my ankle twinges with each hobbled step. It's definitely less painful today but still annoying.

Ollie huffs and lifts me bridal style before I even have the chance to protest.

"What are you doing?" I struggle against him. "I can walk, dickhead. Plus, I'm, like, heavy and shit."

He leans in, so his mouth is close to my ear. "Need to keep your foot elevated, remember?"

A shiver runs through me from memories of last night.

My eyes scan the quiet street, but paranoia for Ollie sets in. "What if someone's watching?"

He does the same glance over the street I did. "Let them see. You're just an injured guy being carried by a super-hot, super-strong hockey player. I'm being chivalrous."

I laugh. "If you say so."

"And you're not heavy. I bench press more than you daily."

"Okay, big guy, I get it. You have muscles."

Ollie's voice takes on a husky quality as he says, "Muscles you traced with your tongue last night."

"Truth."

I don't know what game Ollie's playing, but it's working. Reminding me of last night has me hardening and my worries of our future muted.

But my hard-on dies completely when Tommy's door opens, and instead of Tommy or his wife—or hell, I'd settle for either of his kids—Damon, my friend and Ollie's agent, stands there looking at us with a furrowed brow.

His dark hair is styled casual messy like it always is, but instead of the suit I'm used to seeing him in, he's in jeans and a T-shirt. That's when I remember his boyfriend is Tommy's brother-in-law.

"Shit," I gasp as Ollie almost drops me. I struggle the rest of the way out of his grip and tell my brain to come up with an excuse. Any excuse. "Umm, I injured my foot, and my magazine wanted me to interview Ollie and do a follow-up to all those articles I wrote about him earlier in the season, and now that the Dragons are out—"

Ollie bursts out laughing. "It's a good thing for me that you suck at lying." He throws his arm around me. "Hey, Damon, you know my boyfriend, right?"

Damon's eyes are the size of saucers, and they probably match mine.

"Boyfriend?" I croak.

"Boyfriend-type-person," Ollie says with a wave of his hand. "You know what I mean." He kisses the side of my head and walks past Damon into Tommy's house.

Damon and I stare at each other with mirrored dumbfounded expressions.

"Did he just come out to me?" Damon asks. "Oh, God, has he come out to the world without telling me first?" He whips out his phone from his pocket, but I step forward and cover it with my hand.

"Your professional world isn't imploding, but I fear Ollie's head might be. I had no idea he was going to do that."

We make our way inside, Damon faster than I can manage on my ankle, only to find Ollie in the kitchen talking to Tommy as if he didn't just come out to his agent.

Ollie claps Tommy on the shoulder. "Ready for the game, old man?"

"Of course," Tommy says as his wife and Maddox enter the room.

"Why do you guys look like you're trying to do math?" Maddox asks Damon and me.

The dynamic hockey duo turns to us, as if just realizing we'd followed them in.

"Oh. That," Ollie says. "I think they're freaking out because I told Damon that Lennon and I are a thing."

Maddox cocks his head at Damon. "Why would that shock you? We saw them flirting at the benefit."

"I'm trying to work out if I should be in friend mode or agent mode," Damon says.

Ollie finally loses his calm composure, and he frowns. "You guys already know I'm gay?"

Damon shrugs. "Suspected."

"Lennon, did you give me your gay vibes?"

I laugh.

Damon takes out his phone again. "Does this mean … like, do you need me to do a press release, or—"

"No," Ollie says quickly. "Not ready for that, and I hadn't planned on telling you today, but I'd planned on it eventually."

Damon nods. "Whenever you're ready. OnTrack Sports and I will support you one hundred percent."

"Yeah. After Matt, I figured," Ollie says.

Tommy slaps Ollie on the back. "I'm gonna be totally lame here and tell you I'm proud of you."

Ollie nudges him. "'Cause I totally did it for you, bro." His eyes flick to mine before looking away again and speaking quietly. I don't think I'm supposed to hear it, but I do. "Not making the same mistakes this time."

He continues to refuse to look at me, but I can't tear my eyes away from him. His long body makes me want to go to him and wrap myself around him, like how we were last night.

Maddox pulls me out of almost doing something indecent in front of everyone.

"You could totally tap into the queer market," he says to Damon. "Represent all the gay guys in sport."

Tommy leans against the kitchen counter, next to Ollie. "He might already be there with Matt and Ollie."

Damon scoffs. "Trust me. There are way more gay guys in sports. It's just a fact that it's still hard to come out in our world."

"Exactly," Ollie says, and even if he's still not ready, he's taken another important step, and as selfish as it is, my stupid brain and heart think he's done it for me—something he wasn't willing to do for Ash.

But as fast as that happens, guilt replaces it, because the last thing I need is the pressure of being the guy he comes out for.

Of course, Ollie knows everyone at the arena. This used to be his playground. He fist-bumps his way past all the security and into the press box with me, despite my protests about being in the vicinity of several other reporters who'll be interested to know why he's sitting with me instead of in his old team's owner's box or in the stands with family and friends.

He assures me it's fine and he's allowed to have friends. No one should suspect otherwise.

I'm legitimately beginning to worry that topping for the first time means he lost a severe amount of brain cells when he came.

Sex makes you dumb, people.

He's taking risks he hasn't allowed himself for years.

I'm sweating. Is it hot in here?

This is a lot of pressure.

It eases a little when the game starts and I have to concentrate, but he's got that whole awareness thing about him again, and I feel him everywhere.

"Stop it," I mutter.

"Stop what?"

When I turn to him, his eyes are on the ice, and I begin to wonder if the heat from his gaze has been imagined, but nope. His lips twitch upward.

"I have to work."

"So do I," he says. Then he leans to his right, bringing him closer to me so no one else can hear but not so close it looks suspicious. The scent of his cologne is stronger and somehow reminds me of sex. In particular, sex with him. "I have to work at getting you back to your hotel room and out of your clothes as soon as this game's over."

Kill. Me. Now.

Seems Ollie's goal all day today has been to drive me crazy. Or try to make me come without him even touching me. He's exceedingly good at both, and if he's not careful, I'll *have* to go back to my hotel room, but it won't be to fool around; it'll be for a new change of pants.

I would've thought he'd be more inconspicuous than this, but maybe I'm being overly paranoid. Maybe he was like this with Ash, but I got the impression he hid as much as possible with him and didn't allow for silliness in public.

I have to admit, it's a huge turn-on not being able to touch but subtly dropping hints about what'll happen later. I wish I could concentrate on the ice instead of the unfairly hot, talented, somewhat awkward when he's uncomfortable guy who not only makes playing hockey look good but also makes the game interesting.

I thought I was having an off night when Ollie was with his family instead of at the game. Turns out my interest in hockey solely revolves around one hockey player.

As if sensing me watching him instead of the game, he glances my way, and the smile he gives me reminds me of a promise—a promise for more. And not just sex, but everything. I wish I was rational enough to dismiss it, but whether it's my inner nerd wanting this since I first started liking boys or whether it's my stupid side, a huge part of me knows I'm already in too deep. We might've only admitted aloud yesterday that we want each other, but if I'm completely honest, I've been gone for this guy since the day we met.

It's the reason I kissed him that day in the stairwell. It's the reason I started watching his games and following his career. And ultimately, it's the reason my boss transferred me to hockey. Because my passion for the game—a.k.a. Ollie—shone through in the articles I wrote about him.

"Whoa," Ollie says, his gaze snapping back to the ice.

I tear my eyes away, only to be confused by what's happening below.

Two New Jersey players have gotten into a fight ... with each other. Not Boston.

"That's new," I say as I watch the two giants drop their gloves and try to pummel one another.

The reporters surrounding me start tapping away furiously, probably live tweeting and googling the players' stats and entire careers.

Sorensen and Healy by the names on their jerseys. I open Google, but Ollie beats me to it. "Caleb Sorensen and Kip Healy."

The home crowd roars with cheers, presumably because the enemy is fighting between themselves.

"What's their deal?" I ask.

"I have no idea. I've faced Healy a few times, and he can be a bit of a dick, but not any more than the usual trash-talking shit that goes on or the sneaky penalties we all try to pull off. Not sure about Soren. He was traded from the West Coast last season."

Other players from New Jersey pull their teammates apart, and when they skate back to the bench, their coach sends both players off.

"That's weird, right?" Granted, I'm new to hockey, but I don't think I've heard of teammates fighting during a game before.

"Fights break out all the time during practice," Ollie says, "but we're always told to leave that shit off the ice. Maybe their egos are too big for their helmets. Apparently, us hockey players are known for that. Who knew, right?"

The squabble between teammates is quickly forgotten when Boston gets the breakaway and flies down the ice. Tommy lands a slap shot to the top right of the net, and from that first goal, all the way through to the third period, Boston doesn't let up. New Jersey puts up a strong fight, but the thirst Boston's had all season doesn't waver.

I'd think Ollie would be distracted, watching his old team kick ass, but he's more interested in distracting me.

While the game seems close, and both teams take about the same amount of shots on goal, Boston dominates, sinking three of them. Boston's goalie is on point, not letting a single shot through.

I don't see New Jersey turning this around.

While the after-game press conferences drone on and on, all I can think about is Ollie in my hotel room waiting for me. I sent him with my room key as soon as the game finished so we wouldn't be seen together, and as promised, as soon as I get back to my hotel room, Ollie greets me with no words but his mouth on mine, his fingers working my shirt buttons, and an obvious mission to fulfill his annoyingly hot promises he kept hinting at throughout the game.

"Please tell me you got your article written and sent off," he says breathlessly.

"I purposefully stayed back to get it done."

"Good. Because I need your ass again."

"I've created a monster." Not that I can hate that.

"Nope. I just like having a new toy, so I'm gonna play with it as much as possible."

I snort. "My ass is your new toy. I'm sure that's supposed to sound wrong somehow, but right now, I can't think of why."

And speaking of my ass, he grabs my cheeks over my suit pants and brings me closer to him.

"Warning you now," he whispers. "This isn't going to be like last night. I'm gonna take you hard and fast, because all I've wanted all day was to be back inside you, and I don't have the fucking patience for you edging me."

I try to say "Same here" or "Hurry up" or some other affirmative, but all that comes out are mumbling sounds that make no sense.

It's obvious he understands anyway when he strips off the remainder of my clothes and pushes me on the bed on my hands and knees.

In a daze of want and need, I don't know where the lube comes from, and I don't care. When one of Ollie's fingers breaches my hole, there's no exploring like last night. No going slow. He aims for my prostate and immediately starts pegging it.

My cock goes from happily interested to achingly desperate.

"Fuck, fuck, fuck, fuck, fuck," I hiss.

My ass clenches around his finger as if trying to trap it inside me.

"Not yet," he says playfully, but I get the feeling he's gritting his teeth as he says it. "As much as I said hard and fast, I'm not going to make it painful for you."

"A little pain is good. I need … just need more …"

He adds a second finger, the sting of stretching a welcome ache. Last night, we went so slow, and Ollie was so cautious, I barely felt it this morning. After tonight, I want to ache for days. I'm going to leave for game three and four in New Jersey, and I doubt Ollie's coming with me, so I want to feel him until I see him again for game five.

Ollie gives me exactly what I want. He somehow manages to get himself sheathed one-handed while his fingers continue to prep me and turn me into a quivering mess.

My forehead falls onto the mattress as I rock back and forth onto his fingers. "You need to hurry up before I come already."

I whimper at the loss of his fingers until he eases inside, and the noise coming from me turns into a grunt.

Ollie whispers under his voice, words I don't understand, which turn into rambling about my ass having the ability to kill him and that death by sex would be worth it if he'd already won a

Stanley Cup. Then he starts rattling off hockey stats, and it takes a minute for me to realize he's trying to distract himself.

We're both fighting against our own control, both getting lost in the empty thoughts running through our heads where we can only concentrate on one thing, and that's the feeling of each other. His heat, my want, our combined urgency and need.

Ollie's cock pulses inside me, harder than steel, and my hips move on their own. Stretching out, I raise my hands above my head, slipping them under the pillow and gripping the sheet tight as I continue to fuck myself slowly on his dick.

Ollie starts moving, his quick detour from hard and fast over with, and he meets my movements, thrust for thrust—the reason I love bottoming. There's no better feeling than being turned out until I'm walking funny and I can't remember my stupid name.

Soon he's taking me at a punishing pace, and hard breathing and the slapping of our bodies are the only sounds to fill the room. Ollie's grip on my hip tightens, and I lose myself to him a little more. It's not that I get off on pain but more the possessive way in which he takes my body. It's the claiming bruises, the lasting aches. Last night was sweet, but this is primal, and I'd be happy to take Ollie either way. Last night, I was cared for. Tonight, I feel *needed.*

And when he wraps his hand around my cock while shouting his release, it only takes a few strokes for me to fall over the edge after him.

We stay like that, Ollie slowing his thrusts inside me as he continues to empty into the condom. My chest and the bedding are covered in cum, but instead of making a move to clean up when Ollie pulls out of me, I roll onto my back and collapse onto the bed.

A warm tongue licks at my spent cock. I moan as Ollie laps at the overly sensitive flesh, but I don't stop him.

"Mmm, babe, you taste amazing, but fuck, you came hard. I think you might need to shower."

"Shower sounds good," I say, but my eyes drift closed.

Ollie laughs against my skin. "We're totally the reason these hotels need black lights. You're lying in a pool of cum."

I wave him off. "Legs jelly. Brain broken. Sleep now. Bodily fluid cleanup later."

"I love it when you're romantic."

"Sunshine, flowers, candy, semen … it's allllll romantic." I'm rambling now, and I don't even care.

I'm vaguely aware of Ollie leaving the room and coming back with a wet towel to finish cleaning me and the bed up, and as he rejoins me and wraps his arm around me, something niggles at the back of my mind, but I'm too sated to let it come to the foreground.

It's like that sense when you leave the house and can't remember if you turned the iron off, or when you needed to do something but totally forgot.

Sleep pulls me under before I remember exactly what it is or why it's important.

The incessant buzzing of a phone comes from somewhere in the room. A grumble comes from beside me as Ollie rolls over and throws an arm around my waist.

"You should get that," he mumbles but holds me tighter. "I've been ignoring it for, like, ten minutes now."

"How do you know it's not yours?"

"Mine's dead. Died last night, and I forgot my charger."

"I don't wanna," I complain.

"I know. But I guess we better get up. When's your flight?"

My eyes fly open. "Shit, what's the time?"

"It's early. I think." Ollie slowly releases me and clambers to his feet. On his way to the bathroom, I admire the view, especially when he bends down and picks up my pants off the floor.

I sigh when he throws them at me and they smack me in the face.

"I'm gonna shower. Hurry up and check your messages so you can join me."

My protest is weak, but after the water starts running, I force myself to get this done, because a wet, naked Ollie should never be passed up.

I pull my phone out of my pants pocket, and my stomach rolls at the sight of numerous notifications on my screen. As someone who doesn't have many friends, it's never a good thing when your social media is lit up like a Christmas tree and you have missed calls from your boss, your coworker … and Damon.

But it's the notification with the preview of a news article that catches my eye. I squint and click the link and hold my breath.

There I am splashed all over *Sporting World News* staring at Ollie next to me in the press box like he hung the damn moon. I look love struck, Ollie looks smug, and that means we're both completely screwed.

I only catch the headline *Strömberg Switching Teams?* when my phone starts vibrating with another incoming call.

Kevin.

"Hawkins," I say into the phone, my voice thick from sleep and worry.

"He's gay, isn't he?"

My stomach sinks, and I want to vomit. "What are you talking about?"

Do you really think playing dumb will get you out of this?

"We just need confirmation, man. The article's already written and ready to go."

"You can't do that!" I bolt from the bed and start pacing until pain shoots through my foot and I remember my stupid ankle.

"Why not?" Kevin asks.

"You can't out someone. Harry won't go for it. We're not that type of magazine. Do not print that article."

"He practically outed himself with the shit he pulled last night."

I knew sitting with me in the press box was a dumb idea.

My legs give way, and I land my ass on the end of the bed.

Ollie's going to hate me. Six years he's played professional hockey. He hid a relationship for four of those, and one night after we get together, his news is all over the damn internet.

"Besides," Kevin says, "Harry's already signed off on it."

"Well, he's not going to get it from me."

"What the fuck, Lennon? Is this some sort of us against you people thing?"

You people? I want to scream, but I don't have a voice.

"Just confirm yes or no."

"No," I rasp.

"No as in it's not true, or no as in you won't confirm?"

"If Harry runs that story, he can expect my resignation in his inbox within the hour of him publishing it. That's all I have to say." I hit the end call button and resist the urge to throw my phone across the room.

I bite back a sob. Not for me—I can worry about what this means for my job later—but for Ollie. This is the one thing he didn't want—to be thrown out of the closet the same way Matt was. He wanted to do it on his own terms, but I somehow came along and screwed that up without even trying.

I stay perched on the end of the bed, but I can't bring myself to look at my phone anymore.

This is it. This is all I'm going to get from Ollie. A couple of nights of smoking hot sex, a connection I've never felt before, and what I'm sure is going to result in a broken heart when he tells me he never wants to see my face again.

The shower turns off, and I can't catch my breath. The second Ollie steps out of the bathroom with nothing but a towel around his waist, his smile drops. There's no mistaking the guilt written all over me. I think it's coming out of my pores.

All I can do as I contemplate Ollie hating me is beg. "I'm sorry. I'm so fucking sorry."

CHAPTER TWENTY-THREE

OLLIE

My first thought is something has happened to Lennon's parents or his family or something, but he's apologizing to me. Why would he need to do that if—

"What happened?" I ask, more frantic than I intend. My mind jumps to the worst conclusions, all of which involve him and his stupid magazine.

"There was a photo," he whispers. He can't even look at me.

"Photo?" I croak.

Images of Matt Jackson getting a blowjob flood my mind before I shake them away. I haven't done anything in public.

"What kind of photo?" I say cautiously.

"Of you and me."

"No, I was careful. I'm always careful."

Ask Ash. He was constantly bitching at the lack of PDA.

The treehouse springs to mind, but paparazzi wouldn't have been able to see in, and that's if they even knew where my parents lived and if they had a reason to follow me. Which they don't.

Lennon still refuses to give me eye contact. "The game. The press box."

"All we did was talk."

"People are already speculating, and the photo … I look half in love with you, for fuck's sake."

"Only half?" I mock.

There has to be some mistake. They can't come to the gay conclusion just because I sat next to Lennon during the game.

Lennon thrusts his phone in my direction, and it's open to an article about me supposedly switching teams. And he has a point. The way he's looking at me … hell, it makes me fall for him even more.

I'm not sure I'm ready for what that means though, and the way my heart beats erratically in my chest, I know I can't deal with this right now.

That doesn't stop me from reading the article.

I huff. "Babe, did you actually read this article?"

He lifts his head. "No, but—"

"One of the guys near us in the press box must've seen us being close or whatever and figured I was asking questions about being a journalist. It speculates I'm leaving hockey for journalism." I give his phone back to him to let him read. "Apparently, I only set off gaydars of the queer variety."

Damon and Maddox already knew, and Jet figured it out, but whoever wrote that article is oblivious.

Just when I think I can relax, Lennon shakes his head.

"I got a phone call from my coworker. They're running a story. They said you were gay and wanted me to confirm."

All the air leaves my lungs. *His* magazine is running the story?

"Can't you stop it?" I yell and then hate myself when Lennon winces. "I'm sorry. I'm not yelling at *you*. I'm freaking out."

"Yell at me," he whispers. "Yell at me because I deserve it. You've been risking more than you used to, and I don't want—"

"That was *my* choice. This is neither of our faults, and right now, we need to focus on the more important thing of either beating this story to the press or getting your editor to squash it."

Lennon stares at me with an expression I can't read. Surprise, maybe? Shock? All I know is he doesn't start moving.

"Do you want to call your editor or should I?"

Finally, he snaps out of whatever's holding him back and he starts tapping away on his phone. His finger hesitates over the number.

"Damon," he says. "We should call Damon first and see what he knows. I don't want to give away anything to my editor if we don't have to. If we call and tell him to squash it, he'll ask why we need to."

"Yeah. Do that. Call Damon and put him on speaker."

It rings a few times before Damon picks up. "Where's Ollie?"

No *hi,* no *how are you*, just *where's Ollie*. That can't be good.

"Uh, I'm right here," I say. "You're on speaker."

"You two have got to be more careful. That photo of you guys—"

"It's so hot," a voice calls out from the background. I think it's Maddox. "It's like foreplay porn."

"Ignore him," Damon says, "but he has a point. Unless you want this to come out—"

"Well, that's just it," Lennon says. "It has. Or … it will. I got a call from a guy I work with. He's running a story about it, but they want confirmation from me. Which I didn't give. Obviously."

Damon hesitates, and I can practically hear his gears turning from here.

"Where did the story come from? If this photo is the only source, there's no way they can print that without opening themselves up to a lawsuit, because it's nothing. You're smiling at each other. Yeah, we know it's more, but that's only because *we know*."

"Wait, so there's been no talk in the media this morning about this?" Lennon asks.

I don't let the hope trying to claw at me take hold, because no news means they haven't beaten us to the punch yet.

"I have Google alerts for all my clients, and this was the only thing this morning."

"I want to beat them," I say.

"Like, beat them up?" Damon asks. "I know that's a hockey player's MO, but I don't think it'll work off the ice."

Lennon smiles, but it quickly falls when I glance at him. He also looks away as if I've scolded him. I want to reassure him, but at the same time, I can't even focus on us right now. I need to get my head in the zone. I need to salvage my career.

My worst fear for the past six years is happening, so I need to focus on that first and foremost.

"No," I say. "I mean I want to come out before they can out me. It's been the one thing I've wanted—control over how my news comes out. They can't force me out like they did to Matt."

"Okay," Damon says, slipping into full-on business mode. "First thing we need to do is get you back to New York. We need to track down your PR department and the GM, and then we'll need the head coach for the press conference. If we do this right, we can have it over and done with by tonight."

"I have Ava's phone number—the PR rep," Lennon says.

When I cock my head at him, he shrugs.

"We've kind of become friends."

"Give me the number." Damon's voice is authoritative, and this is exactly why I knew to hire him the moment I met him. "Then get a flight to New York, and I'll call you."

"Are you still in Boston?" I ask.

"Nah, Maddy and I drove back last night after the game. Stay off all social media just in case, try not to draw attention, and I hate to say it, but maybe you guys should go separately to the airport. I dunno if you're coming out and announcing your relationship, but you don't want to add fuel to the fire before you can tell everyone yourselves."

Way to put the pressure on something that's too new to define for real. Yesterday, I may've called him my boyfriend, but as Lennon was quick to point out, it's too early for that. I also don't know how telling everyone we're dating will affect Lennon's career. In all this time, I've never even asked if he was allowed to get involved with an athlete he reports on.

"Think about it," Damon says when I don't say anything. "And if there is any paparazzi, always say *no comment*. It's going to be okay."

I don't know if I believe him, but I want to. Matt won the Super Bowl the same year he came out. Surely, this won't hurt my career too much. Maybe.

"What about my editor?" Lennon asks. "He'll probably call again."

"Don't answer," Damon says. "Only answer my calls, and we'll speak soon."

Silence descends as Damon ends the call, and now I'm the one avoiding eye contact with Lennon.

I need to wrap my head around the prospect of this actually happening. Years of trying to avoid this moment all comes down to a single photo and a rumor.

That's kinda fucked up.

X

As per Damon's instructions, Lennon and I leave the hotel separately and head for the airport in different cars.

I go home first to return my parents' car and to get my charger and grab my shit to go back to my place in New York.

Ma and Dad look worried as they drop me curbside for the flight.

"I need to go to New York to talk to my agent, guys. It's not a big deal."

Yeah, I'm back to lying to my parents. If this comes down to press conferences and a media circus, I'll give them a heads-up, but I don't want to worry them for no reason or get Ma excited about the possibility either. If there's a way out of this, I'm sure as hell going to take it, because this isn't the way I wanted it to happen. Not by a long shot.

"I'll be home in a few days. I might catch the game while I'm there, and hang out with Len—uh, Clark."

Lennon thinks it's hilarious my family won't drop the name, but I find it hard to remember. He was only Clark to me that very first night I met him. In the six months following, he was the random guy who gave me hope, and now ... now he's the guy I want to have a future with if this doesn't all blow up in our faces.

I'm about to invite the whole world into my life, and I don't know two things: one, whether Lennon would be up for that, and two, if he even wants to continue this in the first place. We both travel for work, and unless he gets assigned to my team every year, our schedules are gonna clash. All I know is I want to try, and once this mess is over, whether I come out or not, I'm gonna make damn sure he knows how much I want to try. I think there will be a lot of naked time in the convincing process, and if that's what it takes, then I guess I'll have to be okay with that. It'll be such a hardship.

I manage to get on the same flight as Lennon, but it fucking kills me to walk past him at the gate and pretend I don't know him. It hurts even more when I glance back and see this complete and utter look of remorse on his face.

I sit across from him, a few seats down from where he is, and take out my phone. Shit. Still dead. When I move to a seat in the corner beside a wall with a power outlet, I feel Lennon's burning gaze follow me.

The phone takes forever to power up, and my leg bounces while I wait.

Me: *I WISH I COULD SIT WITH YOU RIGHT NOW. I WANT TO HOLD YOUR HAND.*

Lennon*: IS THAT ANOTHER BEATLES JOKE?*

Me: *NO, I JUST REALLY WANT TO TOUCH YOU. AFTER THESE LAST FEW DAYS, I CAN'T IMAGINE NOT TOUCHING YOU AGAIN.*

There's a pause where he stares down at his phone before he starts typing. With how fast his fingers move and how long it takes, I'm expecting more than the two words that come through.

Lennon: *ME TOO.*

I don't know what to think of that. Especially when he refuses to look up at me.

Me: *YOU LOOK LIKE YOUR CAT DIED. MOST GUYS WOULD LOVE THEIR ... BOYFRIEND TYPE PERSON TO COME OUT FOR THEM.*

I watch for Lennon's response as he reads my message, but when his eyes meet mine, he scowls.

Me: *TOO SOON TO JOKE ABOUT IT?*

Lennon: *IT WILL ALWAYS BE TOO SOON. I MAY HAVE FUCKED YOUR CAREER.*

Me: *MY CAREER WILL BE FINE.*

Lennon: *I MAY HAVE FUCKED MY CAREER TOO.*

Me: *ARE THERE RULES AGAINST US BEING TOGETHER?*

Lennon: *NO. AT LEAST, I DON'T THINK SO. I DON'T KNOW HOW IT'LL WORK FOR A MALE REPORTER IN A SAME-SEX RELATIONSHIP*

WITH AN ATHLETE, BECAUSE IT'S NEVER HAPPENED BEFORE, BUT FOR WOMEN, THEY'VE BEEN DISCREDITED IN THEIR "BIASED" ARTICLES AND HARDLY GET ANY WORK.

Fuck. We've been so focused on my career we didn't discuss his. I've been selfish in the past about my obsession with hockey, but I've never felt as bad about that as I do right now.

Lennon doesn't make eye contact again, and I know this because I don't take my eyes off him until the flight is called.

Being in first class, I board early, and then I sit and watch every person get on the plane, because I need Lennon to acknowledge me as he walks by. A smile … something.

When he appears, something warms my gut, and a sense of desperation takes root, but all that's squashed when he walks by without even looking at me.

All I want to fucking do is talk to him, Damon and the media be damned.

I get the sinking feeling this is more than Lennon feeling guilty over possibly, maybe, ruining my career.

If my private life is going to be splashed all over the media, I want to at least have something to look forward to. But maybe he doesn't want that life. He said his family are private people and want him to hide who he is. Maybe some of that has rubbed off on him. If it were up to me, I wouldn't want the media breathing down my neck either, but that's the career I chose. Lennon didn't choose to be on this side of it.

The entire flight to New York, I keep overthinking everything. From what the media knows to what Lennon's thinking and everything in between.

And when we land at JFK and find Damon waiting for us, I know for certain all my overanalyzing was for nothing because whatever's going to happen has already begun.

Damon greets us with a grim smile. "Ava's getting a hold of the GM and coach, and we're meeting them all at the arena."

Yup. There's no stopping this.

I will not vomit. I will not vomit … Okay, I'm probably gonna vomit.

CHAPTER TWENTY-FOUR

LENNON

I've been trying to remain calm this whole time, but I'm about to freak the fuck out.

This is too much. Too much pressure, too fast, too … everything.

Ollie needs to not take me into account. If he makes his statement today and then we don't work out, how much resentment will he hold toward me?

Ollie didn't take this step with Ash for a reason, and after a few months of back and forth between us, and two days after we hook up, he's being forced to face the media.

Two days.

It's like the universe really does want to cockblock us, because this can't end well. He comes out, he'll resent me for putting him in this position. He stays closeted, we'll be constantly paranoid about being found out.

My head is screaming at me to leave. Get out now before I make the same pathetic mistakes adolescent Lennon made, but I'm too far gone for him to let go.

When we arrive at the arena and head through the back corridors to the pressroom, Damon heads inside, but Ollie pulls me back.

"Are we cool?" he asks.

We haven't spoken since before we left Boston, because I basically don't know what to say to him. Everything is on the line. For both him and me, but right now I'm only focused on what it could mean for Ollie.

I finally find my voice. "Don't do this for me."

"What?"

"If you get a chance to squash the rumors in there, take it."

Ollie lets out a loud breath. "I'm so fucking confused. I had one guy who pushed me to do this, and now another who doesn't want me to do it."

"I want you to do it for *you*."

"A bit late for that now, isn't it?" The bite in Ollie's voice makes me step back.

"I can't handle being the one who got you outed when you've been able to keep it a secret for six fucking years. I don't want to be responsible for ruining your future."

Ollie looks confused. "That's your issue? This is in no way your fault."

"You say that now, but—"

His arms go to my shoulders, and he steps closer. "I will never see it that way."

It's hard to believe that when he's caught up in this moment where he has no choice in the matter.

"This isn't the way I wanted this to happen, but now that it is, we can only look forward, and when I see my future, I see you."

My breath catches in my throat. "How? We both live out of suitcases, our schedules are nuts, we don't have anything in common except for our love of sports even though hockey still leaves something to be desired—"

Ollie kisses me and kisses me hard. My back pushes against the brick wall of the cold corridor, and when his tongue pushes into my mouth, I moan.

When he finally lets me up for air, he whispers against my lips, "That's how."

I stare up into his eyes, unable to find the ability to fight his flawed logic.

His giant hands cup my face. "We'll take this one step at a time. I know there's shit we both have to work out in terms of our careers, but you're the only person who's ever understood me, and it's not you who's pushing me over this line. It's the media. I want this. Us."

I want to accept what he's saying so badly that I hold onto the tiny wisp of hope he's giving me and kiss him again.

"Oh, thank God." The voice comes from the entry to the pressroom, and as Ollie steps back, the coach appears in my line of vision. "I was sure it was gonna be a drug or prostitute problem. Maybe a DUI."

Ollie huffs a tiny laugh. "No, sir, just your run-of-the-mill homosexuality."

The coach waves him off. "The league's been preparing for this day, because you're certainly not the first."

"Just the first foolish enough to get caught?" Ollie's light tone doesn't match the sad look on his face.

"There's nothing to worry about," his coach reassures him.

Ollie takes a deep breath and holds my hand. I don't stop him.

Inside the pressroom, there's no media yet, but all the key players are here. The GM, the coach, Damon, and Ava.

She's on the phone in the back of the room, pacing behind the chairs set up for people in the press.

The GM leans against the long table at the front where the players and coaches sit during conferences. "We thought we'd sit down first and talk about what you want to happen here and how we go about it."

Ollie's hand tightens on mine. "I really don't know. I'm a little out of my element."

"Ideally, we would've told the rest of the players first," the coach says. "But they're scattered all over the country now."

"Ideally, I could've come out after we won the Cup, but that didn't happen either," Ollie says.

"Next year," the coach says with resolve.

"None of this is ideal," Damon says. "But what do you want to get out of it? Are you telling them your whole life story about knowing you were gay when you were five years old and painting a picture of a lifetime of secrecy, or are we going the whole 'it's not a big deal' route? Are you announcing to the world you're gay or introducing them to your partner?" He gestures to me.

"I'm not part of this," I say before Ollie can respond. "I can't be. This has to be Ollie's thing."

Damon nods in understanding, but he seems to be the only one. Makes me feel like a dick, but there's no time to explain myself. This is about Ollie.

Ava approaches, now off the phone, her lips pursed together. "Can I ask where you got your sources from about Ollie being outed?"

"My coworker at *Sporting Health,*" I say.

"Did he mention Ollie's name?" Ava asks, her tone cautious.

I try to recall. "I answered the phone, and his first words were 'Ollie's gay, isn't he?'"

Ava glances down at her phone and then back at me. "Are you sure about that?"

"What's going on?" Damon asks.

"I've been calling around some other friends in PR. Rumor

mill is circling around New Jersey and what happened during the game last night between Sorensen and Healy."

"So, there's a chance this isn't happening?" Ollie asks, his face alight with hope.

I shake my head. "I don't get it ... he said the article is ready to go."

"But not Ollie's name specifically?" Ava asks.

"I ..." I feel all eyes on me. "I ... I don't know. I saw the article about us, and then got the call asking if Ollie—" I remember now. "Kevin never said Ollie. He said *he*. *He's* gay. Who else could he have been talking about?"

"Well," Ava says, "as of this morning, Kip Healy is on suspension, and Caleb Sorensen isn't. There's talk of a press conference happening in New Jersey, and the unconfirmed rumor is they got into a fight over Sorensen's sexual orientation. Is it possible your coworker got a scoop on *that* story?"

My mouth opens and closes like a fish. Fuck, not only did we screw up in public, but now I've made him come out to his complete management team?

"Call your editor," Damon demands. "Now."

It takes a few seconds for me to make a move, but when I finally do, my hands shake. My fingers tremble as I pull up my contacts and hit dial.

"It's about time you called me back," Harry growls into the phone.

Like Damon asked, I've been avoiding my phone calls.

"Did Kevin tell you I'm not confirming anything?" I ask.

"Why the hell not? It's your job to report, so be a damn reporter."

"It's not my job to out athletes, and I won't help you do it."

Four pairs of eyes burn into me, but I don't know how to ask who he's talking about without giving Ollie away.

"I thought we were better than that," I say.

"If we don't report on this, someone else will, and they'll get the online hits and revenue."

Harry's always been interested in numbers and hits and generating money for the magazine, but he's never, not once, asked me to write an article or publish an article that could be considered tabloid-y.

"How did Kevin find out anyway?" I ask.

"Are you admitting you already knew and never said anything?"

"I already told you I'm not going to be a part of this."

Come on, come on, come on, give me a name.

"Sorensen outed himself when Healy called him on his shit and the gloves came off."

A relieved breath leaves me in a whoosh. "Gotta go. Bye." I can't end the call fast enough, but when I'm met with the expectant stares from everyone in the room, I feel about two feet tall. "Uh ... so, it's not Ollie."

All the shoulders in the room sag and relax.

"Thank fuck," Ollie says under his breath, but then he lifts his head. "Who is it?"

"It is Sorensen. What Ava said seems to be the story. Healy somehow found out Sorensen is gay and taunted him or whatever. Maybe provoked him on the ice."

"Would explain why Healy's the one to be suspended when Sorensen threw the first punch," Ava says.

Damon reaches for Ollie, who's staring at the floor. "You okay, man? This is over. Done. You don't have to do this anymore."

Ollie looks like he's going to vomit though. "Yeah. I do."

He still wants to come out?

"Why?" I ask. "You said you weren't ready, and this is your out." I told him to take the out.

Suddenly the pressure is back, sitting on my chest and dragging me down.

He shakes his head. "I don't think I am ready, but after today, with this close call … I know I need to take control if I want this to come out the way I want it to. And I know if it was me being the one forced out today, I would kill for someone to stand behind me and say 'me too.' I can't let Soren do it on his own. It's lonely enough as it is in this industry."

The admiration I have for Ollie grows, and I have to do everything in my power to remain standing a few feet away from him instead of what I really want to do, which is go to him and wrap myself around him.

Damon claps Ollie on his shoulder. "Then let's do this."

"I'll call Jen, the PR rep for New Jersey, and set something up." Ava holds up her phone and walks over to her pacing spot at the back again.

"You're sure?" the GM asks Ollie.

Even though Ollie's still pale, he nods.

"Then we'll do everything we can on our end to make sure this is as smooth and painless as possible for you."

So hard not to blurt out "Just like losing your virginity," but now's not the time for jokes.

CHAPTER TWENTY-FIVE

OLLIE

When Ava gets off the phone, she tells us the press is already arriving at the arena in Newark, so we don't have much time to get there. The New Jersey management team is gonna stall for us as much as they can, because they agree this will be better for the league if we do this together.

"Are you sure you want to do this?" Ava asks one last time.

I really do.

At the same time, I really don't.

I'm not ready, but I know if I don't do this now, I probably never will. I'll hide behind hockey forever until I can retire, and that's no way to live. Not when I've found someone who takes me out of the game long enough to realize there's a whole other world out there that doesn't involve my skates and hockey stick.

"I *need* to do this."

They're the magic words to get everyone moving. Ava and Coach go ahead of us while the GM heads up to his office, prepared for incoming calls.

There isn't enough time in the organization of it all to freak out until we start heading down the cold corridor again on the way out.

"Come with me to the press conference?" I whisper to Lennon.

"Where else would I be going?"

"I dunno. You've been weird all day and keep trying to run away from me, telling me to take the out, so yeah, I wanted to double-check."

Lennon stops before we reach the exit to the stadium. "I haven't been trying to run away …"

"Maybe not *fast*," I mumble.

He smiles. "I'm proud of you, and if you need to do this, then, of course, I'm going to support you, but my position hasn't changed. You can't come out for me or for a possibility of us, because if you do, there won't be an us in the long run. Coming out to support a fellow athlete is a completely different thing, and I admire you for showing solidarity to someone you don't even know all that well."

"I know him. I know him better than I know anyone else, because he's me."

Lennon steps forward and presses against me, his arms wrapping around my back. "It's going to be okay. I promise. Let's deal with today, and then we can see where we're at tomorrow."

I kiss the top of his head. "Tomorrow."

Somehow, somewhere along the line, I've started falling for Lennon. Hard. The thought of him walking away from me to save my career makes me want to say "fuck hockey." I realize that's all Ash ever wanted from me, but I couldn't bring myself to give it to him. Here I am offering it to Lennon on a silver platter, and he's telling me not to.

And I think that's the reason I want to do it. Because he's right. I need to do this for my own reasons.

I want a chance at everything with Lennon even though it still feels out of reach.

At least this next step will bring us that tiny bit closer.

With a small, chaste kiss from him and a loud complaint from me about it being too short, we head to the car, and I try to put Lennon and me at the back of my mind and focus.

Easier said than done. My thoughts drift to what I have to do, what Soren's going through, and I speculate what Kip Healy did to warrant getting punched. I begin to worry about the fallout from all this. Not just from the press but teammates, fans, ticket holders, and everyone else and their dog.

It's been a constant fear for years, and now I'm going to face it head-on. That's what you're supposed to do with your fears, right? I don't know why. If someone is deathly afraid of the zombie apocalypse, I'm not gonna dress up in bloody makeup and try to scare the shit out of them to prove a point. That's a good way to get stabbed in the fucking head.

Are you really comparing coming out of the closet to being stabbed in the head?

I tell my conscience to fuck off even if it has a point. If I make this a dramatic thing, the rest of the world will too. This isn't a big deal, and when everyone can accept that, then it takes away the fear.

"Do you know what you want to say on camera?" Damon asks. "I've been making notes in my phone all day if you want me to draft a proper speech or something, but it's up to you. As long as you don't say anything stupid."

"No pressure."

Someone's waiting for us outside the staff entrance when we pull up to the rink. We're ushered inside quickly to try to avoid being seen by any possible lurkers from the media.

The press conference has already started when we sneak in the back way. Only a few reporters turn our way, and as soon as they see me, they furiously start typing on their phones, tablets, or laptops, and some are even old school with notepads and pens. Lennon gasps when he spots one of the reporters.

"Who's that?" I whisper.

"Kevin. I guess my editor sent him when I refused to dig any deeper into the story."

Kevin turns back to the front when the GM of the New Jersey Bobcats starts talking. That's when I follow his gaze and see that Soren looks like he's about to shit a brick.

"As of this moment, Kip Healy is on suspension for the rest of the season, and his contract is pending against a behavioral review. One thing this league takes pride in is our You Can Play motto. All players should be able to go out on that ice with trust in their teammates. That trust is broken when certain players believe they have a right to discriminate against others."

Their coach goes on to drone about inclusivity, and I'm sure their words reflect whatever Ava and the Dragons' management team scrounged together for almost the exact same press conference they were planning.

The more they talk, the more Soren pales and looks visibly ill. They're kinda dragging it out, but maybe that's the point. By the time it's Soren's time to talk, the press won't be shocked at what's coming. In fact, I'd be surprised if it wasn't already all over Twitter even though nothing's been confirmed yet.

I find myself staring at Soren objectively. His honey-colored eyes shine, only emphasized by his scruff on his cheeks and dark hair. He's a veteran player—only has a few years left in his career, max. It makes me wonder why or how this thirty-ish-year-old decided to come out. Or maybe it was an accident like how Tommy found out about me, only Kip Healy didn't react as well as Tommy did.

His eyes catch mine, and confusion crosses his face before he breaks his gaze.

When it's his turn to talk, he opens his mouth, but only a rasp comes out. He clears his throat and tries again.

"There's one thing I've been terrified of my entire life, and it's not sitting up here and telling the world I'm gay. My greatest fear is having a life full of regrets. This industry isn't easy for someone who identifies as anything other than straight. The reason I've kept quiet about my orientation for so long is not because I haven't been ready but because I've feared the sport wasn't ready. But I owe it to myself and anyone else out there struggling with their identity to be honest."

A lump forms in my throat, because it seems like such a waste. I've been playing for the NHL for over three years, Soren's been here for ten, but neither of us had anyone … Well, that's not true, I had Tommy, but it's not the same thing.

Maybe Ma was right all along, and this is what the league needs for people to start coming forward. Solidarity. Kinship.

Questions are thrown at Soren, each one more invasive than the next and without time in between for him to actually answer.

"How long have you known you were gay?"

"When was your last relationship?"

"Why did you wait so long to come out?"

His GM answers. "Caleb won't be answering any more questions."

My brain and feet decide it's a perfect time for me to make my move toward the long table of microphones.

As soon as Soren's coach sees me approaching, he moves, vacating his seat next to Soren for me. I guess he was given a heads-up about my arrival. Soren still looks confused as to why I'm here.

"I might be able to help with the answers to those questions." I turn to Soren. "At least, for me."

His eyes widen, and I reach over to squeeze his shoulder briefly before facing the media, where cameras are going off in our faces. Ten bucks says the front page of the sporting section tomorrow will be that photo. Me reassuring Soren for a total of three point two seconds. No doubt the article will speculate when we'll get married.

"Sorry to gatecrash the press conference," I start, "but I couldn't sit by and watch this happen while living the exact same story as Soren. I've known I was gay since I was fifteen years old. My last relationship was with my childhood sweetheart, but it ended because I never had it in me to take this step. That's not his fault, and I do regret the way things ended. But the reasons I waited so long to come out pretty much reflect the same reasons Soren had. In a lot of ways, the NHL appears ready for this, but in a lot of other ways, it doesn't. My biggest fear was coming out and having no support and feeling alone in all this. When I found out what Soren was doing here today, I didn't want to let him experience my fear."

"So, did you know about each other before today?" someone asks.

"No. Honestly, when I heard an NHL player was about to come out, my first thought was someone found out about me and was going to run my story. I don't care how the rest of the world sees it, but we're entitled to come out how and when we want. No one should take that from another person."

I feel Soren staring at me.

"You don't think the public has a right to know?" another reporter asks, but I don't see where the question comes from.

My heart kicks up a notch, and anger tries to take hold. What the fuck kind of question is that? No! No one has a right to know what I do in my bedroom. I go to open my mouth to say that, and out of the corner of my eye, I see Damon shaking his head and mouthing *no, no, no, no, no.*

Before I say something I really want to but shouldn't, Soren's GM beats me to it.

"What happens in any player's private life is just that— private. If it doesn't affect their game, it's no one's business but their own. Just because they're public figures, that doesn't mean anyone has a right to pry into their lives off the ice."

"They signed on for that life, though," the same reporters says. I see him this time and realize it's the fucker Lennon works with.

"Actually, I signed on to play hockey," Soren says. "And if you ask every single player on all thirty-one teams, I guarantee not one signed on saying 'I can't wait until my privacy is compromised.' We're all here for the love of the same sport."

"It's the same as celebrities," Kevin says. "It's a known condition of fame. Fans want to know everything."

The PR rep for New Jersey steps in. "If no one else has any relevant questions, we'll gladly call this press conference to a close. Thank you all for your time."

Soren and I are quickly ushered away and led into the back corridors of the New Jersey arena. The GM and coach each give us pats on the back and tell us they're going to go field phone calls. When they leave, I'm left alone with Soren. I go to ask him if we could bring my people back here as well, but he beats me to speaking.

"You're an idiot." There's no real malice behind his words, only pure defeat.

"Uh, why?" I ask.

"You didn't have to do that."

"I know, but if it were the other way around, I wouldn't have called you an idiot for it."

He sighs. "You're not an idiot, but I hope your team accepts it better than mine have."

I cock my head. "Your GM and coach seem to be handling it well."

"Healy," he says through gritted teeth.

"Oh."

"I feel like the idiot. I heard this song—one stupid fucking song at some stupid charity benefit my sister made me be her date to—and it made me think I could have everything. I realized I don't want to retire in a few years without having played as myself. A Stanley Cup win doesn't count unless you win it as yourself, right? It's not the same."

"I've never thought about it like that. I've always hoped that coming out after I win one would prove I really belong here."

Soren scrubs a hand over his tired face. "Yeah, that was another theory I was hiding behind too. Anyway, I came out to the team first, and most of the guys were great about it—or at least quiet. I don't know what Healy's problem is other than he's a twatwaffle."

"What did he say to make you snap?"

"The usual. But he'd been doing it all fucking night even before we hit the ice. All under his breath, of course. Even when we got reamed by coach about the fight, he tried to deny it. Said I was looking for attention after my announcement."

"Ugh. What a dick."

"At least he won't be a problem next year."

"How so?"

"He hasn't been suspended like they said; he's been released from his contract. He still gets all his money he doesn't deserve, but he's no longer gonna be playing. At least, not for us."

It's too early to determine how the fallout of all this will go, but the league taking appropriate steps with the Healy situation might mean it won't be as bad as when Matt came out in the NFL.

"That's promising at least," I say.

"Yeah, it's a start. We'll see how the rest of the league handles it."

"My coach said they've been waiting for this to happen, so maybe the transition will be smooth."

The awkward silence that follows shows how much neither of us truly believe it even though we want to.

"So, what's your deal?" Soren asks. "Closet full of exes back home who all left because of the whole hiding thing?"

I get the feeling Soren's and my stories are similar.

"Uh, just one of those. You?"

"Only one that mattered," he mutters.

The door behind us opens, and Lennon's the first person I see as he, Damon, and Ava step through.

I must make a face or smile or something because Soren says, "I guess that answers my question about current relationship status."

Here's hoping anyway.

CHAPTER TWENTY-SIX

"You two might want to stay out of the public eye for a while," Damon says to Ollie and Soren. "Lay low for a few days, and maybe don't go back to your apartments."

Soren nods. "I can get a hotel room or something."

"Not under your own name," Damon says. "If you get stuck, you can come to Brooklyn and stay with me and my boyfriend."

Surprise etches itself onto Soren's face. "Are you taking on new clients? I've been trying to get a hold of my agent all day, and he's not answering the damn phone, and here you are running your client around and offering your house to someone who isn't even one of your players?"

Soren doesn't know it, but that's just the type of guy Damon is. Last year, I interviewed him, and it was easy to tell the world how great he is and how he's an agent for all the right reasons, not for the ten percent of multimillion-dollar contracts. *Sporting Health* didn't publish it because it wasn't strictly sports related, but I was able to shop it around to other publications, and it was picked up by *Sports Illustrated*. It put Damon King on the map and was my first massive publication.

Damon breaks into a half grin. "Come stay with me, and we'll talk." He turns to us. "Ollie, you got a place to stay?"

"He can stay with me at Noah and Matt's," I say.

They're back from Fiji now, but I'm sure they won't mind Ollie crashing for a night or two until shit settles down.

Damon purses his lips. "As long as I don't have to explain to the press tomorrow about Matt Jackson shacking up with his boyfriend and the newly outed hockey player—because we all know that's how they'd spin *that*—I'm cool with it."

"I think everyone's under the impression Matt and Noah are still on vacation, and no journalists came around the house while I've been staying there," I say.

Ollie leans in. "You say that as if you're not one."

"After this, I don't know how long I will be one." And that scares me more than anything else that's happened today.

My threat to quit if Harry ran a story outing someone against their will was real, but now we'll never know because we beat them to it. Having said that, I don't know if I want to work for someone who even contemplated it.

But what other options do I have? Everyone knows print media is dying. Jobs are rare, and wages are low. I need to play this smart and bite my tongue until I can figure out what to do.

"Whoa," Soren says, "you're dating a journalist? You're brave."

"Nah, I'm just super irresistible. Clearly." I gesture to my nerdy self.

"He's being self-deprecating, but he doesn't realize how true that is." Ollie's lips land on my cheek, and even though I put up a front by rolling my eyes, I'm giddy on the inside, and that mushy feeling I woke up with this morning is back.

Damon offers us a lift back to the city, seeing as he has to go that way anyway, so the four of us climb into his car.

It doesn't take even five minutes for Ollie's hand to start wandering over my thigh, and I have to stop him from practically groping my dick numerous times.

Damon and Soren talk in the front, seemingly oblivious, but still. I give Ollie my best scowl, which only makes him smile. Of course. His new favorite thing is torturing me, it seems.

"Should've caught a cab," Ollie mutters.

"I wouldn't have let you touch me in a cab, either, Mr. Grabby Hands."

"But I'm totally allowed to now. Whenever and wherever I want."

"Uh … not to eavesdrop or anything," Damon says from the front, "but that's not a good idea. Especially in public."

"Wait, I'm out now, and I still can't touch my boyfriend in public?" Ollie asks.

My heart skips a beat at the boyfriend label again. I have no idea how we're going to make this work, but fuck, I want to.

With my job in limbo right now, I don't know what that'll mean.

"Let things die down a bit first," Damon says, and I frown.

I understand it, but I feel sorry for Ollie. He finally gets his chance to be out and he's told to still hide it.

Ollie's hand grasps mine. "What are you thinkin' so hard about over there?"

"Nothing to worry your pretty little head about."

"There you go calling me *pretty* again," he grumbles.

"You are kinda pretty." Soren turns to us from the passenger seat with a charming smile showing off the dark scruff on his face.

Ollie chuckles at me. "I think you're growling. Are you trying to growl? Fuck, that's adorable."

"I'm not growling," I argue. "I'm not that dumb. Soren could snap me in half."

"I'm not after your man," Soren says. "I'm after my own."

"Any guy in particular or any random one?" I ask.

He barks out a laugh. "An ex. Broke up because I wasn't out. That's fixed now, so I guess I'll make myself grovel to get him back."

Damon pulls up to Noah's house and double-parks to let us out. "I'll call if there's any developments you should be aware of, but I doubt anything unexpected will pop up."

We're no sooner out of the car before Ollie's dragging me to the steps leading to Noah's front door.

Climbing stairs without paying attention to where my feet are going is harder than I'd thought it would be, but I don't care when I have Ollie's mouth on me. His hands are all over me, and his lips trail down the back of my neck.

We make it to the landing, and I go to push open the door, but it's locked.

"Awesome," I say.

"Why's it being locked awesome?"

"Because they only ever lock it when they're out."

"And how are we getting in?" he asks nervously, as if I'm about to ask him to break into Noah's six-million-dollar mansion.

"I have my key, and I have plans for you."

That perks him up. "Plans? What plans?"

I fumble with my keyring and open the door. "Why don't we go shower, and then you'll find out?"

Ollie dips his head, his breath ghosting along my skin as we stumble inside. "Can't I find out now?"

I shut the door with my foot and pull Ollie toward the stairs. "No. We both have plane on us, and I want you clean for what I want to do."

Ollie's eyes light up. "Are you going to fuck me?"

I was worried he might ask that, but I'm hoping what I have in store will make up for it. My lips land right by his ear as I whisper, "I want to fuck you with my tongue."

"Sweet Neil Patrick Harris in a harness," he mutters, and I laugh.

"Did you steal my line?"

He starts moving faster, and suddenly he's the one dragging me. "Like you said. Sometimes *fuck* just isn't enough."

I have to laugh at how fast he runs up the stairs. The sound of the shower hits my ears before I even reach the top step.

Ollie hasn't shut the guest bathroom door, and the sight of him getting undressed has my feet moving as urgently as his were.

But before I know it, we're both naked and under the spray of the hot shower. The water beats down on us, and Ollie pulls me in close.

I moan into his mouth as he kisses me while his hand trails down my back.

Pushing him off me, I turn him so he faces the wall. "This is about your ass. Not mine."

He says something under his breath I can't understand but braces himself on his forearms against the wall and sticks his ass out, ready for me.

My hands lather some body wash and massage it into Ollie's shoulders and neck. His head lolls to the side and he hums in contentment, but as I work my hands lower, going slowly over his shoulder blades and then down his sides, his calmness is replaced with whines of want and impatience.

A soapy finger trails down his spine, and he shivers.

"Pull your ass cheeks apart for me," I order.

Ollie obeys immediately and rests his forehead on the tiles in front of him.

My finger moves down lower and circles Ollie's hole. He grunts, and instead of giving him what he wants, I toy with it some more and refuse to put him out of his misery.

I pour more soap on my hands and work his front, including every inch of skin above his waist.

"Lennon," he whines.

"Mmmhmm …"

"God, I hate you. I hate you. I hate you."

I laugh. "Oh, sorry, is this what you want?"

Finally, I bring my hand back around and slowly press my middle finger inside him.

"Yessss." His whole body shudders, and he sticks his ass out even more.

"Impatient."

"Of course, I'm fucking impatient. You can't promise me a tongue fucking and then take your time. That's like …" He breathes heavy as my finger works him over, inching that little bit farther inside him before I pull it back and then slowly torture him again as I do it again.

"Like?" I ask.

"Like bad."

I love him like this. Incoherent and begging. I pull away, and he whimpers.

"Where are you going now?" he whines.

"We're going to bed. Because I'm gonna make this last way too long for me to get on my knees on the cold tiles."

"Fuck," he hisses and grips the base of his cock hard. "Or it's gonna be all over before you barely even do anything."

I chuckle. "Or that."

We both rush to make sure we're properly clean and quickly rinse off. Toweling off is even quicker, and I have him on his hands and knees on my bed faster than he could skate during a power play.

Our towels are discarded on the floor, and my cock wishes I was the one on my hands and knees.

No, this is about him.

As much as I want to take my time, Ollie's not into the whole *wait for it to build until you come so hard you go blind* thing that I love.

The first flicker of my tongue over his hole has him begging for more. I suck two fingers into my mouth, coating them in saliva. When I go back working him over with my tongue and loving every reaction I pull from him, I can barely contain my own arousal.

I add a finger and then two, working him over with both my tongue and my hand, and he turns into a blubbering mess.

His hands fist my comforter, he groans loud enough to wake the dead, and I've never been more thankful to be home alone.

My mouth moves lower to his sac and then his long cock hanging heavy between his legs while my fingers peg his prostate.

His ass clenches around my fingers, and his balls draw up tight. Right when I think he's gonna lose his mind and shoot all over my bed, he rasps, "Stop."

I freeze, my fingers still lodged inside him. "What's wrong?"

"I want … I want …" He breathes too heavy to get it out.

For a moment, I wonder if he's asking me to fuck him. I'd do it for him, but I'd probably last a whole one point six seconds inside his insanely tight ass. It's a snug fit for my fingers. My dick has no hope.

"Don't wanna come yet," he says, and I smile.

Guess he's not so against edging after all.

"Let me know when you're ready to go again," I murmur and place slow kisses up his back.

He nods. "I'm good now."

I don't change anything—just continue to mouth his hot skin along his spine.

"I said I'm good." His voice, so gravelly, makes my dick ache.

Instead of going back to massaging his prostate, I withdraw my fingers and go back to licking and teasing, using my hands to spread his cheeks apart so I can dive in.

Fuck, I wish I had more hands. I need to touch my cock. I need to touch his cock. There's a whole lot of neediness that I can't get to right now.

Ollie's hips start rocking back, trying to take my tongue deeper, and as much as I'd love to put the brakes on again and torture him some more, *I'm* the one getting to the point of no return.

A light breeze could have me coming in moments.

The way he writhes beneath me, his body begging for more, and knowing I'm the one doing it is probably one of the hottest things I've ever experienced.

My fingers go back to his ass and slip inside with ease. My free hand snakes around his front and starts stroking his cock.

I find myself involuntarily grinding against the back of his thigh.

My name on Ollie's lips as his cock swells in my hand has me wishing for my own release, and as soon as Ollie collapses on the bed completely spent, I use his cum as lube and take myself in my hand.

With Ollie's hot body underneath me, all sinewy muscles and tattoos … I get close with only a few strokes. But when Ollie turns his head and sees what I'm doing, he breathes a loud, "Fuck yeah, come on me."

Who knew that would be enough to send me over the edge? I convulse as ropes of cum hit his back and the top of his ass, and if

I thought Ollie was hot covered in his own cum, it's nothing compared to knowing it's mine marking his skin.

When I'm completely empty, I try to climb off, but Ollie rolls over and pulls me down on top of him. My limbs become weightless and my mind fuzzy as he wraps his arms around me.

Complete satisfaction doesn't begin to describe this moment.

CHAPTER TWENTY-SEVEN

"Water," Lennon croaks.

"I'll get it," I say but can't fucking move.

He rolls off my side and nudges me. "You're not moving."

"Can't."

Lennon's laugh gives me the energy to get out of bed, because after that, I'll get him anything he wants. He could ask me for a pet unicorn, and I'd go find one.

He leans up on his elbows as I grab a towel from the floor and wrap it around my waist.

"So, I'm guessing that was okay?" Lennon's tone is unsure.

I run my hand through my hair. "More than okay." I sense he wants to say something else, but he doesn't. "Is this about the whole topping thing? Because I don't care if you never want to top me. At all."

"Are you sure?"

I climb back on the bed, crawling my way to hover above him. "I think we've proved multiple times I don't need a dick in my ass to get off."

"And people say romance is dead."

I pinch Lennon's side, and he laughs.

"I'm gonna go get you some water now, but I don't want you to worry about this, okay? Even if you did like to top, I so wouldn't let you until I get bored of fucking you, and I don't see that happening any time soon."

A smile breaks out, and he nods.

After a chaste kiss on his lips, I head downstairs with a spring in my step.

And in perfect timing, the front door opens as I reach the foyer, and suddenly, I'm in one of those nightmares where I come face to face with one of my role models while completely naked. The only thing covering my dick is a towel that's dangerously hanging low and loose.

I'm pretty sure I'm still covered in cum too.

Great.

I've met Matt Jackson before. I've spoken to him on the phone, and I'm friends with his little brother. But that doesn't mean he doesn't intimidate me. He was the first out athlete to play an NFL game.

Noah smirks. "Aww, babe, did you get me a birthday present in the form of a naked hockey player? Because that's awesome."

Matt elbows his husband in the stomach and then glares at me. "Where's Jet?"

Uh-oh.

I stand frozen, unable to form words even if it is to defend myself about not being with Jet. "Umm … not here?"

Matt doesn't seem convinced, and his scowl deepens.

"I swear!"

"Why are y'all hanging out in the doorway?" Jet's voice comes from behind Matt and Noah, and then he pushes past them. Thank God. "Whoa."

"Uh, Lennon?" I call out. "Your roommates are here."

"And Ollie needs some pants," Jet yells.

"I don't think he does," Noah says. "I like my birthday present wrapped in a towel."

Footsteps thump down the stairs, and Lennon throws pants at me, and then he pushes Noah. "He's not your birthday present. I'm not that generous a friend."

Noah gets him in a headlock. "It's not like I'd fuck him. I'd just want him to walk around the house practically naked and fetch me things. Like beer."

"Ooh, I want in on that," Jet says.

Matt joins in. "Yeah, I'd be down for that."

"Umm …"

Lennon wrestles free of Noah. "They're fucking with you. You have your brothers. I have these people."

Noah puts his hand over his heart. "Aww, did you just call me your brother?" But then he screws up his face. "Makes how we met a little gross."

I cock my head. "How you met?"

Jet bounces on the balls of his feet. "You don't know that story? That needs to be rectified immediately."

"As fun as that sounds, I'm, uh"—I grip my towel tighter —"gonna go get dressed first."

I head for the stairs, but Noah's voice makes me pause.

"By the way, welcome to the club."

"Club?" I turn back.

"The everything's gay club. Meetings are weekly, and on Wednesdays, we wear pink."

I laugh and shake my head. "Sorry to disappoint, but I've been a card-carrying member since I was fifteen. And I look wicked hot in pink."

Noah turns to Lennon. "I like him, Beatle."

As I walk away, Lennon complains, "Don't call me Beatle."

Followed by Noah saying, "Okay, Ringo."

In Lennon's room, I use my towel to finish cleaning myself up before I throw my clothes back on. By the time I get downstairs again, the guys are in the living room watching *SportsCenter*, but Lennon isn't with them.

"Where's—"

Lennon appears around the corner from the dining room, and he pales as his phone shakes in his hand.

"What's wrong?" I ask. My mind conjures shit about what the media could've already printed about me.

"Guess I don't have to worry about resigning anymore."

So, not about me. "They fired you?"

Lennon nods.

"Because of us?" I ask.

He shakes his head. "They don't know we're together, but they're pissed I didn't tell them I knew about you. Or Soren. Because they're convinced I knew of that too. You know, with my gaydar superpowers." He huffs a humorless laugh.

"That's bullshit," I say.

He didn't want to out someone so they let him go even though he's one of their best reporters?

"Hey, guys," Matt says, staring at his phone. "Why is Ollie all over the news, being 'shipped with some other hockey player?"

"Huh?" I step forward to the back of the couch and look over his shoulder.

"Caleb Sorensen," Matt says.

Noah leans in and blocks my view of the phone. "Damn. Need me to beat him up for you, Lennon?"

Lennon's still looking at his phone, but he looks up at that. "*You*?"

"Okay, fine. I'll get Matt to do it."

"Soren's cool," Lennon mumbles and goes back to staring at his phone as if wondering if he really got fired.

Matt turns to look at me. "You came out publicly?"

I swallow the lump in my throat. "Yeah."

"How is your phone not blowing up?" Matt asks.

"Don't have it on."

"Ooh, smart."

As Matt finishes reading the article, the story appears on the TV. Footage from the press conference is played, and it's weird watching it. It's like having an out-of-body experience, and the adrenaline that was pumping through me at the time has already faded the memories around the edges. As TV me speaks, I can't recall saying half the shit I did. I told them about Ash?

I didn't name him, but he might be pissed.

Oh, fuck. Speaking of pissed, I turned my phone off from the world, but I also just remembered I never got a chance to give my parents a warning.

I take my phone out and go to turn it on when a glass of dark liquid appears in front of me.

"If you're gonna do that, I might suggest this first," Jet says.

"Good point." I throw it back and then hit the button.

I hold my breath as it reboots and notifications start popping up. Missed calls from unknown numbers, my family members, and Ash immediately fill my screen.

Then the messages come.

Ma: *I KNOW YOU'RE BUSY, SWEETIE, CALL US WHEN YOU CAN. LOVE YOU, AND SO PROUD. Xx*

Dad: *YOUR MA SAYS YOU SHOULD'VE WORN A SUIT BUT DIDN'T WANT TO MEDDLE SO IS MAKING ME DO IT.*

I snort at that one. My brothers have sent through their own messages, mostly congratulations and one from Vic being a smartass that says:

WAIT, YOU'RE GAY!?

I send out a quick group text to let them all know I'll call them when I can, but I need time for everything to settle first.

Kessler and Petrov and a few other teammates have sent texts of support. There's one from Bjorn, and I know I shouldn't open it. I tell myself not to, but my fingers have other ideas.

Bjorn: *SO I UNDERSTAND WHY YOU'VE BEEN AVOIDING ME SINCE THAT DAY IN THE LOCKER ROOM WHEN I SAID SOME HURTFUL WORDS. WELL, ONE WORD. I TRULY AM SORRY FOR MY STUPIDITY AND WANT YOU TO KNOW I FULLY SUPPORT YOU AS A TEAMMATE AND RESPECT THE HELL OUT OF YOU AS A FRIEND … IF YOU DON'T WANT TO PUNCH ME, THAT IS. IF YOU WANT TO PUNCH ME, GO AHEAD. FREE SHOT. I'M SORRY FOR BEING AN IGNORANT PRICK.*

Whether he's being sincere or not, I don't know, but at least I know he's not going to make a problem for me next season. He probably saw what happened to Healy and is saving his ass, but at least he can admit when he's wrong, or at least pretend so there's no drama. I decide to give him the benefit of the doubt.

Me: *HEY, AT LEAST YOU DIDN'T FUCK MY SISTER. APOLOGY ACCEPTED.*

Bjorn: *LOL! THANKS FOR BEING COOL ABOUT IT.*

The next one in line is from Ash. I hold my breath as I read over his words.

Ash: *I'M STUPID TO THINK ANY OF THIS COULD'VE BEEN FOR ME, AREN'T I? WHY HIM?*

I can't deal with that loaded question right now, so I shoot him a text and apologize for mentioning him at the press conference and tell him we can talk when everything dies down. I can see how he'd assume I did this for Lennon, but it's not that at all.

Okay, maybe a part of me is excited that I get to have Lennon for real now, but if it weren't for Soren, I would've taken the out today like Lennon asked.

My phone starts ringing in my hand as an unknown call comes through. "And so it begins."

Instead of answering, I switch my phone off again. If Damon needs me, he can call one of his friends, and if someone from the Dragons needs me, they can call Damon, so there's no real point torturing me with phone calls I don't want to deal with.

When I look back up, Lennon's gone. I didn't see him slip away while I was distracted.

"Where'd Lennon go?" I ask.

"Drink?" Jet holds up another glass.

"Why are you avoiding answering my question?"

Jets eyes don't hold their usual spark. "He asked to be left alone for a while and went upstairs."

Something tells me to respect his wishes, but I go after him anyway.

I bound up the stairs but hesitate outside his room. He just lost his job. He probably wants to be alone to wrap his head around that.

Then why do I get the impression he came up here to get away from me and not everyone else? I don't have any clue why I think that, but it's like intuition or some shit.

"Are you okay?" I ask, slipping inside his bedroom and closing the door behind me.

He's sitting on his bed using his laptop, and he doesn't look up at me as he grunts his response.

"What are you doing?"

"What do you think I'm doing? I'm emailing everyone I know to see if they've got any jobs available."

Okay, he's freaking out. "Everything's going to be okay. You'll get another job easy."

Lennon's fingers stop tapping away, and he glares up at me.

"Do you know how many jobs there are for sports journalists out there?"

"Probably about the same amount as there are on the NHL roster," I point out. "I know about having an unstable job."

"Then you should know that everything won't be okay."

"Weren't you thinking of quitting anyway?" I ask and immediately know it's a mistake.

Lennon grits his teeth. "If I quit, I'd have to give two weeks' notice, and I'd have time to find something else. I would've finished out the playoffs and had an opportunity to wrap my head around it. Right now, I'm up shit creek without a paddle."

"But you're a great reporter. Any magazine or publication will be lucky to have you."

"There are a lot of great reporters out there, and media as an industry is practically obsolete."

"Lennon—"

"Fuck, do you really not understand this? Imagine if what you did tonight cost you your career. Hasn't that been your fear all along? We've been so worried about what coming out will do to *your* career, we didn't even think about mine."

"Wait, now you're blaming me for this? Are you saying if you knew you'd be fired, you would've said something to your editor sooner?" I don't mean to raise my voice, but I think I'm subconsciously meeting his tone.

"No, but maybe … shit, I dunno, maybe I would've distanced myself? Not gotten involved in"—he waves his hand between us —"whatever delusion we're under."

"*Delusion*?"

"Even before I lost my job, this was never going to work. I was going to go back to Chicago, and—"

"Noah and Matt make the New York–Chicago thing work."

"They can move around together. We don't have that luxury."

"Then maybe losing your job wasn't a bad thing, because now you can stay here." I would love it if that happened.

"And if my next job is in Atlanta? Or Seattle? Or—"

"New York," I suggest. "Don't write us off because you don't know what's going to happen."

Lennon shakes his head. "I can't help thinking if this was you in my position that you would hold a little resentment over us, but you're telling me to stay calm."

"I think you're prematurely freaking out. You've got time to find another job, and if money's an issue, I could always—"

"No. I'm not taking money from you."

"It'd be a loan or whatever. I'm just saying there's no need to panic yet."

Lennon sighs. "I need some time to wrap my head around this and put some feelers out there so I don't feel completely helpless right now. Can you … can you just let me do my thing and we'll talk later?"

I want to keep arguing, because I have no doubt he'll be grabbed by any sporting magazine looking to hire, but then it occurs to me that no one might be hiring, and if I was staring down the end of my hockey career, I'd be high-strung too.

Still, I don't want to leave him. I want to stay in this room and prove to him we're not a delusion. What we have is real whether he's ready to see that or not.

If he's not ready, and I push, I'm gonna lose him. If I keep telling him it'll be fine when he doesn't believe it, I'll lose him.

He's right that if this had happened the other way around and I lost my career tonight, I'd be inconsolable and would most likely take it out on anyone and everyone who tried to rationalize it to me.

And that's why I know I have to give him space, even if I don't like it.

I turn on my heel, and head downstairs.

"God, again?" I complain as Soren and I come up on the screen again as soon as I sit down. "Don't they have like other shit to report on?"

"You'll get used to it," Matt says. "At least y'all got each other. I'm still waiting for someone else in football to say somethin'."

Jet feeds me another drink, and when I down that one, he runs off to get me another.

Matt and Noah talk about shit like nothing's wrong, but they can all obviously sense the tension after Lennon's and my fight.

He called us a *delusion.* Like he has no faith in us ever working out. That it'd be impossible to have a relationship with me. And as much as I keep telling myself he doesn't truly believe that—it was said in the heat of the moment and in the middle of a freak out—I can't help running worst-case scenarios in my head.

What if he really can't forgive that I'm partially responsible for him losing his job? What if he decides being in the limelight isn't worth it? What if he thinks *I'm* not worth it.

Ash realized I wasn't worth waiting for. Maybe Lennon will realize I'm too much effort. Especially if being with me will interfere with his career.

I figure when he calms down he'll come to find me, but he still hasn't, and it's getting late.

"You know, you could always take my seat," Jet says from where he sits across from me.

"Huh?"

"Well, with how many times you're turning your head to watch the stairs, I'd say it'd be safer to prevent injury."

Matt stares at me, concern etched in his scrunched brow. "How was he when you went up there?"

"I'm surprised you didn't hear him yelling at me."

All three of them suddenly lose eye contact with me.

"You did hear."

"It'll be fine," Noah says. "Matt and I made long distance work."

Jet coughs and splutters. "For a few weeks when you were all mopey and broken up. Then you moved for him."

"Long distance isn't even the issue right now," I say. "He's ready to throw us away because of a possible job that could possibly be in another city. He's lashing out at me because it's my personal shit that cost him his job. And the more I think about it, the more I think he has a right to be upset. I just don't wanna lose him over it."

"Maybe he needs some space," Noah says. "Time to clear his head."

"And what if when his head clears, it tells him to walk away?" I ask, but it's more to myself than the others. "We'll be over before we've even really started."

"Then maybe it'll be better that way." Noah shrugs. "Because once you're in, you're all in, and then it's so much harder when you have to walk away."

I stand quickly, because I need to fix this, but I come to the conclusion Jet's been feeding me doubles as my legs wobble more than after a grueling skate. But I'm not belligerent drunk or angry drunk. I'm just sad drunk.

Sad because the same night I come out to everyone, the rest of my world crumbles.

Sad because we should be celebrating, and instead, I'm worrying about the future and what it could possibly hold for Lennon and me.

CHAPTER TWENTY-EIGHT

Fuck, fuck, fuck, fuck, fuck. That's the sound my panicky brain makes as I check my bank balance and work out how long I can survive while being unemployed.

It's funny. Until I got the call from Harry, I thought I held all the cards. We'd beaten them to outing Soren, so I thought it was over. Apparently, that makes me "not a team player" or whatever.

In retrospect, I should've seen it coming. If Harry's going to stoop low enough to out someone, he wouldn't bat an eye at firing someone even if I was pulling in more views than Kevin. The gap between our readership isn't big enough to argue the better reporter defense.

When I threatened to quit, I had the security of giving at least two weeks' notice to find something else.

Now … I have nothing and am starting at square one.

And after a quick search online, it's obvious there's no jobs. My kind of position is rarely advertised. It's all about who you know and your connections. So instead of a frivolous job search, I open my email contacts to put some feelers out.

Shit, I'm gonna need a new résumé, get all my past articles

together … Crap, what if Harry takes them all down? Is that a thing?

Sporting Health was my first job straight out of college. I don't know the protocol with this.

I open my folders on my computer where they're saved, but three years of articles, I have no way of knowing if they're all there. Sometimes, I'd upload straight to the work cloud.

Before I can really get a hold of one thing, another thought pops up, and before I know it, I have about fifteen tabs open with no real direction.

Welcome to the life of being a reporter.

I slump back on my bed and take a deep breath. The sheets still smell like sex, reminding me I'm gonna have to apologize pretty fucking hard after dismissing Ollie the way I did.

Realistically, though, where can we go from here?

Ollie's out now. He can date and have a boyfriend. But that boyfriend can't be me. I'll never work as a sports journalist again, and it's all I've known.

Then again, aren't we making our own rules? Soren coming out, Ollie standing behind him … this is uncharted territory, and we could pave the way for gay men in sports, which has been my goal ever since becoming a journalist.

I grab my phone and send off a text.

Me: *SOREN STILL WITH YOU?*

Damon: *YEAH, WHY?*

Me: *I HAVE AN IDEA FOR A STORY …*

Within seconds, my phone vibrates with Damon's name flashing on the screen.

"Hey," I say into the phone.

"What's the story?" Damon asks. "Soren's here on speaker."

"I want to do Soren's coming out story."

I'm met with silence.

"Hear me out. You guys know people will be pushing for this, but I'm the only reporter who'll do it fairly without trying to use gimmicks and without stereotyping."

"Uh," Soren says, his voice hesitant. "I don't really want to do a favor to the magazine that was going to out me."

"Oh, right. Probably should've led with they fired me, and I'd be shopping this around to other magazines. I have a contact at *Sports Illustrated* after writing that article about Damon about a year ago."

"They fired you?" Damon asks.

"Yep."

"I'll do it," Soren says.

"Really? I didn't think it'd be that easy. Do you need to ask your agent?"

"His soon-to-be agent is right here, and he approves," Damon says.

Soren's chuckle comes through the phone. "Lennon, how long have you known Ollie's gay?"

"About eight months."

"The fact he only just came out means I can trust you."

"Umm, I should say upfront I don't have any money to give you. Other places would offer you compensation."

"Dude," Damon says, "you'd sold him already. Don't back down."

Soren laughs again. "I'd rather have the story I want out there instead of more money I don't need."

The stress over my career eases with the promise of Soren's story, but my work is far from done.

And now with some semblance of a plan, my head breaks out of reporter mode and back into boyfriend mode.

Oh, fuck. I need to grovel.

As if sensing my readiness, there's a knock on the door, and

Ollie steps through.

"I'm sorry," I whisper.

Tension in his shoulders relaxes.

"I'm really sorry."

Ollie smiles. "It's okay."

"No, I was a dick."

"You were scared."

"Doesn't mean I should've said all the shit I did. I freaked out. I don't regret standing by you yesterday. Not at all."

As Ollie approaches the bed, I close my laptop and shove it on my nightstand. He climbs on top of me and lowers his head to kiss my mouth.

"Is this your way of forgiving me?" I ask against his lips.

"If our fight has proved anything, it's that I don't want you to walk away. I want to find a way to make us work."

"I want that too."

Ollie kisses me the same way he did back in the cold corridors of the Dragons' stadium when he was convincing me that we can be together.

My tongue sweeps into Ollie's mouth, and his whole body relaxes on top of me. We make out a little but don't make a move to go any further. I can't help being self-conscious about getting it on in a house full of people again.

When we finally come up for air, I land soft kisses along his jaw and neck before rolling him off me so we're side by side.

"Did you come up with a job solution?" He braces himself, almost like he's expecting to be yelled at again.

I run a hand down his arm. "I thought of going to the game tomorrow anyway and writing about the first NHL game with an openly gay player on the ice and then trying to shop it around. But there'll be a million other articles published on the exact same thing, so I asked Soren if I could interview him instead."

"Soren …" Ollie says. "Is there a reason you asked him and not me?"

I hesitate. "Honestly? It didn't cross my mind."

Ollie tenses under my hands.

"But not because I don't want to," I rush on. "Hell no. It's more an ethical problem. We're sleeping together. The article would be biased."

"You've already proved you can be brutal if you need to be. I must be a sloppy kisser for you to have written those articles about me back then."

A small laugh escapes. "You're a really sloppy kisser. Like, I think you might need to practice." I bring my finger up to tap my lips.

"Just for that, I think I'm gonna hold out."

I lean in, bringing my mouth so close to his. "Let's see how long that lasts."

Ollie groans and whispers, "I hate you."

"No, you don't."

"Okay, no, I don't. But everyone else will when they find out you're the thing coming between me and Soren. The media is totally pushing for Sorenberg."

"Sorenberg? That's terrible."

Ollie laughs. "That doesn't make you mad? Me being 'shipped with Soren?"

"About a stupid celebrity couple name? No. If anything, I'm glad Kevin didn't figure us out and thrust me into the spotlight."

He pulls back. "You don't want people to know we're … uh, together or whatever? Even if you're not going to write the article about me?"

"I don't want other publications to see tabloid opportunities if I'm with an athlete."

"Makes sense."

But fuck, I hate the hurt in his eyes. "Is … is that okay?"

Ollie nods. "Just major role reversal here. We were worried about my career and my secret, and now you're in the exact same position, and I'm the one thinking it sucks."

"If it comes out, it comes out. It's not like I want to hide it, but if Soren's providing a good distraction, I'm okay with that."

"So, what now?" Ollie asks and moves in closer.

"I have the best idea." I roll Ollie onto his back and climb on top of him.

He tries to kiss me, but I pull away and reach for my laptop.

"I look for a job."

Ollie slumps back on the pillows. "I hate you again, Blue."

As soon as Soren and I get approval to do the article, I follow him around like a puppy for the rest of the playoffs and query publications that'll most likely pick the story.

Offers pour in, but there's only one I'm interested in. That's how I've ended up here, sitting at *Sports Illustrated* headquarters in New York. I'm so nervous I'm fairly certain I'd have pit stains in my shirt, so I make a mental note not to take off my jacket, even if it's ninety degrees in here. Every time I shift in my seat, the leather beneath my ass squeaks, so I try to sit as still as possible as Greg Follett makes my lifelong dream come true.

He leans back in his seat. "We've been wanting to do a spotlight on gay athletes in sports, and that article you wrote for us last year about Damon King was a great start. The fact you already have Soren on board has us all excited."

"I've also spoken to Matt Jackson about a possible article on him too." Sure, it was a passing comment, but he did offer.

Greg's face lights up. "This could work. We could maybe

feature one athlete per month over a few months. Matt Jackson and Ollie Strömberg are clients of King, right? Maybe we could use that connection to get Strömberg too."

The tips of my ears burn. "Umm, well, I'm sure I could get Ollie too. Uh … as long as you'd be okay with there being a conflict of interest when it comes to me."

He cocks his head.

"He's, uh, he's my boyfriend."

Greg's lips quirk. "Impressive."

I frown. "What is?" Is this guy seriously judging me right now on my ability to get hot guys? I mean, I can totally see his point, but—

"I wouldn't have guessed that from any of your recent articles about his team. In fact, you were pretty harsh on him in your earlier articles."

I roll my eyes. "Like I don't hear that from him enough."

Greg laughs. "You were harsh but fair. You were right about him getting out from under Boston's hold."

"Thank you! That's what I said."

He purses his lips. "Can I ask why you haven't offered up his article?"

"I didn't want to use our relationship to get ahead."

"I admire that, but we could really use him. The more gay men in sports are normalized, the more accepting the industry will become."

"That's exactly how I feel." My heart won't stop pounding because having any magazine tell me they want me to write my dream articles is amazing let alone *Sports-freaking-Illustrated.*

"Here's the catch," Greg says.

Of course. Too good to be true. "Catch?"

"You mentioned in your email you're looking for permanent work. This would be a maximum of a couple of articles over a few months unless closet doors start flying open at a rapid rate."

"There are always other, less popular sports with gay athletes. I could approach them too and see if anyone's interested in being featured. I think as long as the articles are positive and factual and paint the lives of gay and lesbian athletes the same way we would any hetero athlete, others will sign up."

"We'd definitely be interested in those if these first few articles do well. We promise to pay you well for the articles we do run, but if we're talking a permanent arrangement here, that's not something we can offer right now."

"That's completely fine," I say quickly. What they're offering is more than I ever expected, and it'll give me time to line something else up.

"But, we do have a separate role that might fit what you're looking for. It's covering baseball."

My eyes widen. "Listening."

"On the West Coast. Based out of L.A."

"Oh." My heart sinks. Taking a job on the West Coast would mean the end of me and Ollie.

My conscious yells at me that it's a permanent job, and I'm not exactly in a position to be fussy. And it's *Sports Illustrated* for fuck's sake. Ollie would understand. He's put his career ahead of everything else for six years.

"You need some time to think about it," Greg says.

"Yeah. Uh, yeah. I'm not sure about relocating right now."

"I don't have to tell you the spot won't be available for long, but you've impressed us, and we want to work with you."

Greg's right. I can't turn it down. This is my foot in the door to one of the most reputable sports magazines in the world.

I nod. "I'll get back to you by tomorrow."

"Good man." Greg stands. "Until then, ask that boyfriend of yours if he's in."

So many sex jokes ping in my brain, but I remain professional and only grin like an idiot a little bit.

I shake his hand. "Thank you so much for this opportunity."

When I leave his office, I take out my phone and stare at the text Ava sent me a few hours ago. We had lunch last week, and she mentioned a job available with the team.

Ava: *I SPOKE TO THE GM, AND THE MEDIA JOB'S YOURS IF YOU WANT IT. I KNOW IT'S NOT JOURNALISM BUT IT'S STILL IN SPORTS.*

The Dragons want me. *Sports Illustrated* wants me. One keeps me in New York and super close to Ollie. The other is something I've wanted my entire adult life but sends me across the other side of the country.

I've never had a serious relationship before because I keep moving for my job, but I also never felt what I do for Ollie with any of the other guys I've dated. It's been easy to choose my career over them. It's not so easy when it comes to Ollie.

He's ... everything.

So, do I follow my head or my heart? My head tells me it's stupid to turn down a promising job for a guy. My heart tells me to stop being greedy in the career department. *Sports Illustrated* wants my articles. At least three of them and more if I do a good job. And I can still write freelance.

With any luck, more gay athletes will start coming out now, and they'll want to work with me too after I do these articles.

Fuck, sometimes I wish I wasn't so rational, because I can't shake the feeling of possible regret when I turn down the job and then Ollie and I break up.

What if you don't break up?

Full job security with a company I've been chasing for years or a low-paying media job writing fluff for my boyfriend's hockey team.

Ugh. I sound like a puck bunny. I gasp. I'm Ollie's puck bunny! I chuckle at myself, because even though I'm joking, I don't actually mind the sound of that. Moving to L.A. doesn't feel right. Leaving Ollie would be like leaving my heart here and only taking a shell of a human with me. I'd be taking my dream job but giving up my ultimate fantasy.

Deep down, I believe Ollie walked away with a piece of my heart that very first night in Boston, but is it enough?

I have no idea what to do.

The buzzing atmosphere around the stadium is because it's game seven in the last round of the Stanley Cup, but there's another reason adrenaline's fueling the nerves in the pit of my stomach.

You don't say to a guy you've been officially dating only a few weeks "I gave up my dream job on the off chance you and I work out. No pressure! Wanna fuck?"

L.A. might have the type of sports reporting I always thought I'd do, but New York has important networking connections like Damon and a series of articles that mean so much more to me than following baseball on the West Coast. Plus, it has Ollie, and that's the real selling point. The more time I spend with him, the more I know the truth—I'm stupidly in love with him.

It took a shot or two of scotch and a phone call to Noah for me to make up my mind. I decided almost immediately that I didn't want to take the L.A. job, but I wanted someone else to tell me I was doing the right thing. Noah said if it was him he wouldn't take it because nothing was worth leaving Matt for, but it was different for me because Ollie and I aren't in love.

When I'd opened my mouth to protest but quickly shut it, he'd said "I think you have your answer."

He knew I was about to defend Ollie and me, and he was right.

Now I just need to tell Ollie.

Damon used his agent connections and managed to score eleven seats for tonight's game all together in the family section, and we're all here to support Soren, even Tommy, after getting his ass handed to him by New Jersey in the last round.

Two teams had two gay players in the playoffs this year. That's an achievement in itself, and we're all here to celebrate it.

If New Jersey can secure the win over Vegas, we'll win two for two in the gay athlete coming out only to go on to win the whole season of their sport.

Good luck, Soren.

We find our seats, which are situated over three rows, and I'm surprised to find Matt's teammates sitting there waiting for us. You'd think being a sports reporter, I'd get used to being around athletes, but Marcus Talon isn't just an athlete. He's *Marcus Talon* —a quarterback god. The next Tom Brady.

Ollie does his hovering-by-my-side thing—giving those *I want to touch you so badly* vibes I still haven't gotten used to. If I close my eyes, I can imagine him slipping his hand into mine and holding tight.

We still haven't come out to the world about our relationship, but it's not like we're hiding it too hard. And with the news I'm sitting on, it won't matter who knows about us soon.

We get settled in our seats, but Maddox turns around from his and Damon's in front. "By the way, we're going to hit up that new gay bar in the city afterward if anyone's interested."

"Oh, thanks, but we can't," I say. "We have that thing."

Ollie frowns. "What thing?"

"That thing where I don't want to go."

Everyone laughs.

"I met you in a gay bar," Noah says, confused.

"Yes, but that was to find a hookup. I no longer need to do that." My hand reaches for Ollie's. "Bar means dancing and that's a whole bucket of nope for me."

"Hang out with Miller and Talon," Ollie says. "Don't think they're gonna get down in a gay bar."

Talon and Miller share matching smirks.

"That's not a challenge you want to set for Talon," Miller says. "Trust me on that one."

He doesn't get a chance to clarify before Jet's pulling on my arm from beside me.

"You have to come," he says, almost panicked.

"Uh, why?"

"Just … because. You *have* to."

Something in his urgent tone tells me to agree, but I don't know why yet.

"Umm, okay," I say. "Apparently, being a friend means doing things you don't want to, so for you, I'll go."

"Yay, you're learning," Jet says and throws his arm around my shoulder for a side hug.

Ollie nudges me. "Besides, I've never been to one, so you have to do the boyfriendly thing and make sure to keep all the twinks off your man."

"If they're groping you on the dance floor, you're on your own." That doesn't stop that stupid warm and fuzzy feeling attacking when he calls himself my man. I don't think I'll ever get used to it.

"Lennon, calm down. Your possessiveness of me is a little extreme."

"Sorry." I link my arm with his. "Please don't dance with

anyone else tonight? I can't take it when guys fawn all over you."
I also throw in some batted eyelashes for good measure.

"That's better," he says.

When the game starts, New Jersey doesn't hold any punches.
Literally and figuratively. They're out for blood and in it to win.
They have more to prove than Vegas.

Three fights break out in the first period alone, yet the score-
board still reads 0 – 0 by the time it ends.

I think all of us are hoping New Jersey takes the Cup. "Maybe
if the first NFL team to have a gay player wins the Super Bowl
and the first NHL team with one wins the Stanley Cup, more
athletes will be willing to come out. Surely, there's more than
Ollie, Soren, and Matt," I say to no one in particular.

Miller starts choking on his drink, and Coke comes out his
nose. Talon playfully pats him on the back with a laugh.

During the break, Ollie leans back in his seat, no longer
jumping up every two seconds to yell at the ice.

His arm goes around the back of my chair. "Are you okay?
You seem like you're not really here."

Damn it. I was hoping he wouldn't notice.

"It's hockey, what do you expect?" I try to deflect, because I
know he's right. I'm nervous about telling him I'm staying in
New York. Not only that, but I turned down my dream job for
him. That's a lot this soon, right?

God, did I make the right decision?

One look at him, and I know I did, but what if he's not there
yet? Awkward.

He stares at me as if trying to decipher something or work
something out, and I'm wondering if it's written all over my face.

Jet taps me on the shoulder. "Uh, guys." He points up to the
screen where the kiss cam is on. And it's aimed at me and Ollie.

Fuck.

The game announcer says something about a special request from Caleb Sorensen to make Ollie kiss the nearest boy.

"I'm gonna kill him," Ollie mutters.

"Umm …" I must look horrified because Ollie's expression softens.

The crowd, surprisingly, appears encouraging. Well, there's no booing I can hear, at least. That's something.

"We don't have to," Ollie says. "You're not ready for everyone to know and—"

I swallow hard and go for it, because I won't even be working in journalism anymore. Not really. And *Sports Illustrated* has already said they don't care if I'm with Ollie. We don't have to hide.

Our mouths meet, and the arena breaks out into hollers and applause.

It's probably the most surreal moment of my life.

I wish it was one of those times like in a shitty rom-com movie where the world fades away, and it's just me and him and love and all that shit, but no. I can't get past nerdy Lennon kissing a jock in front of sixteen thousand people. And they're cheering.

Yes, folks, I finally got my shit together. Thanks for the encouragement.

The kiss is brief and PG-rated—I feel only the barest flick of Ollie's tongue against my lips—and when Ollie pulls away, the kiss cam's moved on to other people.

Ollie stares at me dumbfounded. "You didn't have to do that. You've probably thrust yourself into the media spotlight."

"I, umm, have something to tell you."

"What?"

"I got a job. In New York." I mumble the next part. "With the Dragons."

His brow furrows. "Huh?"

As if I had my very own spidey senses, I know everyone in our group is eavesdropping right now.

"Ava wants help in the PR department. She wants someone to write press releases and manage the social media accounts and basically write fluff for the team."

"But … you're a journalist. You write stories and articles, not fluff."

I swallow hard. "Right, but the job's here." *With you.* I fumble over those words and can't get them out.

"You turned down *Sports Illustrated*?" Noah asks.

And fuck, I knew there was a reason I should've been bothered about them listening in. He's the only one I've told.

Ollie's face lights up. "*Sports Illustrated*? You got offered a job with *Sports Illustrated*? That's amazing."

"That job's in L.A.," I say.

The excitement from a second ago disappears, and he responds the exact same way I did to the offer. "Oh …"

"I turned it down and accepted the job with Ava."

Ollie blinks rapidly. "I'm going to ask this very slowly, because I need to know. Did you … I mean, did you turn it down … for me?"

"Fucking duh," Jet says beside me. "And people say I can be oblivious."

"Yes?" I don't mean for it to come out as a question.

"Are you asking me or telling me?" Ollie asks.

"Telling you. I turned it down. For you. So I could stay in New York. *For you.*"

He doesn't tear his gaze away but doesn't say anything either, not even when the next period starts and the players take to the ice once again.

"You … and you … but you …"

I want to laugh, but I'm too scared to. "It's too much? It's too much. Never mind. I'll get a job somewhere else. I don't have to work for the Dragons."

"Too much?" Ollie asks, his tone soft. "Are you kidding me? It's *everything*. Part of me is telling me I don't deserve it. I … I lo—" His mouth slams shut. "Are you sure? You didn't want to compromise my career for you, so why do you get to do it for me?"

"It's completely different. I'd be miserable in L.A. knowing you were back here."

"We could make it work, and—"

I shake my head. "No. It'd be too hard. And I'm not really compromising anything. *Sports Illustrated* still wants me to write freelance for them, and actually, they want me to write your coming out article. And Soren's. They also want me to do an article on Matt."

I glance over Ollie's head at Matt.

"I'm in," Matt says.

"I thought you said you couldn't write about me if we were together."

"The editor I'll be working with has already said he doesn't care about that. This way, I still get my dream job—writing about gay athletes for a massive publication—but I get to stay in New York. I can travel for other stories during your off-season. I'll get the best of both worlds."

He's still not convinced. "You won't resent me for you turning it down?"

I understand where he's coming from, because I was scared of the exact same thing when he came out, but this was completely my decision.

"Even if *Sports Illustrated* is my dream job, you're my actual dream. Giving us a real shot is what I want."

His eyes widen slightly. Oh, God, I'm freaking him out.

"Unless you don't want that. In which case I'm joking. Ha-ha, I'm hilarious. Ooh, look, hockey!"

He's on me in an instant. "Fuck, I love you."

Ollie's mouth crashes to mine, and this time, the world does fade around me, because the only thing I can focus on are those three little words I've never heard directed at me before.

It's like I conjured this guy from pure wishing, and I don't know what I did to deserve him, but I'm not going to question it. All I want is for us to be together.

We're finally pulled apart when the crowd starts screaming. The lamp on New Jersey's end flashes, and Soren's being attacked by his teammates with back slaps and glove bumps.

He might've just scored the winning goal of the fucking Stanley Cup. Maybe. Could still go either way, but with the lack of score so far and how hard everyone's fighting for it, I think it's going to be a low-scoring game.

When the commotion dies down, I lean in and whisper to Ollie. "I love you too. Just in case that wasn't clear by my rambling and job sacrificing and all that."

Ollie stands and grabs my hand. "Sorry, guys, we're bailing on going out. Tell Soren good game, and—"

Jet gets out of his chair and blocks us off. "You can't."

"JJ, what's going on?" Matt asks, his tone firm.

I tug Ollie back down into his seat, and Jet wrings his hands together.

"Okay, fine, I was going to do this later at the club so we could all celebrate with drinks, but ... we did it."

"We did what?" Noah asks.

"The band got signed, and we're recording 'He's Mine' and a few other songs, and then we're going on tour."

"Noah's and my song?" Matt asks. "And a *tour*?"

"National first, but they're talking about going to Australia for some huge music festival in a few months if we do well."

I've never seen Jet look so nervous. "Why are you freaking out?" I ask.

He shakes his head. "No reason. I mean, they want to change a bunch of crap with the band, but so what? Fallout is just a name. It wasn't even a name I picked. It came with the band. So I shouldn't care that we'll be known as Radioactive from now on, right? It doesn't matter … no big deal." He breathes deep.

"You're worried about your artistic control," Ollie says.

"Does that make me a spoiled shithead?" Jet asks, and I worry for a moment that he might not be ready for a record deal. He's young, and—

In a split second, the doubt is gone, and in its place is the Jet I've seen on stage. Confident and happy.

"Oh, fuck it, it's just a name. I've got a record deal, bitches!"

We all jump up and hug the crap out of him, even though it happens to coincide with Las Vegas sinking the puck.

Everyone around us thinks we're traitors, but we don't fucking care. Jet's gonna be famous.

"Damn," I say, "I was kind of hoping to keep you as a roommate." Then I turn to Matt and Noah. "At least until I find a place of my own."

Noah waves me off. "Stay as long as you want. We're going back to Chicago in a few weeks, and with Jet leaving, we'll need someone to look after the place."

"Really? I mean, I can pay rent. Obviously not as much as it's worth, but—"

Noah throws his arm around Matt. "Do we look like two people who need more money? Pay us by managing the upkeep, and you've got a deal."

"Leaving," Jet says as if it's just sinking in. "Holy shit, I'm leaving." He pales a little and has to take his seat again.

"You're gonna rock it," Ollie says.

"Pun intended," I add.

After that, none of us can sit still. We're all buzzing with celebratory energy, even when Vegas sinks another one.

Damn it.

I huff. "Okay, so maybe my theory of the first gay guy in each league winning won't come true."

Ollie wraps his arm around me. "I don't think Soren will hate it so much. I mean, if he loses, fuck yeah, he'll hate it, but no more than a regular player losing the Cup. He's already told me making it to the final feels like he doesn't need to prove anything more."

"Yeah, I know. Still, would be nice."

But niceties and wishing don't always come true, because life isn't always fair.

When Vegas sinks a third in the third period, Jersey can't recover. And when the final buzzer sounds, we remain seated in a depressed heap of loserdom. When the team you root for loses, you take it as if the loss is on *your* shoulders. It's one of the things I love about sports. Even if you can't play, you live the wins through your team but also experience the losses.

Tonight is doubly sucky.

"At least Soren can come out with us," Ollie says. "If they'd won, he'd be out celebrating with the team."

"Are you sure he won't want to commiserate with his team instead?" I ask.

"Maybe, but I doubt it. When you lose, you kinda want to be far away from the people who want to point fingers and blame. Do you still have a press pass? Maybe you can go back to the locker rooms and ask him."

"No sweat." I stand.

Jet jumps up to let me past. "Can I come?"

"Okay, fine. You can be my assistant if they ask."

Jet and I break away from the group, but as soon as we're let into the back corridors, we're aware we've overlooked one very important detail.

"Lennon Hawkins," other reporters call out. Some I know, but most I don't. They're on us before either me or Jet can blink, and they don't seem to care about leaving their spot outside the locker room as they come after me.

I turn to Jet, who looks as scared as I feel. "Gonna have to get used to this type of attention, rock star."

"What's your relationship with Ollie Strömberg?" someone yells.

"How long have you been together?" someone else asks.

All this from one little kiss Ollie was publicly dared to do? Then I realize that our seats were behind the players and right in the press box's line of sight. We probably had eyes on us the whole game.

Ollie's and my normal shyness over public affection wasn't there tonight, and even though I'd hoped this wouldn't happen, I know I can handle it. My family, on the other hand ...

Mom's gonna kill me. I already know how that conversation will go. I'll emphasize nothing bad will happen, and she'll say "You don't know that!" The argument that I don't know if I'll be hit by a bus either is pretty thin by now with how many times I've used it. I understand she worries, but she also has to know I'm a grown man and don't want to hide for the rest of my life because I had bad experiences as a teenager.

Ollie won't hurt me. I'm certain of it.

"Can you get Soren on your own?" I ask Jet.

"Sure. I mean, I haven't met him yet, so he'll think some weird, scrawny dude is asking him out but ..." Jet shrugs.

"Thanks. We owe you." I throw him my press pass and then hightail it out of there and mutter no comment to anyone who catches up to me. I'm outside and meeting up with the others before I can even register I'm referring to Ollie and me as a "we" now.

I see Ollie waiting for me when it does sink in, and I can't help smiling.

I'm a *we* person now.

If I wasn't so damn happy, I'd hate myself.

CHAPTER TWENTY-NINE

OLLIE

Lennon gave up his dream job for me. I still can't comprehend that even as I stare at him from across the crowded bar.

As soon as we got here, Jet dragged me onto the dance floor seeing as it's a rite of passage or whatever to get sweaty with half-naked men. With Lennon's big fat *no* stance on dancing, Jet's taken pity on me and vowed to show me the way.

And while the dance floor is proving to be an awesome experience—to freely admire the bodies around me, the porn-like make-out sessions from others, and all-round freedom of everyone in here—I don't like being away from my man.

The only thing making me take my eyes off him is the wicked harsh scowl Soren's sending my way.

Jet leans back against my chest and reaches up behind him to wrap his hands around my neck. He turns his head and whispers in my ear, "What's your friend's deal?"

"My friend?"

"Caleb. Soren. Whatever his name is."

Soren's now standing, arms crossed, and looks like he's about to murder me. Or maybe Jet.

"What happened?" I ask.

Jet turns in my arms, and his lithe body continues to move against mine. "Dunno. It was weird. When I asked him to come here, he was all 'It's *you*.' But then he looked me over and almost looked disgusted with me. Or himself. I'm not sure."

That is weird. "I have no idea what that's about. Unless you're already famous and didn't know. You're gonna have to get used to randoms recognizing you."

"He did mumble something about the Rainbow Beds benefit." He glances over at Soren and gets this whole intrigued look in his eyes. "Is he single?"

"Jet," I warn, "he's way too old for you."

"Hmm …" He still looks interested.

"You're leaving and going on tour."

"Exactly." Jet waggles his eyebrows.

"He has an ex he wants to get back with," I say.

"*Ex* means fair game."

I don't like this, but I don't know why. Maybe it has to do with me bringing Soren into this group. If Jet gets crushed, Matt will kick my ass, and I've made it a life goal to never have one of my role models hate me. "I'll tell Matt and Noah you're crushing on a hockey player ten years older than you," I blurt.

"You'd tattle on me? Real friendship goals, Oliver."

Apparently, my highly offensive threat is too much for him, and he stalks away.

He's barely out of my eyesight when I'm swarmed by other guys trying to get my attention. Can't say that I hate it, but I do hate that none of them are Lennon.

And then I see him, the guy who means so fucking much to me it's scary and who's changed my life so much already.

He's showed me what selfless love is all about, and I wouldn't change him, how we met, or how we got here.

I wouldn't even change the angry jealousy written all over his face right now.

Not at all.

"Hey," I say to him when he reaches me. "You kinda look like my boyfriend, but he assures me he wouldn't be caught dead on a dance floor."

"He sounds like a smart guy."

"He is. Although not too smart to know there's no way I'm interested in anyone but him so he really didn't need to come fetch me."

"Yeah. He did." His arms snake around my back, and he pulls me close. He doesn't start dancing though. That's probably too much to ask.

"Why did he?" I mock.

Lennon's mouth lands on my ear. "Because I may not be able to dance, but I can fuck, and watching you and Jet together was too hot for words. I need you. Like yesterday."

And it's home time.

I drag Lennon toward the bar entrance, waving goodbye to the group of guys at our table from afar so none of them try to stop us. I don't even look in their direction to see if they acknowledge us leaving. They'd understand.

When we reach outside, the warm summer New York night makes my T-shirt stick to my skin with sweat. Either that or I'm still sweating from all the dancing.

"Your place is closer," I say to Lennon.

"Yours is more private."

Damn it, he's right.

I take out my phone and order an Uber to come pick us up and then turn to Lennon. "So … what are your plans for me for when we get home?"

If I'm honest with myself, the urge to ask Lennon to move in with me as soon as he announced he was staying in New York was strong. Too strong for a couple who haven't been together long. I'm glad I managed to keep my mouth shut about that, but that didn't stop the *I love you* from falling out.

I knew I couldn't hold it back much longer but have been too scared to throw it out there. We might not have been together officially for long, but he's all I've been able to think about since that night at the Honey Bee.

"I don't know," Lennon says. "I gave up my dream job for you, so I'd think you'd be the one to have plans for me."

I smile. "You know, there'll be a time in years to come when you can't use that against me anymore. *I gave up my dream job for you, so do the fucking dishes. I gave up my dream job for you, so rub my feet.*"

Lennon cocks his head. "Years to come, huh?"

Oh fuck. Way to not show my hand too fast.

But Lennon doesn't seem fazed. "How optimistic of you."

Apparently, my mouth thinks it's a good idea to dig a deeper hole for myself. "Confident. Because I know there will never be another guy who understands me like you do. Who doesn't only support me but encourages me to do what's right for me. You're the most selfless person I know, and you're perfect for me. If I could give you the world, I would."

Under the street lights, I swear Lennon's cheeks tinge a cute pink.

"Until I can afford the entire world, I'll give you whatever the fuck you want."

He stares up into my eyes, and with the most serious voice, he says, "I want you to kidnap the president. And the Declaration of Independence. *National Treasure* style."

I laugh. "Fuck, I love you." Damn, there it is again.

Lennon closes his eyes and takes a deep breath.

"What are you doing?" I ask.

"Trying to convince myself this is real," he says quietly.

I kiss him, pulling him close and breathing him in. His vanilla-spiced scent that's all Lennon fills my nostrils, and I can't believe this is real myself.

"I promise this is real," I whisper.

He pulls back again, and his stoic face makes me think he's going to say another joke, but when his voice comes out quiet and unsure, I know he's being serious. "I know what I want from you."

"What?"

"Happiness."

I huff a loud breath of relief. "That's the easiest thing you could've asked for."

"But it's sometimes the hardest."

Truth. "All you have to know is I'm going to make it my life's work to make sure you're happy."

"After hockey, maybe."

I shake my head. "No. You put me before your career, and until I met you, I never understood why or how someone could do that for someone else. With you, I get it. It makes more sense than anything I've ever experienced before, and I can't even explain it. I thought hockey was everything. All the rest was just extras. And while hockey is still a major chunk of my life, you've become my priority."

"Are you sure?" Lennon's still uncertain, and I don't know how to take that away.

I try to come up with something that's an easy way to explain us, but what comes out is a jumbly mess. "Think of me like a cake. Hockey is the base—the plain sponge that's the core element. You're the icing—the best part. The reason you eat the cake to begin with."

"I don't know whether to be turned on or hungry."

I know he's deflecting with humor again because it's hard for his inner teen to believe anything I'm saying is true.

I sigh. "One day."

He smiles up at me. "One day?"

"One day, you won't question it. Even if it takes twenty years for you to realize what we have is real, I'll continue to prove it."

"I love you. So fucking much."

"I love you too … Clark."

He punches me in the arm, but he's gonna have to get used to his new name. Especially if he's going to be part of the Strömberg clan.

When it's the right time, I'll make that happen. Without a doubt, I know he's the one for me. The hockey player and the sports journalist making a life together … yeah, I'll make it happen.

THANK YOU!

Thank you for reading Deke. This was technically going to be the last book in the series, but some characters who weren't even supposed to exist are attention whores.
cough cough **TALON** *cough* **JET.**

So even though there are more books coming in this series, they will NOT contain a fake boyfriend trope, because there is no way in hell I'd be able to tell Talon or Jet what to do. These boys are definitely leaders of their own fate.

Talon and Miller's book, *Blindsided*, is next up.
Jet and Soren's book, *Hat Trick*, will follow.

To keep up to date with these boys and other Eden Finley news, join my reader group on Facebook:
https://www.facebook.com/groups/1901150070202571

Alternatively, you can join my mailing list:
http://eepurl.com/bS1OFH

BOOKS BY EDEN FINLEY

FIND EDEN FINLEY BOOKS HERE

https://amzn.to/2zUlM16

https://www.edenfinley.com

FAKE BOYFRIEND SERIES

Fake Out (M/M)
Trick Play (M/M)
Deke (M/M)
Blindsided (M/M)
Hat Trick (M/M)

STEELE BROTHERS

Unwritten Law (M/M)

ROYAL OBLIGATION

Unprincely (M/M/F)

ONE NIGHT SERIES

One Night with Hemsworth (M/F)
One Night with Calvin (M/F)
One Night with Fate (M/F)
One Night with Rhodes (M/M)
One Night with Him (M/F)

ACKNOWLEDGMENTS

I want to thank all of my betas: Leslie Copeland, Jill Wexler, Crystal Lacy, May Archer, Grace Kilian Delaney, Anita Maxwell, and Kimberly Readnour.

Deb Nemeth for the wonderful editing and making Lennon and Ollie shine.

Thanks to Kelly from Xterraweb editing.

To Lori Parks for one last read through.

And Kellie from Book Cover by Design. You are always a rockstar.

Lastly, a big thanks to Linda from Foreword PR & Marketing for helping get this book out.